The
Ragged
End
of Nowhere

Roy Chaney

The Ragged End
of Nowhere

MINOTAUR BOOKS
NEW YORK

A THOMAS DUNNE BOOK FOR MINOTAUR BOOKS.
An imprint of St. Martin's Publishing Group.

THE RAGGED END OF NOWHERE. Copyright © 2009 by Roy Chaney. All rights reserved. Printed in the United States of America. For information, address St. Martin's Press, 175 Fifth Avenue, New York, N.Y. 10010.

www.thomasdunnebooks.com
www.minotaurbooks.com

Design by Jonathan Bennett

Library of Congress Cataloging-in-Publication Data

Chaney, Roy.
    The ragged end of nowhere / Roy Chaney.—1st ed.
        p. cm.
    ISBN 978-0-312-58253-1
    1. Relics—Fiction. 2. Murder—Investigation—Fiction. 3. Las Vegas
(Nevada)—Fiction. I. Title.
    PS3603.H35726R34 2009
    813'.6—dc22

                                                          2009012749

First Edition: November 2009

10 9 8 7 6 5 4 3 2 1

For Janet—
from Edinburgh
and Bath to Venice

The
Ragged
End
of Nowhere

PROLOGUE

IN THE DARKNESS he stepped up to the open car window and fired. One shot. The silencer attached to the barrel of the automatic reduced the pistol shot to a dull pop.

The head of the man sitting behind the wheel whipped sideways with the force of the impact but the seat belt held his body in place. After an interminable moment the body slumped forward, the head resting against the side of the steering wheel. The dead man looked like he was searching the floor of the car for something he'd dropped.

The shooter lowered the pistol. His arm felt strangely numb. He stared at the dead man inside the car. He was surprised by what he'd just done. He hadn't intended to shoot right off, right then. But he'd lost his cool—he knew that. He'd lost his head.

His nerves jumped and sparked. He took a deep breath and tucked the pistol back inside his jacket. The silencer felt warm against his body. His fingers felt stiff inside the black leather gloves.

Three o'clock in the morning—the roadway behind him was quiet. But it wouldn't be quiet for long. He worked quickly in the darkness. He searched the backseat area of the car, then moved around to the passenger side and searched the front. He felt a wave of nausea rising in him as his gloved fingers came into contact with spattered blood and small pieces of bone and brain matter.

Searching the car trunk he began to feel desperate.

It wasn't here. How could that be?

They'd had an agreement, he and the dead man.

They'd made a *deal*.

Somewhere across the river a piece of machinery came to life with a shriek, metal against metal. It echoed through the canyon like an alarm. The shooter fought the urge to pump another bullet and then another into the hunched-over corpse. Make it jump, make it talk.

But it was too late for talk.

He climbed into his own car. He tucked the gloves and the automatic into a plastic bag and slid the bag under the seat. He pulled out of the overlook and drove down the hill, his headlights scraping the concrete and stone embankments that lined the road. His thoughts pounded in his head. This should've been easy. This should've been simple. But the dead man had turned the tables on him.

The dead man had double-crossed him.

You can't trust anyone these days. . . .

I.

"SO WHAT FORM OF SATAN brings you to Las Vegas?" said the clerk behind the rental car counter at McCarran International Airport. He was an older man. Black brush bristle hair, one sleepy eyelid. A sly smile crossed his face as he tapped away at his computer terminal.

Bodo Hagen got the joke. What little there was of it. Las Vegas— gambling, drinking, hookers, dope. All the accepted vices were here for the asking, and a few others besides.

Hagen was back in Las Vegas. After more than ten years.

Hagen was back home.

He'd left Berlin more than twenty-four hours ago. Berlin to Paris. Paris to New York. New York to Chicago. Chicago to here. He'd gotten a little sleep on the Paris to New York leg but not much. He was worn-out and groggy. Too many cups of burned airline coffee had given him a headache.

Twenty minutes later Hagen drove a silver Buick LeSabre sedan off the rental agency lot, headed out into the harsh sunlight and blast furnace heat of the southwestern desert.

He turned left on Tropicana, then right onto Las Vegas Boulevard. Behind him was a casino hotel built in the shape of a pyramid, with a tall sphinx looming over the Strip, its eyes staring at the runways of the airport across the street. To his left stood a Statue of Liberty and a Coney Island roller coaster. Farther down the Strip he passed an Eiffel Tower, a fully rigged pirate galleon, and an Italian campanile looming over a narrow canal where gondolas floated on still, blue waters. They were all casino hotels and Hagen hadn't seen any of them before, except as pictures in magazines or on television.

The Strip had changed a lot in the last decade. The names of the casino hotels alone told the story—the Luxor, the Excalibur, New York New York, Paris Las Vegas, the Venetian, Mandalay Bay, Treasure Island. Las Vegas had been busy in recent years. Busy trying to turn itself into a billion-dollar version of someplace else. But then the Las Vegas that people came to see had always been an illusion. It was simply the scale that had changed. The illusion had grown larger in every way and now walked with giant's feet across the flat desert of the Las Vegas valley.

Hagen checked his watch. He had a little time. On a side street off the north end of the Strip he pulled up in front of a small bar, half surprised to see that it was still there. The white stucco walls were cracked. The red script on the electric sign that hung over the oak door read HIGH NUMBERS CLUB.

The barroom was cool and dark. Two men with sun-parched faces under battered cowboy hats sat at a table in the center of the barroom, silently drinking. A country-and-western song about picking up and leaving town, some town, any town, played on the jukebox.

Hagen stepped up to the bar. Ordered a short beer and a shot of bourbon.

The High Numbers Club had always been a dump. But it was a comfortable dump. The barroom was dark and the beer was cold and the clientele was usually local. And for comedy relief there were the wedding parties that stumbled in from the Desert Rose Chapel next door, freshly pressed and starched and still giddy from a fifteen-minute, two-hundred-dollar Las Vegas wedding. Hagen had spent quite a bit of time in the High Numbers Club years ago, before he left for Berlin. His old man was sick then, sick with the cancer. Hagen didn't hang around long enough to help bury him.

He let his brother Ronnie do that.

The bartender set the glass of beer and the shot on the counter. Hagen downed the bourbon in one splash, then went to work on the beer. A few minutes later he signaled for another round. "Another quick one."

The bartender set the second round in front of Hagen.

"Let me guess," the bartender said. "You're in a hurry to get to a wedding."

"No," Hagen said. "A funeral."

Bodo Hagen had already been in Berlin for several years when he received a letter mailed from Castelnaudary, France. It was a note from Ronnie, telling Bodo that he'd just enlisted in the French Foreign Legion.

Bodo was surprised but not too surprised. Their father had once served in the Legion. He'd never talked about it much, but once or twice, when he was in his cups, Hagen's father had unlocked the wooden footlocker he kept in his closet and shown his two sons his old dress uniform cap—the *képi blanc*, his medals for service in Indochina, and a wooden plaque that had once hung in a Legion command post in Na San, in the mountains of northwest Vietnam, in 1953. The plaque bore the unit crest of the Deuxième Bataillon Étranger de Parachutistes. Engraved underneath the crest was the Legion motto. *Légio patria nostra*—

The Legion is our country . . .

A year later the Deuxième Bataillon Étranger de Parachutistes had been destroyed at Dien Bien Phu.

Hagen's father had been there too.

Bodo received a few more letters from Ronnie after he joined the Legion. The training was tough, his younger brother wrote him, but "sweat saves blood." It was an old Legion maxim that Bodo had heard his father also invoke.

After initial training in Castelnaudary, Ronnie was assigned to a Legion detachment in the Comoro Islands, north of Madagascar. Later he was transferred to the Premier Régiment Étranger in Aubagne, France. Less than two weeks ago he'd gotten out of the Legion and flown home to Las Vegas.

Five days later he was dead.

Bodo Hagen got a phone call late on Friday night in Berlin from a man who had been a close friend of their father. His name was Robert Ipolito but Hagen had always known him as the Sniff. The Sniff didn't know the details, only that Ronnie was killed out at the Hoover Dam. A gunshot to the head.

Hagen asked the Sniff if he'd take care of the funeral arrangements. On Saturday the Sniff faxed him documents to sign that allowed the Sniff to take custody of the body. On Monday the Sniff called to give him the details of the burial and the phone number of the funeral home so that Hagen could pay the tab.

On Tuesday, his affairs in order, Hagen packed a bag and caught a morning flight out of Berlin Tegel Airport for Paris, on his way back to Las Vegas to bury his only brother.

Now it was Wednesday.

The stop at the High Numbers Club had taken some of the edge off and Hagen felt better. He'd needed a drink. He'd probably want a few more before the day was over.

At the cemetery Hagen parked, pulled his gray sport coat on and walked through the front gates. Dried-out flower arrangements littered the brown grass around the grave markers. Hagen spotted a priest and two other men standing at a grave site on the far side of the cemetery.

The priest looked up from the leather-bound Bible he was reading from as Hagen approached.

"The Ronald Hagen service?" the priest said to Hagen, nodding toward the bronze-colored funerary urn that one of the other men held in his hands. The priest sounded hopeful—an audience of three was better than an audience of two. The priest wore a short-sleeve black shirt with a white priest's collar. A crucifix hung from his neck on a gold chain and a rosary with purple beads hung from his hand. A Catholic priest? Ronnie hadn't been Catholic. Maybe the Sniff was Catholic. But it didn't matter, Hagen knew.

6

"He was my brother," Hagen said.

"May I offer my condolences." The priest pulled his sunglasses down on his nose, looked over the tops of the rims at Hagen. "Would you like me to start over?"

"No, that's all right."

The priest returned to his Scriptures. Hagen looked across the small hole dug in the ground at the other two men. He didn't know the short Asian man in the green suit who held the funerary urn before him as though it was a trophy he was showing off. Must've been a cemetery employee. Maybe this was his sole function—holding the ashes of the deceased at graveside services that no one showed up for.

But Hagen recognized the other man. A tall gaunt man in his fifties. A tan linen suit topped by an austere bolo tie. A white Stetson cowboy hat. A pair of dark aviator sunglasses hiding his eyes. His name was John McGrath and the last Hagen had heard he was a cop. A detective. Las Vegas Metro.

McGrath nodded to him.

The priest read on. Hagen watched the sweat roll down the side of the priest's face. Must've been a hundred and ten degrees. The heat made Hagen feel sluggish. Hagen lowered his eyes. The freshly dug earth in the grave at his feet looked parched. The Ronald Hagen service—it was difficult to believe that Ronnie was dead. His only brother. Dead at thirty. He'd survived five years in the Legion only to come home and die.

The priest closed his Bible. McGrath coughed. The man holding the urn looked uncomfortable. The priest turned to Hagen.

"Would you like to say a few words?"

Hagen shook his head. "No."

When the urn was in the grave the priest picked up a handful of dirt and let it fall between his fingers over the urn. Then Hagen did the same. He felt no emotion. The urn was only an urn and the ash inside wasn't much different than the warm earth that now slipped between his fingers. The ash wasn't his brother.

As soon as the priest departed the Asian man handed Hagen a business card, told him to call when he was ready to make arrangements for a grave marker. Then the Asian man hurried off and McGrath stepped up.

"How are you, Bodo?"

"Hello, McGrath."

"I'm sorry about Ronnie."

"What do you know about it?"

"We can talk about it when you're ready."

"I'm ready now."

"Suit yourself."

The two men started off toward the cemetery gates. McGrath lifted the Stetson off his head, smoothed his thin gray hair back on his scalp.

Hagen said, "Are you working the case?"

"I took it over yesterday."

"Would've thought you'd be retired by now."

McGrath tucked a cigarette into the corner of his mouth, lit it. "I'm a tired old dog, Bodo, but I've still got a few teeth left."

McGrath suggested that they go to the station. McGrath could show him the police file. At present there weren't any leads in the case. No witnesses, no hard clues other than the bullet that killed Hagen's brother. The fact that Ronnie had only been in town five days didn't help matters much.

"How did you hear about it?" McGrath said.

"The Sniff called me. He heard it on the news."

McGrath nodded. He knew Robert Ipolito from the old days. He must've also known that the Sniff had taken custody of Ronnie's body. "What else did the Sniff say?"

"Nothing. I asked him to make the funeral arrangements."

"But he didn't show up."

"Why did you show up, McGrath? You weren't close to Ronnie."

"No, I wasn't. But I'd like to know who was. I was hoping that some of them might turn up for his funeral."

"There's only you and me."

As they approached the cemetery gates McGrath said, "Come to think of it, you weren't here for your old man's funeral. He's buried here in this same cemetery. Did you know that, Bodo?"

McGrath offered to show Hagen the grave. The two men followed the low rock wall that surrounded the cemetery, then veered off toward a small barren tree. After a few minutes of searching they found it. A small bluish metal plate lying flat on the ground.

The inscription read simply:

WOLFGANG KARL HAGEN

1926–1991.

2.

WOLFGANG KARL HAGEN WAS CONSCRIPTED into the German Army in 1943 at the age of seventeen. He didn't believe in Hitler. He didn't believe in the Reich. But he believed in his ability to fight and stay alive on a battlefield and he excelled at soldiering.

In April 1944 he was assigned to the Second SS Panzer Division based in France. Six weeks later the Allies invaded Normandy and from that point forward Wolfgang Karl Hagen and his comrades in the tank corps were on the run.

During Von Rundstedt's offensive in the Ardennes in the winter of 1944 the tanks bogged down in the mud, ground themselves to pieces for lack of oil, fell silent when their fuel tanks ran dry. Hagen and his tank crew became foot soldiers, dragging themselves through the mud and snow, Hagen's fingers frozen around the stock of his Mauser rifle, the toes of his boots held closed with twine, his daily rations reduced to what he could find in the rubble of the burned-out villages they passed through. Comrades who weren't killed quickly by a bullet or hand grenade or artillery shell died slowly of sickness and exposure. Hagen decided early on that he'd rather die quickly, die fighting, but through luck or lack of it he survived the war.

There was nothing to go home to afterward. The village along the Rhine River where Hagen grew up had ceased to exist. Hagen wandered through the ruins of what had once been Germany. He met many other people on the roads, all of them sickly pale, half starved and bone-weary as they carried what remained of their belongings in their arms, on their backs, in wheelbarrows and dogcarts.

In time Hagen found himself on a work crew in Frankfurt, moving piles of debris from one place to another. It was there that he decided he'd had enough. Let the others rebuild their Germany. He wanted no part of it. He set out on a journey that eventually led him to Sidi Bel Abbès, Algeria, at that time the home of the French Foreign Legion.

The Legion was quite willing to accept Germans into its ranks. Soon Hagen found himself in Indochina with many other former Waffen-SS soldiers, fighting for the colonial interests of a country that only a few years before he'd helped to occupy at gunpoint. But he and the others didn't see it that way. They weren't fighting for France. They were fighting for the Legion. The Legion was their country—they recognized no other.

But then came Dien Bien Phu. Another abject defeat. The Legion pulled out of Indochina in disarray. Among the politicians in Paris there was talk of disbanding the Legion entirely. Suddenly a career in the Legion didn't look so promising and in 1957, after eleven years in the Legion, Hagen left. He emigrated to the United States on a French passport. He traveled across the country and eventually found himself in the deserts of the American southwest. The landscape was vast, harsh and empty. It seemed to Wolfgang Karl Hagen that he'd arrived at the ragged end of nowhere.

And then one day he drove along Highway 91 to Las Vegas. The city on the edge of nowhere. Money flowed freely and the bright lights burned around the clock. The town was wide-open and howling. A man was limited only by his ability to cough up the jack, the scratch, the greenbacks, the cold hard cash. And there was a lot of cash to be made.

Hagen found employment in one casino, then another. With his military background and his professional soldier's physique he gravitated toward security work. He landed a job at the Sands Hotel casino, dropped the name Wolfgang and became Karl Hagen, casino security officer and general enforcer of the rules.

For thirty years Karl Hagen kept watch over the green felt tables at the Sands casino, looking for the dice sliders, the card counters, the pickpockets, the shiners, the crooked card dealers who pocketed chips, the cage cashiers who pocketed banknotes, coin cup thieves, slot machine slug artists, cooler move operators, camera schemes, big six dealers, card daubers, prostitutes who were too obviously plying their trade. Some of them were rousted out of the casino and told never to return. Some of them were turned over to the police. A few of them were taken out into the back parking lot for a quick hard lesson in casino decorum, then kindly relieved of their winnings.

The first rule in Las Vegas is that the percentage always stays with the house. And it was Karl Hagen's job to enforce that rule, whatever it took.

Bodo Hagen kept one eye on his rearview mirror.

He was being followed.

At the cemetery a black Chrysler parked down the street had pulled out behind Hagen when Hagen pulled out to follow McGrath's Chevrolet. At the first intersection McGrath and Hagen turned left. The Chrysler sped up and took the turn too fast, as though the driver was afraid of being caught at the light and losing sight of Hagen. The driver gained ground, then eased off the gas pedal. Dropped back. Changed lanes. Now he was pacing Hagen from forty yards back.

As Hagen passed through the next two intersections the Chrysler held steady behind him. But a quarter of a mile farther on the Chrysler faded back into the traffic, slowed to make a turn, disappeared.

A false alarm. A touch of paranoia. Hagen chalked it up to nerves. He was tired, probably more tired than he realized. This wasn't Berlin. Anyone who might want to keep him under surveillance was half a world away.

McGrath worked out of Las Vegas Metro's substation on Spring

Mountain Road, not far from the Strip. The building looked like a concrete bunker surrounded by ornamental landscaping. McGrath's office was small and tidy. On one wall hung the plaques and awards accumulated over McGrath's twenty-eight years on the force. The window behind his desk looked out on a row of black-and-white Metro squad cars freshly washed and shining in the sunlight.

"What have you been up to since we last talked, Bodo?" McGrath said when he returned from the break room with two Styrofoam cups of coffee. He set one down in front of Hagen, then stepped around behind the desk.

"When was it, the last time we talked?"

McGrath eased himself into his chair, took a sip of the coffee, made a sour face. "About the same time this pot of coffee was made."

Hagen could remember when McGrath was still a patrol officer, twenty years ago. He'd been one of the men who used to come by the house from time to time to sit out on the patio with Hagen's father, drinking scotch and barbecuing steaks while they talked shop, the ice cubes in their highball glasses rattling together like dice in a cup. Casino security officers sometimes worked closely with the police and Hagen's father had made many friends among the Las Vegas Metro force. Bodo Hagen had also worked at a casino for a time, and he'd run into McGrath once or twice then. Those encounters had been on a more professional basis.

While Hagen gave McGrath a brief and not entirely forthright account of his time in Germany, he studied the older man's face. McGrath's dark eyes seemed to have sunk into the heavily wrinkled skin around them. His cheeks were drawn in and gave him a sickly aspect. A heavy line of sweat left by the sweatband of his cowboy hat circled his matted gray hair, making him look even more unhealthy, like a man caught in the throes of a bad fever. If McGrath was still drinking as much as he used to then maybe it was time for him to lay off the sauce. The cigarettes weren't doing him much good either.

McGrath was interested in Hagen's contact with his brother in recent years. Hagen couldn't help him. In the last five years there had only been the handful of letters he'd received from Ronnie, and the letters hadn't told him much.

"When he was in France, how far away was he from where you were, in Germany?" McGrath said.

"Twelve-hour drive. Maybe a bit longer."

"He was there for two or three years?"

"Three years."

"You didn't see him during that time?"

"No, I didn't."

"Why not?"

Hagen didn't have an answer for that. Why not, indeed? He'd intended to visit Ronnie in Aubagne, but it hadn't happened. "I don't know. Didn't get around to it. What are you getting at, McGrath?"

"Just grist for the mill, Bodo. Don't take offense."

McGrath got up from his chair, retrieved two dark brown file folders from a wire basket on top of a file cabinet, returned to the desk. With one of the folders lying open in front of him he proceeded to give Hagen a description of the case as it stood.

It wasn't much of a case.

Ronnie Hagen was killed by a single gunshot wound to the head. He was in the driver's seat of a rented car parked at a scenic overlook on the east side of Hoover Dam at the time of death. The bullet entered just forward of the left ear, traveled through the skull and exited. The round was found deeply embedded in the passenger seat. The trajectory of the bullet was consistent with a shot fired by someone standing beside the open car window. The medical examiner's report set the time of death between midnight and three o'clock in the morning on the previous Friday. The report from the Firearms Examination Unit indicated that the round was .38 caliber. An analysis of gunpowder residue on the side of the deceased's head was consistent with a shot fired at extremely close range. The gunpowder residue pattern and marks on the round were also consistent with the use of a silencer, possibly homemade.

The fact that none of the security guard staff at Hoover Dam heard a shot fired also suggested the use of a silencer. "An unsuppressed gunshot at Hoover in the middle of the night would carry up and down the canyon quite a ways," McGrath told him. "But no one heard a thing."

The body was discovered by a security guard shortly after four o'clock in the morning and reported to Las Vegas Metro. Hoover Dam was federal land and by rights it was a federal case but the Bureau of Reclamation security guards were in no way prepared to launch a murder investigation and the local Federal Bureau of Investigation office wasn't too interested in pursuing it. So while the case was, on paper, an FBI investigation, the FBI had requested the assistance of Las Vegas Metro, the law enforcement agency responsible for all unincorporated areas of Clark County as well as most of metropolitan Las Vegas.

"The FBI boys say the only federal aspect of the case is the fact that the victim was found in a parking lot owned by Uncle Sam," McGrath said. "They've handed it to us. We'll do the legwork and wrap the case up all nice and tight and then we'll give it to the FBI and they'll act like they knew everything all along. But I'm glad I'm working this case, Bodo. I'm going to find whoever killed Karl Hagen's boy and I'm going to nail his ass to the wall."

"No leads on the shooter?"

McGrath shook his head. "Some good prints in the car, but it was a rental that Ronnie picked up at McCarran the day he flew in, so it's likely that those prints belong to the people who clean the cars there. We're following up though. Forensics vacuumed out the interior of the car but they're still poking through the dust, so we don't have a report on that yet either. The trunk of the car and the glove compartment were tossed after Ronnie was shot, which suggests that it was a robbery, but none of the other facts seem consistent with a robbery. Unless the shooter was someone who knew Ronnie and knew that he had something with him worth stealing.

"The only other thing we know is that the day before your brother died he rented an apartment in East Vegas. He paid the deposit and the first month's rent in cash. We don't know where he stayed before that. We went through the apartment on Saturday—didn't come up with anything. His personal belongings amounted to two suitcases of laundry. But it's early, Bodo. Something's going to turn up."

Hagen pointed at the two file folders. "Can I take a look?"

McGrath pushed the two files across the desk. Hagen studied the labels. One of them was the investigation report. The other file contained the medical examiner's autopsy report.

McGrath got up from his chair, closed the door of his office, then stepped over to the window and opened it a crack. "Mind if I smoke, Bodo?"

"Of course not."

"I've been notified by my betters that this building is now a non-smoking piece of property, but I don't give a shit. I just close the door and puff away. The way they carry on, you'd think I was running an opium den."

While McGrath stood by the window smoking, Hagen opened up the investigation file and began to read.

The accumulated reports, what few there were, corroborated at great length what McGrath had just told him succinctly. But the photographs of the crime scene, contained in a manila envelope, came as a shock. A corpse, hunched over in the front seat, the right arm limp, the right hand lying palm up on the gearshift console, everything in the photograph washed out by the powerful blast of the police photographer's camera flash. The facial profile of the corpse from this angle, shooting inside the car from the open passenger-side door, was nothing but an indistinct mass of torn tissue and dried blood.

Could that be his brother? Could that possibly be Ronnie?

Hagen forced himself to study each of the photographs closely.

When Hagen was done with the investigation file he set it aside, opened the medical examiner's report. The autopsy notes were bare. On a sheet of paper were four outlines of an anonymous nude male body—

front and back, left and right side. The medical examiner had penciled in arrows to reflect the trajectory of the bullet and the injuries to the head. Beside these wound location diagrams the examiner had written the essential information—the estimated time of death, a general description of the body. Cause and manner of death were listed as "massive head trauma resulting from a close proximity gunshot wound." The mode of death was listed as "homicide, unknown person(s)." The examiner had noted the presence of a large tattoo on the upper right arm of the deceased—something Ronnie must have picked up in the Legion. A notation at the bottom of the sheet indicated that the results of the toxicology tests were pending.

The autopsy file also contained a small sealed envelope with a microcasette inside—the medical examiner's *portrait parlé*—and a manila envelope containing the autopsy photographs. The air-conditioning in McGrath's office was strong and cold and the chill of the air against Hagen's skin as he studied the photographs gave him a macabre sense that he could actually feel the coldness of the steel morgue table, the coldness of the exploratory scalpel, the coldness of his brother's pale skin.

Hagen had seen enough. He'd seen what he needed to see. He returned the photos to the envelope, closed the medical examiner's file and pushed both files across the desk toward McGrath, who had finished his cigarette and returned to his chair.

"It's tough, looking at those files," McGrath said.

Hagen got up from his chair. "I'd better get going."

"How long are you in town?"

Hagen didn't know. A couple of weeks, maybe longer. He wanted to look up a few people. Hagen told McGrath where he was staying and McGrath told him to give him a call, once Hagen got settled in. McGrath handed Hagen a business card with his home phone number written on the back. Then McGrath made a call to the property room downstairs, and arranged for Hagen to take possession of his deceased brother's belongings on his way out.

McGrath leaned back in his chair, his elbows on the armrests, his fingers loosely pressed together, fingertip to fingertip. Like he was praying. "Give the Sniff my regards, Bodo. Tell him I'll be dropping by to see him soon too. And Bodo, if you hear anything, you'll call me."

"Sure, McGrath. Thanks for the coffee, or whatever it was."

3.

HAGEN COULD RECALL, when he was a boy, watching the Sniff practice with a deck of cards for hours each day—dealing cards, pulling them in, reshuffling, dealing again. His fingers so fast that it seemed impossible to tell whether the cards were coming from the top or the bottom or the middle of the deck. "What do you want to see, Bodo?" the Sniff would say. Hagen would call out a poker hand and seconds later the Sniff would send those very cards sailing out of the deck and across the table to land face up in front of him. When the cards came up different from what Hagen called out, the Sniff would laugh and say that it was on purpose. "Got to deal a little trash or else the marks will wise up. And we can't wise up the marks, can we?"

When the Sniff came to Las Vegas in the 1950s he was already an accomplished card mechanic. But the Sniff hadn't made his money playing cards. With his skills, working the casino tables night after night would've proven dangerous. The Sniff would have quickly found himself in the "Griffin book," the collection of mug shots and modus operandi that the casinos used to identify the more notorious cheats. And appearing in the Griffin book was nothing but a ticket to a beating or a jail cell or worse. Rather than risk his health or his life, the Sniff had sold his expertise directly to the casinos. Because he knew all the tricks himself, he could spot other card cheats at the gaming tables faster and more often than most of the casino security officers. For a time the Sniff had worked exclusively at the Sands with Hagen's father. In later years the Sniff branched out and became a consultant who provided the

19

security staffs of several casinos with ongoing instruction in the art and artifice of the mechanic.

All the while, the Sniff kept one foot in the Las Vegas underworld of grifters, mobsters and racketeers. The Sniff had a lot of friends. Friends who told him things. Friends who the Sniff sometimes did favors for. And the more favors he bestowed, the more favors he collected. It was a game the Sniff played in the same way he played cards—serious and discreet, with his poker face giving away nothing for free.

The Sniff had connections.

The Sniff had *juice*.

The Sniff lived now in a condominium complex that stood at the edge of a golf course fairway. The complex looked new and clean and tranquil in an anonymous middle-class way. It wasn't at all what Hagen had expected. The Sniff had always displayed a taste for high living. This golf course retirement community didn't look like the Sniff's type of gig at all.

But times had changed.

"You look just like your old man, Bodo," the Sniff said when he answered the door. The voice was thin and raspy, like a metal file scratching slowly against a copper pipe.

"How've you been, Sniff?"

"I'm sorry about Ronnie, Bodo. I truly am."

Hagen followed the Sniff down a short corridor and into a living room lined with bookshelves. On one side of the room stood a baize-covered casino blackjack table with one stool behind it and three more along the front. Across the room a set of heavy drapes were pulled nearly closed across a pair of sliding-glass patio doors. A narrow wedge of sunlight cut across the beige carpet.

"Did you go to the cemetery?" the Sniff said.

Hagen said that he had. "Thought I'd see you there."

"Bodo, I don't go to funerals. You understand."

"McGrath turned up there. He's working the case."

"McGrath? Small world. Is he getting anywhere with it?"

"Spinning his wheels."

The Sniff sat down behind the blackjack table. Situated in front of him were two decks of new cards, a glass full of melting ice, a pack of cigarettes, a gold lighter, and a brown glass ashtray half full of crushed white cigarette butts. A bright circle of light from a ceiling fixture shone down on the center of the table. The Sniff pointed toward the kitchen. "Get yourself a drink. Freshen this one up too, will you? Four fingers of soda and a splash of gin. Doctor's orders. How was your flight?"

"Long."

Hagen stepped into the kitchen and made the drinks. When he returned the Sniff was shuffling a deck of cards. The cards fell together in a soft whisper of motion. The sound of sand flowing into the bottom of an hourglass.

Hagen set the drinks down on coasters and sat down across from the Sniff.

The Sniff didn't look bad. How old was he now? Seventy? Hagen wasn't sure. He'd finally lost all the hair on the top of his head and the pair of metal-framed bifocals that hung down on his chest from a gold chain around his neck were new, but the Sniff looked about the same as he'd always looked. His pale blue eyes under his gray eyebrows were still sharp, as sharp as the creases on his starched burgundy luau shirt.

But the remark the Sniff had made at the door—about Hagen looking like his father—had hit home. In recent years Hagen had watched his face in the mirror as it filled out, became squarer and harder. With the addition of a mustache and a bottle of hair oil to sweep his hair back he would look quite a lot like his father. Hagen found it disconcerting, this growing resemblance to his father, as though he was somehow falling into a life that wasn't his, and that he didn't want.

The Sniff cut the cards and dealt. Two cards slid across the green baize, came to rest in front of Hagen. Then the Sniff dealt himself two cards, one up and one down. The backs of the cards were printed with the name CAESARS PALACE inside a round white oval surrounded by a pattern of red diamonds.

Hagen looked at his cards.

Ten of hearts and deuce of clubs.

The Sniff had a king of diamonds showing.

Hagen said, "Hit."

The Sniff tossed another card across the table. The seven of clubs for a total of nineteen. Hagen turned his cards face up. The Sniff overturned his second card. The king of spades.

"House wins," the Sniff said. He collected the cards. "Bodo, I saw Ronnie last week. Monday night—he'd just gotten into town the day before. He wanted to borrow money. A thousand minimum, more if I could spare it. And he wanted me to set him up with a fence."

"A fence? Why?"

"Why does anybody need a fence? He had something to sell that wasn't his. He didn't say it like that but that's what it sounded like." The Sniff picked up his glass, raised it halfway to his mouth, paused. "Surprised?"

Ronnie had always had a way of finding trouble, Hagen knew. He'd had scrapes with the law when he was growing up. But a fence? Hagen had never known Ronnie to be involved with stolen goods. The whole thing sounded even more odd when Hagen considered the fact that Ronnie had only been in town one day. What kind of trouble had he gotten himself into in one day? Or had he brought some trouble home with him from France?

The Sniff took a long drink, set his glass down. "Ronnie wasn't like you, Bodo. He was different. He was all edge. When he was here last week he came on way too strong. At first I was glad to see him—he brought back a lot of memories. But after five minutes I just wanted him gone. I should've pushed him, found out what was going on. Maybe I could've helped him get out of trouble. But I didn't and there it is. Nothing I can do. Maybe that sounds hard but I'm too old to mince words."

The words did sound hard. But Hagen couldn't argue with what the Sniff said. Hagen knew how his brother could be—crass, thoughtless, short-tempered. Like their father had been. But unlike their father, Ronnie never had any charm to help gloss over the rough spots.

Hagen said, "This thing he wanted to sell—what was it?"

"He said it was a little something he picked up in his travels. Some kind of a relic. Said there might be some baggage behind it, but nothing serious. I didn't ask him what kind of baggage, I figured I knew. He gave me a photograph of the thing to pass on. It was a wooden hand, looked like a carving or something. Didn't mean anything to me. Ronnie called it a dead man's hand. I thought he was trying to be funny. He left me a phone number too, said that if I knew anybody who could keep their mouth shut, to give them the picture and his number and he'd give them the particulars. I said I'd do what I could. Then I dealt him a thousand on account and pushed him out the door. After he left I felt bad about giving him the bum's rush, but not real bad. Next thing I hear, somebody's taken him out. That's when I started feeling real bad."

A dead man's hand—Hagen hadn't heard that expression in years. At a card table it usually meant two pair, aces and eights—the hand of cards that the gunslinger Wild Bill Hickok was holding when he was shot dead in a South Dakota saloon.

But Ronnie had been talking about a wooden hand.

"Can I see the photograph?"

The Sniff coughed, a loose chest-rattling cough. Then, "I passed it on, like I said I would. I sent it over to a fellow I know, name of Martinez. Dallas Martinez. He deals in things that are hard to find. This and that. I gave him the number Ronnie left, told him that if he was interested in the dingus in the picture then he should give the number a call. I talked to him again a few days later, just before I heard what happened to Ronnie. Martinez said the dingus wasn't anything he was interested in. Last I heard about it."

"Martinez is a fence?"

"He takes it as it comes."

"I'd like to talk to him."

"I'll see what I can do. He's funny about who he talks to."

"The money—any special reason why Ronnie needed it?"

The Sniff tapped the edge of the deck on the table. Began shuffling. "He said he found himself a game as soon as he got into town, got himself cleaned out in a hurry."

"Who cleaned him out?"

"I didn't ask. A man loses his wad at the tables—it's not big news."

The Sniff shuffled the cards once more, then cut the deck. He dealt Hagen two cards, face down.

Hagen examined the spread. He had a ten of hearts and a deuce of clubs—the same cards as the last hand. The Sniff had a queen of clubs showing.

Hagen said, "Hit."

A third card landed in front of him. Hagen glanced at it. Also the same as last time—a seven of clubs, for nineteen. Hagen tossed the cards into the center of the table. "I don't suppose that's going to be good enough."

The Sniff glanced at Hagen's hand, then turned over his second card. Queen of diamonds for twenty.

"House wins." The Sniff gathered up the cards.

Hagen said, "McGrath said he wants to talk to you about Ronnie."

"How does he know I saw Ronnie?"

"He doesn't. But he's wondering."

"If you want me to tell McGrath what I just told you, Bodo, that's okay with me. I've been thinking about giving Metro a ring. But I wanted to talk to you first. In case you have your own angle on this."

The Sniff set the deck of cards down and eased himself up from his chair. He walked across the room to a bookcase. When he returned he brought with him a black address book, a ballpoint pen, a small pad of paper. He slid his glasses on, thumbed through the pages of the address book.

"Sniff, how did you get my number in Berlin?"

"Ronnie gave it to me. Gave me your address too. I thought I'd send you a postcard, just in case you'd forgotten the old Sniff. And there's something else Ronnie told me. Maybe it means something and maybe it doesn't."

The Sniff found the page he was looking for. He wrote a name on the pad of paper, and underneath it an address and phone number. The Sniff tore the sheet of paper off, pushed it across the table.

The name written on the paper was Jack Gubbs.

"That phone number—it's the one Ronnie gave me," the Sniff said. "He said he was staying with that fellow until he could find his own place. Do you know that name?"

Hagen didn't.

The Sniff went on. "It rang a bell, when Ronnie told me the name, but I couldn't quite place it. I had someone look into it. Turns out Gubbs works for Marty Ray."

Marty Ray was a name that Hagen knew.

Marty Ray and his brother Jimmy—they ran a small casino off Fremont Street called Diamond Jim's. Hagen had once worked for the Ray brothers, and a few years after Bodo left town the Ray brothers had hired Ronnie to do the same kind of work. Ronnie couldn't have worked for them long though, he'd left town to join the Legion a short time later. So what if Ronnie knew someone at Diamond Jim's well enough to stay with him when he returned to Las Vegas?

Hagen said, "What are you getting at, Sniff?"

"Did you know that Jimmy Ray was murdered?"

"When did that happen?"

"Few years ago. He was at home one night and someone broke in, took some cash off of him and shot him. Quite a bit of cash—two or three hundred G's. Skim money. Everybody knew the Rays were skimming. No one ever fingered who did the job. For a while the talk was that it was a mob hit, because of the way he got it—one shot in the back of the head, execution-style. But I've got it on good authority that it wasn't a mob hit. The mob never gave a shit about the Ray brothers."

The Sniff went on, his voice calm, unconcerned. He might have been talking about the weather or a new pair of Italian shoes he'd just purchased. But the hard fast movements of his hands as he shuffled the cards belied the casual tone of his voice. The Sniff was using the deck like worry beads. "Ronnie was still here and still working for the Rays. He left town a couple of months later. Joined the Legion and disappeared. After Ronnie was gone I heard some loose talk that maybe he knew something about what happened to Jimmy Ray and that's why he left town. Just loose talk, from nobody that matters. I didn't place any stock in it. I'd forgotten about it, but when I heard what happened to Ronnie—I just thought you should know."

Jimmy Ray—murdered. And Ronnie was working for the Ray brothers when it happened. The death of Jimmy Ray was certainly a piece of news. And yet Ronnie had never mentioned it in any of his letters. Hagen didn't like the way the Sniff was splitting hairs. Loose talk or no, if Jimmy Ray's murderer had never been caught, and if Marty Ray had ever had the remotest suspicion that Ronnie might know something about it, Marty Ray would have crucified him.

Hagen tried to get more information out of the Sniff, but the Sniff only shook his head and shuffled his cards, stone-faced. He'd told Hagen all he knew. And all he knew was what he'd heard—loose talk among people who had no stake in what had happened to Jimmy Ray. It probably meant nothing at this point, five years down the road. Still . . .

"I'll have a talk with Marty Ray," Hagen said.

There was a long silence. The Sniff studied Hagen's face, like maybe the Sniff didn't quite remember who was sitting across from him at the table. Hagen thought that the Sniff looked much older now than he had only a few minutes ago. Much older and much more frail.

The Sniff shuffled the deck. Dealt four cards face down into the center of the table. Slapped his open palm down on each one, then sat back and waited.

Hagen reached out, turned each card over, left to right.

Four aces.

"The house always wins, Bodo," the Sniff said. "Remember that. You've been away. Maybe you've forgotten the mechanics of this town. You're just a mark now, no different than any other. And when you're a mark, the house always wins. You catching the drift?"

Hagen caught it.

Before Hagen left, the Sniff made a phone call, then handed Hagen another piece of paper with two more names, two addresses, two phone numbers. One of the names belonged to a man who ran a small gun shop on the northern edge of town. The man nervously ran his tongue back and forth over buckteeth as he led Hagen into a dusty back room full of metal shelves and cardboard boxes. The man had a set of doctored sales records ready to cover the transaction.

"What kind of piece?"

Hagen asked for a Heckler & Koch P9. It was a good solid automatic and one that Hagen was familiar with. The man didn't have that model in stock, but he did have one P7 model. Used, but in good shape. Hagen was familiar with the smaller P7 as well—it was one of the standard handguns carried by the German federal police. The man assured him that it had no history that Hagen needed to worry about.

"You want to take it with you or eat it here?" The man laughed at his wit as he wrapped the automatic in plastic bubble wrap and set it inside a brown paper sack, along with a soft black leather shoulder holster, two spare ammunition clips, three boxes of 9-millimeter cartridges, a small plastic bottle filled with gun lubricant, a cleaning kit.

Hagen hoped he didn't need the pistol.

But he knew Marty Ray—and Marty Ray ran with a tough crowd.

Years ago, on the strength of his father's reputation, the Ray brothers had hired Hagen on as a member of their security staff at Diamond Jim's. It was a mundane sort of security work—mostly keeping the peace at the tables and bouncing bad drunks and pickpockets out the front door. But when the Ray brothers saw that Hagen was good at his job they began to give him other duties. He became a sort of personal aide and general factotum to the two hard-drinking, hard-living brothers. The job turned sour after a while and Hagen was happy to leave it when he was offered employment in Berlin.

The Sniff said that the money taken from Jimmy Ray's place the night he was murdered was skim money, and he was probably right. Hagen recalled one evening in the upstairs office at Diamond Jim's, watching the Ray brothers and a few of their close associates divvying up bundles of money. Hagen's job that night was to sit by the door with a loaded revolver under his coat, his eyes fixed on a bank of video monitors patched into security cameras that covered the casino floor, the elevators, the hallway just outside the door. When the counting was done the bundles of money disappeared into briefcases and the close associates disappeared down the back stairs. Hagen knew that it was money skimmed off the profits of the casino. It was a simple tax dodge. Nothing more or less.

Years later Hagen was surprised when Ronnie mentioned in one of his letters from France that he'd also gone to work for the Ray brothers for a time, doing much the same job as Bodo had.

But he hadn't mentioned that Jimmy Ray was murdered.

Hagen wondered why.

Driving back to the highway after picking up the automatic, Hagen noticed a late-model black Chrysler a block behind him—the same type of car he'd noticed behind him when he'd followed McGrath to the police station.

He wasn't so paranoid after all.

Hagen sped up. The Chrysler followed suit. When Hagen pulled onto Highway 95 heading east the Chrysler had closed the gap between them to seven or eight car lengths. Whoever this tail was, they weren't very good. Either that, or they didn't care whether Hagen saw them or not.

Hagen cruised in the far left lane on the highway. The Chrysler stayed behind him. A highway exit appeared on the right. At the last second Hagen gunned the engine and cut across three lanes of traffic. He cut in front of an exiting pickup truck with only a few feet to spare.

Hagen sped into the curve of the exit ramp. He was going too fast. The car began to drift and Hagen pumped the brakes lightly. The brake pedal was spongy and for a second Hagen felt the car pulling even more to the left, toward the guardrail. Hagen got the Buick back under control and glanced into the rearview mirror. The Chrysler had swerved across the highway and was now riding the rear bumper of the pickup truck Hagen had cut off.

The exit ramp came out at an intersection. The traffic light was red. Hagen pumped the brakes hard as he glanced down the cross street to his left. He saw no traffic. He gave up on the brakes and stepped on the gas pedal. He spun the steering wheel into a hard right turn as he slid into the intersection.

For a second Hagen thought he'd pushed the car too hard. He felt the Buick's rear end sliding, heard the screech of tires skidding on pavement. The front end of the Buick shimmied. Shook. Shuddered. Hagen cursed gutless Detroit machinery.

But he managed to keep the car on the road.

Hagen sped down the street. Halfway down the block he hit the brakes and turned into the entrance of a grocery store parking lot. He spun the wheel around and pulled into an empty parking space among a line of parked cars.

He faced the street.

He could see the light at the intersection as it changed from red to green.

The slow-moving pickup truck appeared in the intersection, with the Chrysler right behind it. The Chrysler swerved around the truck and shot forward down the street. Hagen watched as the Chrysler sped past. There were two men inside the car but Hagen couldn't see them clearly.

But Hagen knew one thing now.

He needed to be careful.

And if Marty Ray was involved in this, he needed to be very careful.

4.

HAGEN SAT AT THE TABLE in his hotel room. The Heckler & Koch automatic lay in pieces before him. With the small cleaning cloth he went about the work of oiling each piece with the gun lubricant. Out the window the hotel casinos along the southern end of the Strip shone in the sunlight. Twenty-four floors below, the traffic was snarled up along Las Vegas Boulevard.

The Strip was ugly during the day—too garish and pretentious. It looked much better at night, when the sparkling casino lights up and down the boulevard created a luminous playground with enough shadows to hide the rough edges and the artifice. The Strip was one of the few places in the world where the rise of the sun every morning was viewed as a great injustice.

During his stopover in New York Hagen had called ahead and booked a room at the Venetian. Hagen hadn't realized until he arrived that the Venetian stood on the site of the old Sands Hotel. The Venetian was a grand hotel—the exterior built in a lavish Italianate style, the interior elegantly appointed—but the Sands had been a piece of Hagen's personal history. The place where his father had worked. The place where Hagen had come as a child to run along the carpeted hallways. Eat free meals in the coffee shop. While away long summer days at the swimming pool. He was Karl Hagen's son and that had given him privileges at the Sands. The Sands had been a second home. Perhaps even more of a home for him than his real one.

But maybe it was better that the Sands was gone. Maybe it was better to bury as much of the past as possible, here in this city of the eternal now. History was a liability in Las Vegas, and the future was no further than the next roll of the dice, the next shuffle of the cards. That's what all the best gamblers said. Sometimes they were right. But sometimes the next roll of the dice or the next shuffle of the cards was a dead end.

Or a dead man's hand.

When Hagen got up to his hotel room he'd searched the black Delsey suitcases that he'd picked up at the police station's property room. Two suitcases—not much to show for five years overseas. Hagen found nothing inside the suitcases that told him anything or helped him in any way.

No wooden hand. Not even a photograph of one.

Ronnie told the Sniff on Monday night that he'd been cleaned out. He needed some cash and he had something he wanted to sell—a wooden hand that he called a dead man's hand. Early Friday morning Ronnie was murdered. Ronnie calling the hand a dead man's hand might just be an odd coincidence, a colorful choice of words that in retrospect took on a significance that it didn't deserve.

But Hagen was going to find out, one way or the other.

He owed that much to Ronnie.

Hagen reassembled the pistol. Dry-cocked it. The action was smooth and tight. Hagen counted out eight blunt-nosed 9-millimeter cartridges from the box, pressed them one by one into the ammunition clip. The golden-jacketed cartridges felt cold and purposeful in his hands. He slid the clip into the pistol. When he slipped the automatic into the shoulder holster and checked himself in the mirror there was only the slightest bulge showing under his sport coat, which was as it should be. His sport coat had been cut by a Berlin tailor who knew his way around a shoulder holster.

The road to Berlin began in Panama—

Hagen arrived in-country with the first assault troops from the Eighty-second Airborne Division in December 1989. Panamanian dictator General

Manuel Noriega had become a loose cannon in Central America and the Bush administration decided it was time to take him down to the pavement. On the flight in the soldiers inside the C-130 were silent. Most of them had no combat experience whatsoever—had never shot at a man, had never been shot at themselves. It had all seemed like a big jolly show during their briefing at Fort Bragg but now, a few miles from the coast of Panama, it looked slightly different. . . .

Hagen was a staff sergeant assigned to a Fourth Psychological Operations Group loudspeaker team. Using banks of loudspeakers carried on a jeep, Hagen and his team spent that first day and night broadcasting prerecorded propaganda messages across the shifting front lines. The messages were supposed to convince the Panamanian Defense Force soldiers to drop their weapons and surrender, but most of the time they succeeded only in drawing fire. Hagen's recollection of those first hours in Panama consisted largely of lying facedown in a dirty street while small arms fire sailed over his head and the placid Spanish voice coming over the loudspeakers spoke of surrender, useless resistance and safe conduct passes at 120 decibels.

Later, when Noriega sought refuge in the Vatican embassy, the Nunciatura, Hagen's team was one of the loudspeaker units ordered to take up positions around the embassy and blast raucous rock-and-roll music at the building around the clock. The army brass wanted to create a wall of sound around the Nunciatura that would keep the assembled representatives of the world press from using surveillance microphones to eavesdrop on the negotiations going on inside the building between Noriega and Vatican officials. Late in the afternoon, in the midst of the earsplitting noise erupting from the loudspeakers, two Americans in civilian clothes appeared and began asking far too many questions. Reporters, Hagen thought, but when he reported their presence to the officer in charge he was quickly corrected—the two men were advisors from the Central Intelligence Agency. The CIA men were intrigued by the work of the PSYOPS teams. Warfare designed to work on the mind— it was right up their alley. One humid evening Hagen spent several hours drinking warm beer and talking shop with one of the advisors, a man named William Severance. Six months later Hagen left the Army and returned home to Las Vegas, took the first job that came his way—security officer at the Ray brothers' casino. It wasn't long before Hagen wondered why he'd ever come back—his father was dying, his younger brother seemed to be headed for a jail cell or a drug overdose, and the Ray brothers were just shady enough that Hagen worried about landing in jail himself. He'd been back more than a year when he received a letter with a Virginia postmark and "Career Placement Service" as the return address. The letter advised him that if he was interested in civilian employment related to his work in the military, he should call the enclosed toll-free number.

When Hagen called he found that he was speaking with the recruiting branch of the CIA.

William Severance was putting together a small team to perform some work in the recently reunited Germany. Severance had been favorably impressed with Hagen in Panama and he recalled that Hagen spoke German. Was Hagen interested in employment with the CIA?

A trip to Washington followed. Hagen found himself sitting in a blue plastic chair in a cold concrete building. There were numerous applications. There were numerous questionnaires. There were reasoning tests. Language tests. Psychological examinations. Physical examinations. Polygraph examinations. Security and suitability examinations. The bespectacled doctors and analysts peered at him over the tops of open file folders and made cryptic notations on yellow legal pads. Hagen began to get the feeling that the smoke detectors in the ceiling hid microphones, the paintings on the walls hid cameras. The testing went on and on, the questions often untenable. Do you have trouble distinguishing voices? True or false, I enjoy reading Lewis Carroll's Alice in Wonderland. *Do you experience feelings of alienation and if so, why? True or false, I find that most of my friendships are hollow. Describe your father, in two words. Describe your mother, in two words. If you could live as a member of the animal kingdom, what animal would you be and why? True or false, I don't like large bodies of water. True or false, I prefer winter to summer. True or false, I'd rather steal than lie. True or false, I'd rather kill than betray.*

Somehow he got the job . . .

* * *

"Jack Gubbs?"

"That's right."

The bleary-eyed man in the green cotton bathrobe who answered the apartment door was a couple of inches taller than Hagen and thirty pounds heavier. His round face was puffy and red. The unkempt mustache hanging under his flat nose looked like a dark stain that the man couldn't quite scrub away.

"I'm Bodo Hagen. Ronnie Hagen's brother."

The man's eyes opened a bit wider. "I was real sorry to hear about what happened to Ronnie."

"Can I talk to you for a minute?"

Gubbs ran the tips of two fat fingers over his regrettable mustache. "Yeah, sure."

Gubbs lived in a back apartment in a yellow stucco complex a couple of blocks off Rainbow Road. A long couch stood against one wall, propped up at one end by a piece of wood. The coffee table in front of the couch was littered with old magazines, two overflowing ashtrays, empty glasses and soda cans, a dirty paper plate. Heavy drapes were pulled closed across the front window.

"You'll have to excuse the mess," Gubbs said, nodding toward the far side of the room, as though the mess was something that was just now occurring in that one dark corner. "So you're Ronnie's brother? Marty Ray's talked about you. You live overseas or something, right? Like Ronnie did." Gubbs imbued the word *overseas* with great suspicion.

"How's Marty these days?"

"He's doing all right."

"You work at Diamond Jim's?"

"Yeah. Graveyard."

"Sorry to wake you up."

"You want a drink?"

Hagen declined the offer. He took a seat on the couch while Gubbs walked into the kitchen, his bare feet making sticking noises on the linoleum. Gubbs's movements were slow and shaky. He couldn't have been more than thirty-five or so, but he moved like an old man. Thirty-five, going on sixty. Gubbs returned with a water glass half full of a clear liquor. As Gubbs sat down in an armchair next to the couch Hagen caught the smell of peppermint.

Schnapps—for breakfast. Gubbs had a rough diet.

"I understand Ronnie stayed here last week," Hagen said.

"He needed a place to crash. I told him he could stay here as long as he wanted. He showed up a week ago Monday, I think. Yeah, Monday night. Stayed for a couple of nights and then he found an apartment someplace, I'm not sure where."

As Gubbs worked on his schnapps he told Hagen that he and Ronnie had both started working for the Ray brothers at Diamond Jim's at the same time. They'd hung around together quite a bit back then. But Gubbs didn't hear from Ronnie after Ronnie joined the Legion. Gubbs was surprised when Ronnie suddenly appeared out of the blue the week before. "He gets back into town and a few days later he gets killed. I couldn't believe it when I heard."

"Did Ronnie say anything about being in trouble?"

"Shit, he wasn't here long enough to get into trouble."

"I heard he lost quite a bit at the tables."

Gubbs swirled the liquor around in his glass. "I wouldn't know about that."

"Did my brother leave any of his belongings here?"

"No, nothing. Didn't have much with him. Just a suitcase."

"Just one?"

"That's all I saw."

"Did Ronnie say anything about a wooden hand he wanted to sell?"

Gubbs frowned. "What's that supposed to mean?"

"It means a hand, made out of wood. That he wanted to sell."

"I don't know what you're talking about."

"Why did Ronnie need a fence?"

"A fence?" Gubbs laughed out of the corner of his mouth. His eyes darted around the room, finally landed on a spot on the wall several inches to one side of Hagen's head. "I don't know who you've been talking to, but maybe you've gotten hold of some bad information. All I know is, Ronnie showed up and he needed a place to stay and I told him he could stay here. We had a few drinks and talked about old times, and then he gets a place of his own and he takes his stuff and leaves. A couple of days later I hear that he's dead."

"How did you hear about it?"

Gubbs looked squarely at Hagen now. "Marty told me. He heard it on the news. Listen, let me ask you something—do you always make noises like a cop? I don't dig this interrogation bullshit."

"Ronnie was my brother, Gubbs. Someone murdered him. I'm trying to piece together what happened when he got into town. If I can do that, maybe I can find out who killed him. You're the only person I know of who spent any time with him. I just want to know what you know."

"You've been talking to someone else. Sounds like they know more than I do. You're better off sticking with them."

Gubbs took another drink. From somewhere outside Hagen heard the squeal of small children playing. The lively sound was incongruous with the pall inside Gubbs's apartment. Gubbs went on. "Shit, I was working most of time. I didn't see him that much. That's all there is. If he got into trouble at the tables, I don't know about it. You sure you don't want a drink? You act like maybe you could use one."

When Hagen didn't respond Gubbs pulled himself out of the armchair, walked across the room. He pushed the drapes aside and peered out the window, then came back and took up a position in the kitchen doorway, his glass in one hand. Gubbs wanted to put some distance between himself and Hagen. Gubbs was nervous.

"There's one thing," Gubbs said, like he'd just thought of it. "Maybe you're interested. One night when Ronnie was staying here he showed up at Diamond Jim's. I wasn't there but some other people who were around when Ronnie worked there saw him and I heard about it from them. Ronnie might've spent some time at the tables that night. But if he lost some large, I didn't hear that."

"What night was it?"

"Might've been Tuesday."

"Did Ronnie talk to Marty?"

"I don't see how."

"Why?"

"Marty was out of town."

"When did he get back?"

"Maybe you'd better ask Marty."

"Maybe I'd better."

Hagen moved to get up from the couch. He let his arm brush open his sport coat. Gubbs caught a glimpse of the holstered pistol underneath.

"So you *are* a cop."

Hagen stood. "No, but I've talked to them. They don't know about you. They're running a murder investigation, Gubbs. They'd be interested in talking to you."

"I'll talk to them. Why not?"

"Why haven't you talked to them already? Ronnie was murdered last week. He was your friend. Most people would've called the police and told them what they knew. But you didn't call them, Gubbs. What is it you don't want them to know?"

"Maybe I'm just not civic-minded."

"That's not the right answer."

"Who told you about me?"

Hagen didn't respond. Apparently Ronnie hadn't told Gubbs about his visit to the Sniff and how Ronnie had left Gubbs's phone number with him. Good. It gave Gubbs something else to wonder about. Maybe keep him a little worried.

"Straighten me out, Gubbs. What kind of trouble was Ronnie in?"

"I don't know. I mind my own business."

"Talk to me or talk to the police."

Gubbs set his drink down. He removed a pack of cigarettes and a lighter from the breast pocket of his bathrobe. The cigarette he pulled from the pack was crooked but Gubbs didn't bother to straighten it out before he lit it. Hagen found an empty white envelope amid the clutter on the coffee table. He wrote his name and the Venetian's phone number on the envelope, then stepped over to Gubbs.

"Listen, Gubbs. Ask around. I want to know what kind of trouble Ronnie got into. I think you know where to look. I want some names."

Gubbs said nothing. Hagen waited for him to take the envelope but Gubbs was frozen in place. Hagen tossed the envelope onto the seat of the armchair. Then Hagen grabbed the front of Gubbs's bathrobe. Pushed him hard against the wall. Gubbs's head bounced off the plasterboard with a hollow thud. The cigarette fell from his mouth. Hagen ground the burning cigarette into the carpet with the toe of his shoe.

"I'll give you a day, Gubbs," Hagen said. "If I don't hear from you by tomorrow night, I'm coming back. When I get done with you the police will be right behind me, and they'll have a crack at you too. Understand?"

The fearful look on Gubbs's face seemed genuine.

Hagen left, closing the apartment door softly behind him on the way out.

Walking out to his car Hagen wondered what he'd just set in motion. He'd set Gubbs to thinking. Now Hagen would give him time to think. Let him twist in the wind for a day, wondering what Hagen knew and who Hagen was talking to. Wondering whether he'd rather talk to the police or to Hagen.

Hagen had cast a net.

Now he'd see what he could catch with it.

Ronnie might've turned out like Gubbs. Drinking alone in an empty apartment. The long dark hours preying on his mind while helplessness and self-pity collected in the corners of the room. Weighing him down. Like cement shoes.

A drowning man, sliding down into oblivion.

Ronnie was drinking hard when Hagen got out of the army and returned to Las Vegas. Harder than a twenty-year-old man had any right to drink. And he'd picked up an amphetamine habit. Ronnie hadn't thought anything of it, had even handed Hagen the plastic bag full of green and white pharmaceutical capsules, telling him to take what he wanted. Ronnie ate them by the handful. Mixed them with the booze. Ronnie laughed it off, assured his older brother that he knew what he was doing. Sure, he dabbled in drugs, "But I never stuck a needle in my arm." As though this was the one sure sign of virtue in all things.

Hagen blamed their father. That was what it always came back to. A background in the Waffen-SS and the French Foreign Legion hadn't prepared Karl Hagen to raise children. Things might have worked out all right if their mother hadn't died shortly after Ronnie was born. But she had, and suddenly Karl Hagen had two young sons to raise and no inclination to learn how to raise them. What was there to learn? Karl Hagen had believed that he knew all he needed to know about handling young men.

And Ronnie, being much younger than Hagen, caught the brunt of it.

Hagen could remember when the mere sound of their father's car pulling into the driveway could send Ronnie into a fit of terrified sobbing. Hagen remembered the long red welts on Ronnie's legs from the swift bite of the leather belt, and the small scabs where the metal belt buckle broke the skin. More than once Ronnie had tried to run away from home to escape the angry tirades of their father. But running away only made it worse when their father found him and brought him home.

As Ronnie grew up and their father grew older and more sickly, things changed. Ronnie began to fight back, the two of them often coming to blows. Hagen saw it as a good sign. Ronnie had spirit. He was willing to stand up for himself. Fighting back was better than being beaten down into nothing. But when Hagen returned to Las Vegas from the army he saw the drinking and the pills. Ronnie was looking for peace in oblivion.

Shortly after Hagen left for Germany their father died. Hagen hadn't been able to return to take care of things, hadn't particularly wanted to. Karl Hagen was dead—so be it. Ronnie kept his distance too—a lawyer took care of the affairs of the funeral and the estate. But Karl Hagen was gone, and with him went the source of Ronnie's turmoil. Hagen assumed that the bitter war between Ronnie and their father must necessarily be over.

If only things were that easy.

When Hagen received that first letter from Ronnie, telling him that Ronnie had joined the Legion, it made no sense at first. Then the answer came to him. The Legion had been their father's home and the source of his pride. By joining the Legion, Ronnie was going off to fight one last battle with the ghost of their dead father. If Ronnie survived the Legion, it would be a great victory. He would win at their father's game and in that way prove to himself that he was as strong and hard as Wolfgang Karl Hagen had ever been.

And Ronnie did survive the Legion.

But he didn't survive coming home.

Hagen drove out to East Las Vegas.

He wanted to take a look at the apartment that Ronnie rented the day before he was murdered. He'd made a note of the address when he read the police reports in McGrath's office. An address out on Toledo Road.

The address belonged to a narrow, termite-eaten building that had once been a motel. Weeds grew in the deep fissures that crisscrossed the asphalt parking area. The electric sign out front hung from a crooked post: EL DORADO APARTMENTS—WEEKLY AND MONTHLY RATES.

Hagen found the manager's apartment and knocked. The woman who answered the door was elderly, her face pinched and hard.

Hagen introduced himself. He was here to pick up the belongings of his deceased brother. The woman peered at him. "You have identification?"

Hagen handed the woman his passport. She studied the photograph and the name, then leafed through the following pages, as though the assortment of entry stamps from around Europe would vouch for Hagen's identity in a way that a mere photograph could not.

"I've never seen one of those," the woman said, handing the passport back. Hagen assured her that it was the standard issue. She didn't care whether it was or not. "There isn't anything here that belongs to your brother. The police were here Saturday and took everything. That's the first time we've had police here."

"Did he have any visitors while he was here?"

"He was only here for a day. That's all I know. When the police left I cleaned up after them. It's been cleaned up good. It's back in the newspaper now."

"Can I take a look?"

"I'm busy."

Hagen pulled out his wallet. Just a quick look around. Wouldn't take long. He'd be happy to pay her for her time and trouble.

The woman took the twenty Hagen offered without a word.

The inside of apartment number seven smelled of cleaning solvent. A gray-striped mattress on a metal frame stood on one side of the tiny room. On the other side was a narrow counter with a small sink. A microwave oven sat on the counter and pushed underneath the counter was a small white refrigerator.

Hagen walked around the room. Not many hiding places in here. Even for an item as small as a wooden hand. He looked into the closet, pushed against the walls inside, but the walls were solid. In the bathroom he lifted the lid of the toilet cistern. He prodded the bare mattress on the bed and felt around underneath the sink counter. Nothing. Hagen knew he was grasping at straws. The manager stood in the open doorway, arms folded across her chest. "The microwave comes with the apartment," she said, afraid that Hagen might try to carry it off.

Hagen left his phone number with the woman, asked her to call him if anyone came around asking about his brother. Anyone at all. The woman didn't say yes and she didn't say no, but she took another twenty-dollar bill when Hagen handed it to her.

Driving back to the Venetian Hagen saw no sign of the black Chrysler that had followed him earlier. Maybe his watchers had grown tired—whoever they were. Or maybe better men were following him now. When he returned to his hotel room he found a telephone message waiting for him. It was from the Sniff. Asking Hagen to call him, first thing.

"Bodo, I got in touch with Martinez," the Sniff said when Hagen returned the call. "He doesn't have the photograph. He passed it on to somebody else he thought might be interested in that wooden hand—a guy named Sidney Trunk. I don't know the guy but I've heard of him. He's a fence from way back, and not too particular about the toys he plays with. He operates out of his house in Boulder. Martinez talked to him tonight and Trunk agreed to talk to you, if you want to go out there. One thing, Bodo—Trunk told Martinez something that was kind of funny."

"What was that?"

"Trunk said he talked to Ronnie about the hand a couple of days ago."

"Ronnie was dead a couple of days ago."

"That's what's kind of funny."

5.

HAGEN WONDERED ABOUT what the Sniff had said. This man Trunk had talked to Ronnie a couple of days ago? Trunk had spoken imprecisely, that was all. Or perhaps this fellow Martinez had misreported what Trunk said. Hagen dialed the number the Sniff had given him. He stood at the hotel-room window with the receiver to his ear. Below him the bright lights of the Strip filled the night. A glittering electric highway, cutting through the black desert.

"Hello?"

"Mister Trunk? My name is Bodo Hagen."

"Yes, Mister Hagen?" The voice was deep and muddy. A burst of static came across the line, sounded like bacon frying in a skillet.

"Mister Trunk, I'd like to talk to you about some business my brother had with you."

"What's your interest in this? Are you representing your brother?"

"My brother is dead."

"That's what I've been told. My condolences. But the question remains, are you picking up where he left off?"

"I might be."

"You don't sound certain."

"I don't know where he left off."

"We had a transaction under discussion."

"When did you talk to him?"

"Monday night. I asked him to meet me here in Boulder. I wanted to discuss an item he had for sale. He didn't show up at the appointed time and I didn't hear from him again."

"Mister Trunk, my brother was murdered last Friday."

There was another burst of static on the line. Followed by a long silence. For a moment Hagen thought he'd lost the connection. Then, "Interesting news, Mister Hagen. Mister Martinez informed me today only that your brother had died. I wasn't told when or how. Yes, interesting news. . . ." Trunk's voice trailed off.

"This man who said he was my brother, did you talk to him in person?"

"You ask a lot of questions, Mister Hagen."

"I'm wondering who you spoke with."

"I'm wondering too. But I'm not sure it changes things for me. With all due respect to the memory of your brother, my interest extends only to purchasing the item he had for sale."

"Maybe I've got the item."

"You still don't sound certain."

"All right, let me make it more solid. I'm sure I can get the item. But first we've got to scratch out a deal. And I'm going to want to deal in person. What do you say, Mister Trunk?"

"You'll bring the item?"

"No, I won't bring the item. Not until we talk."

Hagen heard the phone receiver being shifted around on the other end. Trunk sighed. Then the deep muddy voice said that he had other business to take care of right then, but he was free later that night. Could Hagen meet him at one o'clock? Trunk gave Hagen an address in Boulder City.

"Do you always take care of business in the middle of the night?" Hagen said.

"Does it bother you?"

"Just curious, Mister Trunk."

"Don't get too curious, Mister Hagen."

Trunk said something further but his voice sunk down into another ball of telephone static and Hagen didn't catch it. Then the static disappeared as Trunk hung up the phone.

Hagen washed his face, put on a fresh shirt. It was just after nine o'clock. He could've used a couple of hours sleep but he knew he wouldn't sleep now. Trunk must've been wondering if Hagen was on the level but that was all right. Let him wonder. Hagen would string him along until he found out what this wooden hand was, what it was worth. And more than that, Hagen wanted to know where he could find this man that Trunk talked to on Monday night. The man who claimed to be Ronnie.

Hagen dropped ice from the ice bucket into a glass. Filled the glass with water. Drank it down while he sat on the couch next to the window. Hagen wondered about Gubbs, whether or not he was the man. Ronnie had left Gubbs's phone number with the Sniff. Had Trunk been given the same number?

Gubbs—one of Marty Ray's boys. Hagen wondered how close Gubbs was to Marty Ray. Hagen shook the ice around in his glass, poured some ice into his mouth and chewed on it. He had a few hours to kill before his appointment with Trunk but he didn't feel up to a meeting with Marty Ray right now. He was tired. He'd talk to Marty Ray tomorrow. First thing. If he could scare him up.

Hagen pulled out his wallet, removed one of the pieces of paper the Sniff had given him. The one with the two names, two numbers, two addresses. He picked up the phone and dialed the second number.

A woman answered.

The sound of her voice stirred up memories for Hagen. Memories that had lain unstirred for many years. Earlier he hadn't been sure he wanted to call her but right now, hearing her voice, he was sure.

"Hello, Peach."

"Bodo, is that you?"

"Sure it is. How are you?"

"I should be asking you. I read about what happened in the newspapers. I couldn't believe it was the same Ronnie Hagen so I called the

Sniff. He told me it was. I wish there was something I could say. The Sniff said you were coming home so I told him to give you my number. In case you wanted to call. In case you needed anything."

"I'm fine, Peach. I don't need anything."

"You used to say that a lot. It wasn't always true."

"It's true. But thanks for asking."

Maxine Peach said that she was off work for the next couple of days. She asked Hagen if he wanted to drop by her place that night. She'd just moved into a new apartment off Warm Springs Road, out in Henderson. They could have a drink. They could talk. Eat dinner. Whatever. It would be good to see him.

Hagen said he had some things to do later that night in Boulder City but maybe he'd drop by on his way out there. Just for a drink. Just to talk.

Peach said, "What do you have to do in Boulder in the middle of the night?"

"Business. Nothing much."

Peach started to say something. Paused. Said something else. "I was thinking about ordering Chinese take-out."

"Sounds great."

"Then I'll see you in a bit."

Hagen hung up the phone.

Maxine Peach—she sounded just the same. They'd spent a lot of time together, ten years ago. They'd had some fun. But things had fallen apart when he told her he was leaving town, going to Germany. He recalled that last day in Las Vegas. He'd wanted to see her before he left. Put aside the hurt feelings and just be friends again. He was flying out to New York at eight o'clock in the evening and he arranged a late lunch for the two of them at the Aristocrat. But she didn't show. He ate his last meal alone.

It was her way of saying good-bye.

Hagen had just gotten up off the couch when the phone rang. He assumed it was the Sniff again. He was wrong.

"Mister Hagen?" A woman's voice. A French accent. "My name is Suzanne Cosette. I was involved in a business matter with your brother, Ronald Hagen. I was very sorry to hear that he passed on. I'm here in town for only a day or two and I had hoped to meet with him. I was wondering if perhaps you could help me to get this matter straightened out. . . ."

Twenty minutes later Hagen stepped out of the Venetian. The night air enveloped him like a warm blanket. It was nearly ten o'clock but the temperature outside hovered around one hundred degrees.

A walkway led around the side of the hotel and out to the street where a pedestrian bridge arched over the Strip. Hagen crossed over the bridge, then walked down the street and up the long circular drive that led to the front doors of the Mirage, almost directly across the street from the Venetian.

The woman had asked him to meet her there.

Suzanne Cosette—she was some type of an antiques dealer, she'd said. "Antiquities and artifacts"—that's how she'd phrased it. She'd stopped in Las Vegas on her way from Paris to Los Angeles. She said she'd spoken to Ronnie in Paris a few weeks ago about something he wanted to sell. He'd left Paris before she could look into the proposition closely but she'd been in touch with him since then. She didn't say how or when. And she didn't say how she'd found Hagen. But she wanted to meet with him. At the Mirage—in half an hour.

She hadn't mentioned what it was she wanted to buy but she didn't need to. Hagen knew what it was.

The atrium bar inside the Mirage was surrounded by lush rain forest vegetation dotted by orchids and other bright tropical flowers. The glass dome over the atrium rose a hundred feet over the casino floor. Hagen found the woman sitting at a table that stood in the shadow of a tall palm tree.

She was young—not more than thirty years old. Short and thin with a sharp nose and brown hair wrapped in a circular manner at the back of her head. Hagen knew it was her from the blouse she'd described to him on the phone. A black silk blouse with two Chinese dragons embroidered on the front. The curling gold and red dragons were positioned nose to tail to form a yin and yang design. The dragons spit tongues of flame as they chased each other's tails.

"Good evening, Mister Hagen," the woman said as Hagen sat down. She tossed a business card across the table. A hesitant smile crossed her face. The card was printed on expensive cream-colored card stock, the name of her firm embossed in red—AMARANTOS ANTIQUITÉS, 27 RUE JEAN GOUJON, PARIS, 75008. The firm's phone number appeared on the face of the card. A second phone number was handwritten in blue ink on the back.

"Would you like a drink?" the woman said.

Hagen set the card aside. "Am I going to be here long enough for a drink?"

"That is entirely up to you."

Hagen settled back in the chair. The woman studied him from under thin arching eyebrows. The drink on the table in front of her was a colorful one in a fluted glass with a white straw. The tip of the straw was covered with her red lipstick.

"Suppose you tell me how you know who I am and where I can be found. Then maybe I'll know how long I'm going to be here."

"It wasn't so difficult, Mister Hagen." The woman's smile grew larger, more assured. She took a sip from the drink. Her fingers were pale white and thin and delicate. Fragile porcelain fingers. "I went to your brother's apartment house yesterday, the place where he was staying. It was the landlady who told me that he passed away. I asked her if she would call me if anyone else came looking for your brother. She called me this evening to tell me that you had been there. She gave me your name and the hotel where you are staying."

"For a small consideration."

The woman shrugged. "For a small consideration, that's right."

Hagen thought of the elderly woman at the El Dorado Apartments.

Hagen had paid her to tell him the same thing. The woman had a good side business going in surveillance. Hagen wondered how much Suzanne Cosette had given her. Apparently more than Hagen had, since she'd told Cosette about Hagen's visit but hadn't mentioned Cosette's visit to him.

"Let me offer my deepest sympathies, Mister Hagen," Cosette said. "Losing a brother is so tragic."

"Did you know him well?"

"I'm afraid I didn't know him at all."

"But you met him in Paris—that's what you said on the phone."

"I must have misspoken. It was one of my associates who met with him in Paris. I did not have that pleasure myself." The woman's eyes held his gaze. Her accent was heavily French but she'd learned her English well. Well enough, Hagen supposed, to know that she'd finessed the truth on the phone.

The woman fidgeted with the thin black strap of a small purse that lay on the table. "But let me tell you why I wanted to speak with you. Let us get down to the brass tacks."

"I don't think my brother was selling brass tacks."

The woman laughed softly. Hagen cocked one eyebrow and smiled. A cocktail waitress appeared. Hagen ordered a drink, bourbon and soda. The waitress moved off. Hagen studied a swarthy young man in a stiff green blazer standing at the bar. He'd been looking over at the table where Hagen and Cosette sat—Hagen had caught it out of the corner of his eye. The young man's eyes fell to his watch now. He frowned as though he were late for an appointment. Finished his drink quickly, left the bar.

"You know that man?" Hagen said.

Cosette looked confused.

"That fellow who just walked out."

Cosette looked past Hagen's shoulder in the direction of the casino floor but the man was gone. "Who do you mean?"

Hagen let it pass. He was keyed up, suspicious of everything. Maybe he was too suspicious but he didn't think so. Someone had followed him from the cemetery and then later, when he left the Sniff's house. He hadn't imagined that. He had good reason to be suspicious.

Hagen said, "Let's start with Paris and work our way out here. That's a lot of ground to cover. I'm interested in how you're going to cover it."

"I can understand that you have questions, Mister Hagen. Let me lay some of them to rest. Things are not so very complicated as you are thinking."

"I'm glad to hear it."

Cosette sat back in her chair. Her tone was cool and professional, a businesswoman explaining the facts. "Let me tell you something about the firm I represent. Amarantos Antiquités is one of the oldest dealers in rare historical artifacts in Paris. Don't get the wrong idea—my firm is not a little shop where tourists can purchase the broken Louis Philippe tables and the imitation Fabergé eggs. We deal in the truly historic— ancient coins, medieval armaments, religious artifacts, illuminated manuscripts, all of these types of things. Much of our business is with auction houses in Europe and here in America but we also offer our services to private accounts.

"Your brother came to our offices in Paris a few weeks ago and spoke to one of our representatives. He said that he had acquired a certain artifact that he believed was valuable. He had the impression that we might sell the piece for him on a consignment basis, but my firm does not generally work in that fashion. Also, there was a question of authenticity. Research needed to be performed before we could even begin to determine whether or not the piece was of any real value. Before we could complete that research your brother left Paris. However, he left instructions as to where we might contact him in Las Vegas should the firm decide that it wanted to pursue the purchase of the piece.

"As it happens, my firm has decided that the piece might be a worthwhile acquisition. I was on my way to Los Angeles on other business and it was decided that I should stop here and talk to your brother and examine the artifact firsthand. I arrived only yesterday and went to see him at his residence. That was when I was informed that he had passed on, I'm sorry to say. I have a certain flexibility in my schedule so I decided to stay on here for a day or two longer and see if I could contact your brother's family in the hope that the artifact is now in the family's possession. I must admit that I didn't find the prospect of spending a longer time in Las Vegas unappealing. I have never been here before. It is an interesting city, isn't it?"

"It has its ups and downs."

Cosette smiled. "Yes, I understand. All of these games of chance— they can be treacherous."

"This artifact—tell me about it."

"I can do one better, Mister Hagen. Let me show you."

Cosette opened her purse, removed a small white envelope. She slipped a photograph out of the envelope and handed it to Hagen.

It was a small color photograph. A picture of a wooden hand made of dark polished wood. A left hand, with the middle finger broken off at the second joint, the other fingers curled inward slightly, the thumb curled in toward the index finger. A wide black band that looked like it was made of some substance other than wood circled the wrist of the hand. The hand lay on a piece of crumpled brown shipping paper. There was a patch of glare in the upper right-hand corner of the photograph from the camera's flash unit.

Hagen studied the photograph.

"How is your understanding of Russian religious history, Mister Hagen?"

"Not as good as it might be."

"No matter. This is nothing one could easily find in the history books." Cosette stirred her drink with the straw. She nodded at the picture Hagen held in his hand. "That wooden hand—it may have come from a piece of statuary that for many years stood in the chapel of a monastery in northern Russia. The monastery belonged to the Russian Orthodox Church and is located on the banks of a river not far from the town of Vologda. The monastery still exists although it is mostly a ruin now. The statue itself was crafted in the mid-nineteenth century. It was a representation of the adult Jesus and it is noteworthy for one very peculiar reason—the craftsmen who created it gave the statue certain articulated features. The fingers of the hand as well as the wrists, arms, and neck were fashioned in such a way as to allow them to be moved into different positions. It isn't clear what the craftsmen had in mind by doing this—very little is known about them or the monks who commissioned the statue. Perhaps it was only an artistic flourish—something the craftsmen added to the statue because they knew how to.

"But one thing we do know is this—the monastery was looted at the time of the Russian Revolution by a band of local rogues. The statue fell into their hands. The town of Vologda stands five hundred kilometers north of Moscow. The winter months are cold and long and the men who looted the monastery had more practical uses for a wooden figure of Jesus than the monks of the monastery. They cut the statue up into small pieces for firewood.

"Or so it was believed.

"Fifteen or so years ago a man in Vienna purchased for next to nothing a life-sized wooden carving of the head of a bearded man. The carving was not in good shape—the left side of the face bore deep gouges in the wood that were most likely made by the blade of a hatchet. The neck portion of the carving had clearly been roughly cut from some larger artifact, probably with the same hatchet."

Cosette looked at Hagen with a grave expression. "But this particular buyer had a great interest in Russian artifacts. He could see even through the damage wrought to the carving that it bore features that were consistent with a Russian origin and he decided to research the head. During a visit to Saint Petersburg he found a description of the Vologda Jesus in a journal that was kept by one of the monastery monks at the turn of the twentieth century. Based on that description he identified the wooden head as having belonged to the Vologda Jesus. There have been disputes about this identification, as there always are, but one collector of religious iconography was convinced enough of the head's pedigree to purchase it for what was probably a good price— eighty thousand dollars. I assisted him in that purchase and the head now rests in his private collection.

"That sale occurred six years ago. Since that time this collector has actively searched for other pieces of the Vologda Jesus, on the assumption that if the head has survived, other pieces may also still exist. That collector remains a client of Amarantos and we have helped him with his inquiries. We haven't held out a great deal of hope. To see one piece of the statue resurface after seventy years was incredible. To find a second piece would be—well, the odds are clearly against us.

"And then your brother came to our offices in Paris with this photograph of a wooden hand. He wasn't entirely sure of what he had. He mentioned the Vologda Jesus although he did not seem to know much about the history of the statue. He was also less than specific as to how and where he acquired the artifact. An associate of mine spoke with him and told him we would get back to him shortly, and your brother left this photograph with us. I was away from Paris at that time and I didn't get the chance to speak with your brother or examine the actual piece. By the time I returned your brother had left Paris.

"And that is why I am here now."

Hagen's drink arrived. Hagen laid the photograph down and reached for his wallet to pay but Cosette told the waitress to put the drink on her tab. Hagen didn't argue.

"So you're certain this hand came from the statue."

"That remains to be seen—as I've said." Cosette absently scratched the patch of exposed skin at the base of her throat. "I have yet to see the actual piece. But I am the person who brokered the sale of the Vologda head. I am familiar with the raw materials and the craftsmanship that went into the making of the statue. If I could see the actual hand I believe I could determine its authenticity or not with a fair degree of certainty. But judging from the photograph, it is my opinion that the hand could well be from the Vologda Jesus."

Hagen picked up his glass and took a drink. Cosette watched him closely. She had told him quite a story. Hagen tried to imagine Ronnie in Paris, walking into an upscale shop and tossing around a photograph of a wooden hand, not wanting to talk too much about how he had come to possess it. It was difficult. The Ronnie that Hagen knew had been no dealer in antiques. And he'd been no student of history.

"What would it be worth?" Hagen said.

Cosette cocked her head to one side. "The Vologda head was sold for eighty thousand dollars six years ago. I would say that the hand could realize at least that much now."

"And what would it be worth to me?"

"A percentage of our expected sale price."

"What's to stop me from cutting you out and selling the hand myself?"

Cosette smiled. Her blue eyes turned colder. She seemed to have been waiting for this question. "For one thing, you don't know where to find the individual who is interested in paying the top price for it. And if you were to take the step of making it known that you had the hand in your possession and wanted to sell it, you might be taking a substantial risk. You might even find yourself involved with the police. I don't know as yet how your brother acquired the hand. There may be *entanglements*. However, assuming that the hand is genuine, my firm is willing to pay you a percentage of what we think we can realize on the sale of the hand and assume all of the risks."

"You're saying the hand is stolen."

"I am saying only that it is a possibility. My firm is making inquiries right now. But these things must be done discreetly and they take time. On the other hand, if we want the hand we have to purchase it while it is available. Which is right now. So we are in the awkward position of possibly purchasing a piece that we are not entirely comfortable with. But as I say, we're willing to assume that risk." Cosette leaned forward, set her elbows on the table, folded her hands. "And that brings us to the brass tacks. Your brother's belongings—I take it they are in your possession now?"

"Yes, they are."

"Have you seen this piece among them?"

"I might have."

"I would think you would know, one way or the other."

"Right at the moment, Suzanne, I'm more interested in what you know. I still have a few questions. For instance, how did you contact my brother after he left Paris?"

A thoughtful look came over Cosette's face. "I'm not exactly sure, Mister Hagen. I suppose he must have left his address with the gentleman he spoke to at our Paris office. As I say, I didn't speak to your brother myself. I was given his address before I left Paris and told to contact him when I arrived here. I'm not aware of the nature of his communications with us."

"What address were you given?"

"The address for his apartment here. Do you find that odd?"

It didn't sound right at all. Ronnie had stayed with Gubbs when he arrived in Las Vegas. A few days later he rented the apartment over in East Las Vegas. Hagen considered it unlikely that Ronnie knew that he'd be staying at the El Dorado Apartments before he'd left Paris. Highly unlikely. And yet that was the address Cosette had been given. Either Cosette was lying, or Ronnie had contact with Cosette's people in Paris after he'd arrived in Las Vegas and rented the apartment. But if Ronnie was that interested in continuing his discussion with Cosette's people, why leave Paris? Why pack up and fly halfway around the world?

The woman's story didn't quite wash. Hagen thought again of the black Chrysler that had followed him earlier that day. Had Cosette brought a couple of colleagues with her to help clinch this deal?

"Suzanne, my brother was murdered," Hagen said. "Right now I'm wondering if this hand he was trying to sell had anything to do with it. What do you think?"

The question took Cosette by surprise. A pained look came over her, as though the words were a tangible thing that hit her hard. "To be honest, Mister Hagen, I don't know a great deal about what happened to your brother. What little I do know is what I was told by his landlady at the apartment, and she wasn't entirely clear about it herself. All I can say to you is that I cannot imagine anyone going to such a heinous extreme to acquire the hand. If it is truly from the Vologda Jesus then it is a valuable piece of history, to be sure. But when all is said and done it is interesting only to a few people in the world."

Cosette reached across the table, picked up the photograph. She studied the image of the hand, as though wondering herself whether its value were somehow much higher than she believed, high enough to cause the death of the man who possessed it. Then she returned the photograph to the envelope, slid the envelope into her purse.

"Mister Hagen," Cosette said now, slow and quiet, "If the hand is genuine, I think you could realize several thousand dollars on the sale, depending on the condition of the piece. But I'll need to examine the hand first. When do you think you can produce it?"

Hagen didn't want Cosette to disappear on him. Not until he knew exactly what her interests were. He'd have to string her along—like he was stringing along Sidney Trunk.

"I'll need time. A couple of days."

"I'm not certain I will be here for that long."

"Surely you can find something to do in Vegas for a couple of days. Something that's not too treacherous."

Cosette finished the last of her drink before she answered. "All right, Mister Hagen. Two days. My cell phone number is on the back of my business card. If I haven't heard from you by Friday then I will contact you in any case."

Cosette turned over the check left by the waitress, laid a twenty-dollar bill and a ten on top of the check. She pushed her chair back and stood up, slinging the long narrow purse strap over her shoulder. "Please understand one thing, Mister Hagen. My firm's offer to purchase the hand may not stand for long. My advice is to take what you can realize on the hand now."

The gold and red dragons on Cosette's blouse caught the light and shimmered as she left the table.

A wooden hand with articulated fingers from a statue known as the Vologda Jesus. A wooden hand worth eighty thousand dollars or more. Hagen was sure that Cosette either knew the hand was stolen or had strong suspicions that it was. And he was also sure that she didn't care. No, the woman and her employers planned to purchase and resell the hand regardless. The asking price would be much higher than Cosette had let on and the sale would be discreet, no questions asked. Hagen was well aware that there was a black market in antiquities just as there is a black market for anything else of value.

Hagen walked back across the street to the Venetian. It was eleven o'clock. At the valet desk outside the hotel's front door Hagen asked for his car to be brought around. Hagen watched the late-arriving guests pulling bulky suitcases from car trunks and waving for one of the hustling bellmen in their blue-and-white-striped gondola shirts to come over. Vegas—too many overloaded tourists. When Hagen's car appeared he got in and drove south on the Strip, then got on Highway 15 southbound and drove out toward Henderson. In the darkness out on the highway he thought about the wooden hand in the photograph. Then another photograph came to mind. The police photograph of Ronnie hunched over dead in a rented car out at Hoover Dam. This wooden hand, was it worth so much that someone would kill for it?

Suzanne Cosette said no.

Maybe Sidney Trunk had a different answer.

Just past Henderson Hagen stopped at a gas station and bought a map that included a detailed grid of Boulder City. He studied the map in the car, pinpointing the address that Trunk had given him on the phone. Boulder City was an additional twenty minutes down the highway. Hagen reached the town shortly after midnight.

He was early for the appointment—but not early enough.

The address that Trunk had given him was on Cerrito Street in the older section of Boulder. Any other time the street was probably a nice quiet street in a nice quiet neighborhood. But right now it wasn't quiet and it wasn't nice. A policeman stood in the middle of the street. A hundred feet behind the policeman the street was blocked off by three red and white fire trucks, an ambulance, and three police cruisers. Roof bar lights flashed red and blue in the night. The policeman waved Hagen toward a sidestreet.

Hagen turned off and parked, walked back to Cerrito.

Firemen in yellow turnout pants and black boots directed high-pressure streams of water from a pumper truck onto the smoldering remains of a small house. A crowd had gathered on the sidewalk across the street. As Hagen approached the crowd he checked the numbers on the houses that he passed. He felt a sinking feeling in his stomach. Then the bottom of his stomach fell out entirely and hit the ground.

The address Trunk had given him belonged to the burned-out house.

"Is that Sidney Trunk's place?" Hagen said to a balding man with wire-framed glasses who stood at the edge of the crowd.

The man kept his eyes glued to the activity across the street. The words came out quick and nervous. "Not much left of it. I was sitting in my living room when I saw the flames. The whole front of the house went up. I've never seen anything burn so fast. One minute the house is there and the next it's a goner. Nothing anybody could do."

Hagen didn't give a shit about how fast the house burned. "What happened to Trunk? Was he in there?"

"Trunk?" The man looked at Hagen for the first time. The man's eyeglasses reflected the lights from the police cars and the fire trucks. "Sure, he made it out. They pulled him out about twenty minutes ago. They were working on him on the lawn. Then they threw him into an ambulance and took him away. Not that he needed an ambulance. He had a sheet pulled over his head. What he needed was a hearse."

* * *

Hagen drove back out of Boulder City. His thoughts intersecting at odd angles, like the beams of headlights crisscrossing in the darkness.

A wooden hand hacked off a Russian statue. Ronnie murdered on one end, after putting out feelers to sell the hand. And Sidney Trunk dead in a house fire on the other end, while trying to buy it. Their deaths were no coincidence, Hagen was sure. Suzanne Cosette had made her interest in the hand very clear, but Hagen couldn't credit the idea that the petite Frenchwoman had come to Las Vegas to murder everyone who stood between her and the hand. Even if she'd brought help with her. The story she'd told Hagen about the hand and Ronnie's contact with her people in Paris might've been a pack of lies, but one thing was certain. She'd stepped out into the open when she arranged the meeting with Hagen. She and her people were visible now. Too visible and too obvious for people engaged in killing the competition. And right now Cosette believed there was a good chance that Hagen had the hand. So why kill Sidney Trunk?

No, it didn't make sense.

There was some other angle here. But for the moment Hagen was up against a dead end.

When Hagen reached Henderson he pulled off the highway. Peach had promised him a drink. He thought he could use one. Maybe two.

Warm Springs Road—it was one of the main streets running through Henderson. The address Peach had given him belonged to an apartment complex located just inside the city limits. The buildings didn't look impressive but the cars parked out front were new and expensive.

Hagen parked, turned the engine off. He sat there, looking up at the lights burning in the windows of Peach's second-floor apartment. Now that he was here he wasn't sure that he should be. Or wanted to be.

He got out of the car, took off his sport coat. Slid the shoulder holster rig off. Laid the rig in the foot well behind the driver's seat and covered it with the coat.

"Did you get lost?" Peach said when she answered the door.

"Sorry, Peach. I got tied up with something. And then I had to get out to Boulder."

"How's Boulder these days?"

"Dark."

Peach laid her hand on Hagen's shoulder. Gave him a peck on the cheek. Left her hand on his shoulder while she studied his face, her brow furrowed into a look of concern. "How are you doing?"

Hagen said that he was doing fine. But he was ready for that drink. He followed Peach into the kitchen. The kitchen was small and new and clean. Half-opened moving boxes full of dishes and cookware sat on the counters. A breakfast bar separated the kitchen from the living room. Larger moving boxes were stacked around the living room, most of them unopened.

"I just moved in a couple of days ago," Peach said. "They call it a garden apartment, I don't know why. I haven't found any gardens. But when the wind is just right you can catch the smell from the trash bins around back."

"Sounds exotic."

"Nothing but the finest."

Peach stood there, next to the stove. Still studying him. Then she stepped up to him and took hold of his arm. "I'd welcome you home but this isn't much of a homecoming for you, is it, Bodo. I'm so sorry for you. If there's anything I can do, anything at all."

Hagen let his eyes wander across her features. Her blond hair was very different now—cut into some sort of a bob that angled down toward the front, about an inch off her shoulders. But aside from her hairstyle she was just the way he remembered. The watercolor gray of her big eyes. The small nose. The full lips glistening now with lipstick. Even the perfume she was wearing seemed familiar—a soft powdery smell with a trace of spice. She hadn't changed. He smiled. "It's all taken care of, Peach. Right now I'm just worn-out. It's been a long day. But it's good to see you. You look great."

Peach let go of his arm, stepped back. Stood there with her hands on her hips. Smiling now too. "You've put on weight, Bodo."

"A little."

"And you look older."

"I am older. So are you."

"Do I look older?"

"You look great."

"You look great too."

"You're lying. Now how about that drink?"

"Any flavor you want, as long as it's vodka."

Peach rummaged around in a paper grocery bag, pulled out a fresh bottle of vodka. She found a couple of glasses in a cardboard box and wiped them out with a dish towel. Pulled cranberry juice and ice cubes from the refrigerator, Hagen noticing the take-out containers of Chinese food on the top shelf. Hagen stood back and watched Peach mix the drinks. He hadn't been lying—Peach did look great. She was forty years old but her body looked lean and hard. Probably had a health club membership, sweated it out every day on the treadmill. But the curves were all still there. Maybe not as pronounced as they once were but still there, in the right places. Her blue jeans were tight and showed off the curves of her hips. And then the larger curves of her breasts that were now pressing against the thin cotton of her black camisole.

"Try that on for size," Peach said, handing him one of the drinks.

There wasn't any furniture in the living room to speak of, only the stacks of moving boxes. Hagen followed Peach out onto a balcony. Down below them in a long courtyard was a swimming pool. The lights in the pool were on and the deep blue of the water shimmered in the night. Hagen sat down at the small café table in the center of the balcony. Peach lingered by the railing for a moment, sipping her drink.

"Do you want to talk about it?" Peach said.

"There's nothing to talk about."

"There wasn't much in the newspapers. Just that he was shot out at Hoover."

"Then you know as much as I do."

"The police must be working on it."

"I've talked to them. They haven't gotten far."

Peach stepped away from the railing, sat down at the table. Set her drink down. She looked at him in silence and then she smiled again. That same wide smile that he remembered, with just a hint of sadness at the corners. Like there was some great unhappiness in her past that she could never quite shake off. Hagen had always thought the hint of sadness in her smile made her face more attractive, gave it depth. And yet it was off-putting too.

"I hear Jimmy Ray was killed," Hagen said, just to change the subject.

Peach fidgeted with her hair. "You didn't know that?"

"I haven't exactly been around. Do you still see any of the old crew from Diamond Jim's?"

"I can't remember the last time. It's been years."

"Do you remember that you owe me a lunch?"

"I'm sorry about that. That was wrong."

"Why didn't you show up?"

"I tried to talk you out of leaving but I couldn't. So I decided that I didn't want to see you at all. I had no intention of being a good sport about it. I was angry. I think I'm still a little angry."

"That was ten years ago, Peach."

"All right. So maybe I'm not angry anymore. And to settle my debt, I'll buy you that lunch. I've got some things going on today, but how about Friday?"

"Sure, it's your nickel." Hagen spoke now with a lightness he didn't feel. "So what have you been doing for the last ten years, besides skipping out on lunch dates?"

"The usual. Breathing. Paying bills. Watching late-night television. Getting a tattoo. Watering the plants."

"You've got a tattoo?"

"Everybody's got one."

"Let's see it."

"I can't show it to you."

"Is it ugly?"

"It's pretty. It's two roses, with their stems intertwined."

"Sounds fraught with poetic feeling."

"It was either the two roses or Minnie Mouse."

"Minnie Mouse would've been good."

"It was a tough call."

"Show it to me."

"I can't. It's in a private place."

"What kind of private place?"

"Private as in 'none of your business.'"

Hagen took a drink. The cranberry juice tasted a little bitter. The vodka was a good brand though. Smooth and strong. Down in the courtyard the reflections off the water played against the wall of the building opposite the balcony. Hagen recalled another apartment that Peach had lived in. Right about the time she left Diamond Jim's to go to work at Caesars Palace. One of Peach's neighbors in an apartment that faced hers had a taste for peeping into her windows with a pair of field binoculars. Hagen had to go over to the neighbor's apartment one day and have a quiet word with him. And that put an end to the peeping. No doubt because the neighbor found it difficult to use binoculars with his broken nose covered by a metal splint held down with medical tape. Still, it was a better deal for the neighbor than the solution Peach had proposed at the time—load up her Remington target rifle and shoot out his windows, preferably with the neighbor standing behind them. Peach had grown up on a ranch in northern Arizona, and early on in her childhood she'd traded dolls and toy ovens for breaking horses and shooting empty soda cans off fence posts. She'd even won a few shooting trophies over the years—Hagen had watched her win one up at the Pahrump Rifle and Pistol Club, decided right then that she was a better shot with a rifle than he'd ever be.

"Still putting time in at the rifle range, Peach?"

"Now and then. Just to work off some energy."

"How's your eye these days?"

"Set your glass on top of your head and let me take a shot at it, and we'll just see how good my eye is."

"I'll take a pass. I'm not real fond of parlor tricks with a Remington."

Peach shook her head. "I sold the Remington long ago. Bought a souped-up Ruger from a company in England. Lightweight, the whole thing built to fit my specifications. Made out of some kind of composite metal that NASA or someone developed. Very twenty-first century."

Hagen smiled. "Keep playing with guns, you'll scare off all the suitors. Husbands don't generally want wives who wave firearms around at awkward moments."

"Who says I'm not married?"

"So where do you keep your husband?"

"I keep him in Texas. We're separated. You want another drink?"

They finished the first round of drinks and then a second round. Sitting out on the balcony. Talking. When the second round was gone and Peach went inside to make two more Hagen stood up, stepped over to the railing. Looked up at the night sky. Looked down at the swimming pool. He was still standing there, leaning against the railing, when Peach returned with the fresh drinks. He heard her setting the drinks down on the table, stepping up behind him. She placed her hands on his shoulders. Began kneading the tight muscles under his shirt.

"You're tense, Bodo. I can just look at you and see that you're tensed up."

"I'm not tense."

Peach kept on kneading. "Your muscles feel like steel wire."

"Like I said, it's been a long day. That's all."

"You need to get more exercise."

"That pool down there looks inviting."

"Swimming. A good way to relax."

"I didn't bring my swim shorts."

"Well, there's other ways to relax."

"Take a trip out to the rifle range?"

"I was thinking along different lines."

Something in the tone of her voice made Hagen turn around. She was looking up at him, a smile on her face. With just that hint of sadness. He reached out and she moved into his arms and he held her. Looking down at the softness of her face. Wondering if he could work the sadness out of her smile by applying pressure with his lips.

He tried it. It seemed to work.

"You still interested in my tattoo?"

"Sure I am, Peach."

6.

HAGEN AWOKE with a start.

For a moment he thought he was still at Peach's apartment. Thought she was lying right there beside him in bed. Then his eyes focused and he looked around and saw that he was alone in his hotel room.

It was eleven o'clock in the morning.

Hagen shaved and showered. The merciless Las Vegas sun was creeping in through the cracks between the drawn curtains. Hagen's hard-shell suitcase rested on the folding stand near the bed. When he opened the suitcase he paused to inspect the broken combination lock once again.

Someone had been in his room last night. And it wasn't the maid giving him turndown service.

Hagen couldn't be sure when the room had been tossed. He hadn't come back to the room after his meeting with Suzanne Cosette. But when he returned from Peach's place early that morning he found that Ronnie's two suitcases and his own had been opened and searched.

It might have happened while he was at the Mirage, talking to Cosette. Or it might have happened later.

Hagen was inclined to believe the first option.

Cosette had asked him to meet her across the street at the Mirage. Most people pursuing a contact would've offered to meet Hagen at his own hotel, but no, she'd wanted him to come to her. And the Mirage wasn't so far away that he might've balked. He'd been at the Mirage for forty-five minutes—more than long enough for an accomplice to search Hagen's room. Hagen thought of the swarthy young man who'd seemed to be watching him when he first arrived at the Mirage. If Cosette had an accomplice, the swarthy man in the cardboard blazer got Hagen's vote.

But whoever had tossed his room had left without the item they'd come for—the wooden hand of a Russian Jesus.

Hagen called room service for a pot of coffee. When the coffee arrived it was tepid and weak. He drank down a cup before he sat down to make some phone calls.

The first one was to the Sniff, who told Hagen what Hagen already knew. Sidney Trunk died in a house fire in Boulder City early that morning.

"I was supposed to meet Trunk last night," Hagen said. "When I got out there his house was a barbecue pit and Trunk was on his way to the morgue."

"It was on the news," the Sniff said. "The Boulder police say it's a torch job."

"Did Trunk have enemies?"

"Who doesn't."

"Serious enemies?"

"I didn't know him."

"But Martinez knew him. Sniff, I still want to talk to Martinez."

There was a pause. Hagen heard a rattling on the other end of the line, sounded like ice cubes in a glass. Then, "Martinez doesn't want to get involved in this."

"He's already involved. If I go to McGrath right now and start talking about what I know, his name is going to come up. If he wants to stay away from the law, he needs to talk to me. Then maybe I'll keep his name under wraps."

The Sniff agreed to contact Martinez again.

The second phone call was to Diamond Jim's Casino in downtown Las Vegas. The woman who answered transferred him to a man in the back office. Hagen asked if Marty Ray was around. The man said that

Marty Ray wasn't in right now but he might be in later. The man asked for Hagen's name, said he'd take a message.

Hagen didn't leave his name or a message.

Next Hagen dialed a long-distance number. Paris, France. Hagen studied the business card Cosette had given him while the phone line went through several clicks and changes in tone. It would be eight o'clock in the evening in Paris—maybe too late to catch someone at work. Hagen heard a muffled ringing that sounded like it was coming from underwater.

A man answered. *"Amarantos Antiquités."*

Hagen asked in French to speak with Suzanne Cosette. The man said she wasn't available. When Hagen asked if she was still in Las Vegas the man didn't say one way or the other, but he wasn't surprised by the question. When Hagen asked to speak to Cosette's boss the man said that Mister Amarantos wasn't available either. Hagen asked a few questions about the merchandise in the shop. The answers sounded genuine.

Hagen thanked the man and hung up the phone.

Hagen had learned two things—there was indeed an Amarantos Antiquités in Paris and there was a Suzanne Cosette who worked for that firm. The woman's story had sounded far-fetched last night. It seemed slightly less far-fetched now.

As Hagen finished the last of the coffee he felt a presence in the room. He looked around, startled. Half expecting to see Peach standing there in morning disarray. Smiling, looking sheepish.

But there was no one there.

It was raining hard in Berlin the day Hagen arrived.

As the Boeing 757 broke through the cloud cover and began its final approach to Berlin Tegel Airport, Hagen studied the city through the window. Berlin looked vast and grim in the rain. Clusters of pallid brick buildings were hemmed in by thick stands of dark trees. In the distance Hagen could see heavy fog clinging to the landscape.

William Severance met him at Tegel and drove him directly to a small gasthaus *in the Schoneberg District. There Severance and Hagen drank Berliner Pils and ate fresh hot spaetzle while Severance explained the job at hand.*

"What do you know about Die Wende*?" Severance said.*

Die Wende. *"The change." The German name for the collapse of the Deutsche Demokratische Republik—East Germany—in the autumn of 1989. At the time of* Die Wende, *the East German Ministry for State Security, more commonly known as the Stasi, maintained spies throughout the world. Many of these spies—especially those who had worked within West Germany—were highly placed in government, the military or private industry. The Stasi's six million intelligence files chronicled the activities of these Stasi agents within and outside of East Germany, as well as the Stasi's support of numerous international terrorist organizations.*

The Stasi files were too incriminating to be allowed to fall into the hands of another intelligence service. In the midst of East Germany's collapse, Stasi officers around the country—from East Berlin to Potsdam, from Metterheim to Rostock to Zwickau—shredded intelligence files by the box full. When the shredding machines broke down under the strain the documents were burned or torn up by hand. But destroying six million files required more time than the Stasi had at its disposal. As East Germany crumbled teams of agents from the West German Federal Intelligence Service—the Bundesnachrichtendienst, or BND—aided by the CIA and Great Britain's MI6, descended upon the Stasi offices and seized what files they could find. Even the shredded remains of documents were carefully collected and carried away. Garbage bags full of shredded Stasi documents were stored in offices in Berlin and Nuremberg, and a staff of men and women with high-level security clearances was assembled and given the Herculean task of reassembling these documents, one sliver of paper at a time, using nothing but cellophane tape and patience. These men and women came to be known as "puzzlers."

The job that Severance discussed in the Berlin gasthaus *the day Hagen arrived carried the code name* Blau Licht*— "Blue Light." Blau Licht was a joint BND-CIA-MI6 operation. The objective of* Blau Licht *was simple— use the documents reassembled by the puzzlers to identify former Stasi agents* and other "individuals of interest"—a euphemism that included Stasi-supported terrorists and assassins as well as former agents of the Stasi's sister service, the defunct Soviet KGB. In some cases the BND wanted to bring these individuals to justice. In other cases they wanted to place them under surveillance in the hope of learning who they worked for now.

Blau Licht went on for years. Hagen's job was to assess the value of reconstructed Stasi documents and follow up on leads when leads could be identified. Much of the time there were too few details to go on. The documents full of code names and aliases couldn't be made to reveal their secrets, as hard as Hagen and his colleagues tried. When particular individuals were identified and investigations initiated, the investigations more often than not led nowhere. At times Hagen felt like nothing more than a file clerk engaged in the day-to-day grind of papierkrieg—the paperwork shuffle of the petty bureaucrat.

Then one day Severance dropped the Totenkopf documents on Hagen's desk. "Take special care with these," Severance said. "You're going to be spending some time with them."

There were a total of twelve documents. Notations on several of the pages indicated that the documents had all once belonged in the same Stasi file—zentralarchiv file 47-5563/78. Ten of the documents detailed the training of three Stasi operatives code-named Totenkopf, Natzweiler and Hohle at a Stasi training camp near Dresden in 1985. The training reports appeared to have been written by at least two separate Stasi case officers. The remaining two documents appeared to be field reports on meetings with one of these individuals—agent Natzweiler—in Hamburg in 1986.

The first thing that Hagen concluded from reviewing the documents was that the three subjects of the training reports were most definitely "individuals of interest." The nature of their training—weapons, explosives, escape and evasion, target identification and surveillance—indicated clearly that the three operatives were members of a Stasi-sponsored terrorist cell. Just the sort of training that might be sold for a high price on the open market after the fall of East Germany. These were exactly the sort of people that Blau Licht was designed to identify.

The second thing that Hagen concluded was that the Totenkopf documents were workable. The field reports on the meetings in Hamburg included the address of an apartment presumably used by agent Natzweiler. It should be a simple matter to find out who resided at that address at that time.

Hagen and a young BND agent named Johannes Vogel drove to Hamburg to look into the matter. The current landlord hadn't owned the building in 1986, but the records kept by the previous landlord were boxed up in the basement. After an hour of searching through moldy boxes of records, Hagen and Vogel identified the individual who had rented the apartment at 29 Charlottenstrasse in the spring of 1986 as Heinrich Kress. The name meant nothing to Hagen but Vogel recognized it immediately—Heinrich Kress had been found guilty of planting a bomb in a Hamburg nightclub in 1988 that killed three off-duty British soldiers and a Turkish guest worker.

Heinrich Kress was Natzweiler. Now they could use Natzweiler to identify agents Totenkopf and Hohle. But an additional piece of information was soon received from the German Bundeskriminalamt—Heinrich Kress hanged himself in Stammheim Prison in Stuttgart in 1995.

Vogel thought that was the end of it. Agent Natzweiler was dead and the identities of Totenkopf and Hohle would remain a secret. But Vogel was wrong. This was just the beginning. . . .

Totenkopf—

The death's head. The skull and crossed bones.

The insignia of Adolf Hitler's Schutzstaffel—the SS.

Hagen saw the *totenkopf* everywhere. Five, ten, twelve of them, all in a row. Lights blinking around them, bells clanging, wheels spinning. The empty mouths of the skulls hanging open in a silent shriek. Then suddenly the rattle of coins—

Slot machines. Long rows of them. All advertising Pirate Treasure at twenty-five cents a play. The slot machine players mingled around the machines watching one another play, all of them carrying plastic cups full of coins, like an army of street beggars.

Hagen walked past the banks of slot machines. The action at the blackjack tables was thin this afternoon and the nearby baccarat tables were empty. At a craps table a young woman in blue jeans and sandals was shaking her bottom and waving her arms in the air, trying to put some english on the pair of dice in her hand while her boyfriend motioned to a cocktail waitress with long legs clad in fishnet stockings to bring another round of free drinks. Hagen thought of Peach, how she used to look in a cocktail outfit. Strolling across this same casino floor, all legs and cleavage and big eyelashes. Working the room like she owned the joint. She knew how to turn a few heads back then.

She still knew how.

Diamond Jim's hadn't changed much. It still looked to Hagen like what it was—a sawdust joint with pretensions. Like the El Cortez, the Las Vegas Club and the Golden Nugget, Diamond Jim's was one of the older casinos in town, built in the 1940s when Fremont Street was still the center of the gambling action and the Strip was only a long dusty stretch of highway on the way to Los Angeles. But times changed and Diamond Jim's was teetering on the edge of bankruptcy when the Ray brothers bought it in the 1970s for a song. They sunk quite a bit of capital into the operation, tried hard to give Diamond Jim's a little class. But there was one thing they couldn't change and that was the clientele—and the clientele at Diamond Jim's was strictly sawdust joint.

Low rollers. Grinds. Stiffs.

Hagen walked up to the cashier's cage, told the cashier that he wanted to speak to Marty Ray. The cashier called over a manager who eyed Hagen with suspicion. A phone call was made and presently a barrel-chested young man who moved uncomfortably in his pin-striped Brooks Brothers suit escorted Hagen to the private elevator that took them upstairs to Marty Ray's office.

On the fifth floor the elevator doors slid open to reveal a short white corridor. The zebra-striped carpeting was new but the two security cameras hanging from the ceiling at the end of the corridor weren't.

Hagen followed Pinstripes to the door. As the young man reached for the doorknob Hagen heard a low buzzing and a metallic click—the automatic lock on the door being released.

Hagen followed him inside.

The office was large, with a low ceiling and track lighting. One wall was covered with bookcases and filing cabinets. The opposite wall was bare except for a wide rectangular painting of a desert sunset, the modernist shapes of the rock formations and cacti all done up in burnt sienna and dusty rose, the sky several shades of orange. At the far end of the room was an enormous oaken desk. Behind the desk sat Marty Ray, with a plate of food and a glass of red wine in front of him.

"Hello, Sauerkraut," Marty Ray said. "I've been waiting for you."

Sauerkraut—the name the Ray brothers had always called him. It hadn't bothered him ten years ago. But now the nickname rankled Hagen. It spoke of a familiarity that Hagen no longer wanted with Marty Ray.

Marty Ray daubed at his mouth with a white linen napkin as he looked up at Hagen, one eyebrow raised. Marty Ray was sixty years old now but he still dyed his gray hair jet-black. Still combed it back onto his head in a pompadour. Still wore his shirts unbuttoned halfway to his waist. Still shaved his chest so the gray chest hairs wouldn't give him away.

He even dyed his eyebrows black now. But his skin was pale and slack and his eyes looked dull.

Marty Ray looked like a badly primped corpse.

Hagen said, "What made you think I'd be here?"

Marty Ray waved a hand in the air as though brushing aside a slow housefly. "Your brother gets it the hard way, I figure you'll turn up. Who else is going to bury him? And since you're in town already, I figure you'll drop by to see Marty. Maybe talk about old times. Maybe talk about new times."

"So now I'm here."

"So now we talk."

Off to the right a tall bald-headed man with a crooked nose sat in a swivel chair in front of a bank of video monitors that showed split-screen images of the hallway outside the office, the interior of the elevator that had brought Hagen up here, the elevator doors at the casino level, a back elevator and stairway, several different views of the casino cashier cages. The tall man rose from his chair and stepped forward. Motioned with his hands for Hagen to raise his arms for a pat down.

Hagen turned full around to face the tall man. Hagen took one step back, planted his feet apart. Held his hands out at his sides. Ready to make a fight of it if the tall man moved closer.

The tall man stopped, looked at Marty Ray. Waiting for orders. Pinstripes, still standing by the door, looked nervously at the tall man, at Hagen, at Marty Ray.

Marty Ray picked up his silver dinner fork and waved the tall man back to his chair. Then Marty Ray pointed the fork at Pinstripes and he departed quickly.

Now the tines of the fork were pointed at Hagen.

"You'll have to excuse Cleveland, Sauerkraut. He just wants to do his job. I don't like guns in here. I'm allergic to guns. My doctor says I should avoid them. Unless I want to break out in a rash of blood. But you didn't come here to shoot me, did you, Sauerkraut? No, I don't think you did. So we'll skip the pleasantries. Have a seat." Marty Ray returned his fork to his plate of food—green peas, mashed potatoes and gravy, a large half chicken covered in thick red barbecue sauce. "Cleveland is a good man. As good as you were, Sauerkraut. Maybe better."

Before sitting down Hagen pushed the red leather-cushioned chair in front of Marty Ray's desk to one side, so that he could keep Cleveland in sight.

Marty Ray pushed a fork load of mashed potatoes into his mouth, pushed the potatoes from one cheek to the other and back, then swallowed. Marty Ray had once told Hagen that he ate one item on his plate at a time because he didn't like to mix up the flavors. It had always struck Hagen as a childish predilection. But Marty Ray was prone to odd tangents of the mind. Once, back when Hagen worked for him, Marty read in a magazine that the singer Sammy Davis Jr. added a mixture of Lactopine, Hermès and Au Savage colognes to his bathwater in order to rejuvenate himself during his evening ablutions. Marty immediately sent Hagen out to procure the three ingredients so that Marty could bask in the same bathwater that Sammy used. Hagen had felt distinctly like a fool searching Las Vegas for the items. The next morning Marty was visibly disappointed that the bath mixture hadn't done a thing for him except make him smell like the bargain shelf of an all-night drugstore.

Jimmy Ray had been the brains behind the business. He'd had a cool head and a quick mind. If business was going well for Marty Ray, Hagen was sure that someone else was pulling the strings.

"What do you hear about what happened to Ronnie?" Hagen said.

"What do I hear?" Marty Ray said. "Let me turn that question around. What have you heard about what happened to my brother, Sauerkraut?"

"Not a thing. Why don't you tell me about it."

"You're being flip. I don't like flip." Marty Ray rolled his tongue over his front teeth, took a sip of wine. He held the wineglass with his fat pinkie extended straight out from the side of the glass, like a bishop sipping tea at a garden party. Hagen noticed that his fingernails were ragged and broken. Marty Ray still chewed his nails.

"What happened to Jimmy, Marty?"

"Somebody took him out. Right in his own house. Can you imagine that, Sauerkraut? They robbed him and took him out in his own damned house. Jimmy didn't usually keep large at his house, but he had a couple of hundred thousand that night. Big coincidence, right? Bullshit. Whoever took him out knew he was holding. That's what I say."

"So how come the police didn't find your man?"

"Who said it was a man?"

"Have it your way. How come the police didn't find your woman?"

"I didn't say it was a man or a woman. All I say is that whoever killed him knew he had cash in the house that night. And they knew a few other things. Like the surveillance cameras—they knew about those. After they killed Jimmy they took the tapes from the surveillance cameras with them. It was no small-time job. Whoever did that job, they did some planning."

"That doesn't mean it was an inside job."

"You're thinking the way the police thought. That's why they never got anywhere. That's why they never found out who murdered my sainted brother Jimmy." Marty Ray waved his fork at Hagen. "But I'll find them, Sauerkraut. I'm still looking. It's been five years but I'm still looking."

"Maybe the police didn't get anywhere because you didn't tell them where the money came from or who knew about it. Is that the way it was, Marty?"

Hagen smiled. Marty Ray shot him an angry look, then glanced at Cleveland across the room. Cleveland sat with his eyes glued to the video monitors, trying hard to look like he wasn't paying attention to the conversation. Years ago Hagen had spent many nights sitting where Cleveland was sitting now, staring at those same monitors. Hagen had known about the skim operation back then, but what the Ray brothers did with their money after the skim went down Hagen never knew. They'd had some scheme in place for getting the cash off their hands and laundering it, and it must have been a good scheme too, because the gaming commission and the feds never caught wind of the skim action at Diamond Jim's, or if they did they could never prove it. It would've meant jail time for Jimmy and Marty Ray if they had. Hagen had often wondered if the Ray brothers had the mob behind them and that was why the skim operation was successful. He wondered about it again now.

"Get your head out of your ass, Sauerkraut," Marty Ray said. "The money meant nothing. Jimmy's death destroyed me. It tore me all up inside. So when the police didn't do anything I put my own boys on it. I told them to work like Christmas—I wanted to know who was naughty and who was nice. But they let me down. Someone inside the casino was a rat but my boys couldn't shake the rat out. And I wasn't going to start busting caps on people's asses because maybe they knew something and maybe they didn't. I had to know for sure. I'm a reasonable man. I've got morals."

"So what did the boys tell you about Ronnie?"

"You worried?"

"It's what you're working up to."

Marty Ray leaned back, wiped his mouth with his napkin. "Ronnie seemed like a good kid. Jimmy liked him too. Ronnie had a future with this organization. But then about a month after Jimmy got it, Ronnie quits his job and leaves town"—Marty Ray snapped his fingers. Across the room Cleveland turned in his chair, then realized that the snap wasn't for him—"just like that. And he doesn't just leave town. He doesn't just drive up to Reno for a weekend. He leaves the fucking country, Sauerkraut. He goes to the other side of the world. That raised some eyebrows, I don't mind telling you. We were shaking our noggins trying to figure that out. Why did Ronnie want to disappear like that? Maybe he's scared about something. Maybe the heat's getting too hot in Vegas.

"And then the police come around. They wanted to know where Ronnie was too. Suddenly they're real interested in talking to him. So I say, 'What've you got on him? What's the action on that kid?' They didn't want to tell me. They acted cagey. But I could read between the lines.

"So then I want to talk to Ronnie again too. If the cops want him, then I want him. And I want to talk to him first. But where is he? He's gone. He fell off the edge of the earth. I put out a line on him but I couldn't find his ass. He went into that Foreign Legion bullshit and disappeared. Swallowed him right up. But I said, that's okay. I'll keep a marker out. He'll turn up again and I'll be here waiting for him. And then he'll tell me what it was the police had on him because maybe it's something I ought to know about."

It had become warm in the room. Hagen wanted to take off his sport coat but didn't. Why had the police wanted to talk to Ronnie? Then another thought came to him. Hagen didn't like it. He didn't know exactly why, but he didn't like it.

Hagen said, "Who were the cops who worked the case?"

Marty Ray grimaced, as though the act of trying to remember caused him a sharp shooting pain. "The usual fucks."

"McGrath?"

"Might've been. What's it to you?"

"He was a friend of my old man's, that's all."

"Your old man had a lot of friends. He had a lot of enemies. Sometimes they're the same people. You might think McGrath is a friend but he's a cop too. He had business with your brother. He had a bone to pick. He was most displeased to hear that Ronnie disappeared. Most displeased."

Hagen wondered why McGrath hadn't mentioned this. Had it slipped his mind? Jimmy Ray was murdered five years ago. It was probably a dusty folder in a cold case drawer by now. But no, cops had long memories. McGrath had a long memory. What did the police have on Ronnie? Hagen would have to talk to McGrath again. Hagen wanted to know all the pieces of the puzzle, not just the ones that McGrath felt like giving him.

Marty Ray prodded the half chicken into the center of his plate with his finger. "Sauerkraut, I wondered about you too."

"How's that?"

"It wasn't so long after you left town that Jimmy got whacked."

"It was five years."

"Five years is nothing. Five years is yesterday. Ten years is last week. When you left town, you disappeared too. You went to the other side of the world. Then Jimmy got it and then your brother disappears just like you did. It made me think. Maybe you weren't so far away as you said. Maybe you came back to town and didn't want anybody to know. Maybe you and your brother decided to work some kind of *angle*." Marty Ray took hold of the chicken wing with the tips of his fingers. With a quick tug he ripped the wing free of the half chicken and held it up. Red droplets of barbecue sauce landed on the desk around his plate like blood spatter at a crime scene. "If I thought you had anything to do with what happened to Jimmy, Sauerkraut, your bright sunny future wouldn't be worth a turd in a pot."

"You're reaching now, Marty."

"Am I? I wonder."

"While you're wondering, why don't you tell me what happened when you saw Ronnie last week. I didn't come here to watch you play in your food."

Marty Ray kept his eyes on Hagen as he raised the chicken wing to his mouth, pulled a large piece of skin and meat off the bone with his teeth. He chewed the bite of chicken slowly, swallowed. Then, "Nothing happened. Nothing happened because I didn't see him."

"He came here."

"That's right. He was here. But I wasn't. I wish I was, but I wasn't. I was out of town. When I got back I put out feelers. I sent people out to find him and bring him here. But before they could do that little thing he shows up on the news, dead. I was upset, Sauerkraut. I don't mind telling you. I was distressed. I wait all this time to talk to him, and then as soon as he shows up in Vegas he gets himself whacked. Your brother had an all-around shitty sense of timing."

"What have you heard about it?"

An indifferent look crossed Marty Ray's face. "Not a thing."

"You sure?"

Marty Ray found an enticing spot on the wing and took another bite. He didn't respond. Hagen sensed that Marty Ray was telling the truth. And it jibed with what Gubbs had told him. Not that that counted for much. Hagen was sure that Gubbs had already talked to Marty Ray. Probably called him the second Hagen walked out of Gubbs's apartment.

Hagen said, "What did Ronnie do when he was here?"

Marty Ray shrugged. Through his mouthful of food he said, "Damn little, from what my people tell me. He showed up with a squeeze on his arm—nice girl too, I've seen her around. So he hangs out for a couple of drinks and then he takes his squeeze and he leaves. One thing though— he asked to see me, you know that? He wanted to look me up like I was an old friend. How about that? But I wasn't here, so I didn't see him. The next thing I hear is that he's taken up residence inside a body bag. Too bad for him. Too bad for me. Too bad for you. End of story."

"She have a name, the woman?"

"Most of them do."

"What's her name, Marty?"

"Couldn't say. Some kind of dancer. She used to work over at Harry Needles's place."

Harry Needles—Hagen hadn't expected to hear that name. Another name from the past. Another old friend of his father's. Harry Needles had once worked for Hagen's father at the Sands. He moved on to other casinos later, then got out of casino security entirely, got into the restaurant business.

"What's Harry's action these days?" Hagen said.

Marty Ray took one last bite of the chicken wing and dropped it onto his plate. "Runs a strip club over on Industrial. Calls it the Venus Lounge or some such shit. By the way, Sauerkraut. Leave Gubbs alone. He works for me."

"All right. But you can do something for me."

Marty Ray tore the leg off the half chicken. "What might that be?"

"Call off the boys you've got tailing me."

Marty looked up from his food with a blank expression. Then a smile slowly appeared on his face. "You're some kind of comedian now, Sauerkraut? You learn some jokes when you were overseas? Believe me, if I had people following you, you wouldn't know. Until I wanted you to know. But I'm serious about Gubbs. And anybody else who works for me. Leave them alone. You fuck with them and you're fucking with me. So then I have to turn around and fuck with you."

Marty Ray snapped the bone of the chicken leg cleanly in half. More barbecue sauce splattered across his desk. Marty Ray dropped the two halves onto his plate. Across the room the bald-headed Cleveland turned away from the video monitors and gave Hagen a menacing and gap-toothed smile. Ten years ago it would've been Hagen sitting there. Hagen was staring down the business end of his own past.

It was time to go. Hagen got up from the chair.

"Wipe your face, Marty. You eat like a pig."

"Fuck you too, Sauerkraut."

7.

HAGEN WALKED OUT of Diamond Jim's.

It was just past five o'clock.

He climbed into the Buick, slid his sunglasses on and started the engine. He pulled out into the street. At the first intersection he studied the rearview mirror while he waited for the red light to change. He didn't see the black Chrysler. He didn't see anything. Except a lot of faces from his past, slowly catching up with him.

The Sniff. McGrath. Marty Ray. Peach.

And now Harry Needles.

It was old home week in Las Vegas.

The Venus Lounge was located at the northern end of Industrial Road. The flat outline of the green and white building and the absence of any windows gave it the appearance of a warehouse, albeit a warehouse with a black awning over the front door, a uniformed parking lot valet standing underneath the awning, and a plaster replica of the Venus de Milo rising from the center of a circular water fountain near the front door.

The interior of the club was taken up by three runway stages lit up in colored lights. Several more colored lights were trained on the mirror balls hanging from the ceiling, sending shimmering reflections around the room. The reflections were multiplied greatly by the floor to ceiling mirrors behind the stages and along the walls. Loud rock music shook the building as the topless dancers writhed against silver poles positioned on the stage at intervals of several feet.

Hagen pushed his way through the crowd and up to the long bar. He ordered a bottle of beer. A busty young brunette wearing only a sequined G-string with a fluffy pink pom-pom at the rear danced on a circular platform behind the bar. She ran her tongue across her glossy lips and threw what she hoped was a smoldering glance at two middle-aged men standing to Hagen's left. The two men didn't take notice, but a man in a red cowboy shirt to Hagen's right leaned forward and shouted for the dancer to shake her pom-pom. She obliged, twirling around on high heels and bending over, her rear end up in the air. She reached back and slapped one bare butt cheek once, twice, three times. The cowboy tossed a crumpled dollar bill up onto the stage, shouted further instructions.

When the beer came Hagen asked the woman bartender where he might find Harry Needles. The woman pointed to a glassed-in booth at the far end of the bar where a disc jockey was playing the music that now thudded through the room. Hagen paid for his beer and walked over to the booth. Inside a disc jockey wearing a banker's visor tapped away at a laptop computer keyboard, plotting his next musical assault. Beside the door to the booth a thin man with Mediterranean features was trying to listen to what was being yelled into his ear by a young man wearing a black polo shirt that bore the Venus de Milo logo. Hagen got the thin man's attention and asked him where Harry Needles was. The thin man shrugged, told Hagen that Harry Needles might show up any minute and he might not show up at all. Hagen told him it was a matter of some importance, and one that Harry Needles would certainly be interested in. The thin man raised his hands with a flourish and looked up toward the ceiling, as though emphasizing the ethereal nature of Harry Needles and his daily routine. Hagen slipped the thin man a twenty-dollar bill. The thin man wrote down Hagen's name and told him that if Harry Needles did in fact materialize, he'd give him Hagen's message.

Hagen sat down at a table near the wall to finish his beer. Five Japanese men in business suits sat with their wives at the edge of the near-est runway stage. The wives were dressed elegantly in evening dresses and sparkling jewelry. The entourage clapped politely and smiled as the leggy black woman at the edge of the stage rolled her hips, cupped her bare breasts and pretended to moan. One of the Japanese wives stood up and with the encouragement of the others she stepped for-ward and tucked a folded dollar bill under the dancer's white garter, then sat down again quickly, twittering with laughter and relief, as though she'd just fed a morsel of raw meat to a roaring lioness.

As Hagen worked on the bottle of beer he thought about what Marty Ray had told him. How hard did Marty believe that Ronnie knew some-thing about Jimmy Ray's murder? Hagen wondered again if Marty Ray told him the truth about not seeing Ronnie last week. If it was the truth, it might be a very narrow truth. Marty Ray didn't need to talk to Ronnie in person. Marty Ray had other people who could talk to Ronnie. Per-haps the discussion had gotten out of hand. Tempers flared. Guns were drawn. Shots fired.

No, that didn't add up. Ronnie was sitting out at Hoover Dam at midnight. If Marty Ray arranged to have some of his men get heavy with Ronnie, they wouldn't have done it at Hoover Dam. And if Marty Ray simply wanted Ronnie murdered, Hoover Dam still wasn't a likely choice. No, Ronnie was sitting in his car when he was shot. The shooter walked right up to the driver's side window and fired. The shooter hadn't snuck up on Ronnie. Not in an empty overlook parking lot in the middle of the night. The shooter was someone Ronnie knew and who he wasn't surprised to see.

Because he'd gone out there to meet him.

And what did McGrath know? McGrath hadn't said a word about Ronnie being implicated in Jimmy Ray's murder. And yet McGrath had worked that case. Either McGrath was holding out on him or Marty Ray was lying about the police believing that Ronnie knew something about Jimmy Ray's murder.

He'd talk to McGrath again. But first Hagen wanted to talk to Harry Needles.

And the woman too, whoever she was . . .

She was lying on a powder blue blanket in the middle of the lawn. She wore a black leotard and she lay on her shoulders, her arms propping up her back, her legs bicycling briskly in the crisp spring air. She sat up quickly when she noticed them walking up the stone pathway toward the house.

They'd interrupted her exercises, she said. What did they want?

Her name was Ingeborge Stromm.

She'd once been Heinrich Kress's lover . . .

When Hagen and Johannes Vogel returned to Berlin from Hamburg, the long work of researching Heinrich Kress began. All the available databases of the BND, the Bundeskriminalamt, the CIA, and MI6 were searched. The hours of interrogations that occurred after Kress's arrest for the Hamburg nightclub bombing were pored over. A list of names was compiled. Relatives. Friends. Former employers. School acquaintances from Kress's days at the University of Kiel. The Totenkopf files pieced back together by the puzzlers identified three Stasi-supported terrorists. Natzweiler—Kress—was accounted for. He was dead. The other two, Totenkopf and Hohle, were unaccounted for and might still be active, somewhere in Europe, somewhere in the world.

Only one name stood out as a possibility better than the others.

Ingeborge Stromm.

Stromm met Kress in Kiel at the university in the 1970s. At the time of the nightclub bombing in 1988 she resided in the small town of Hochenhiem, only a few kilometers from Hamburg. After Kress's arrest the Bundeskriminalamt had questioned Stromm closely on several occasions. Stromm expressed profound shock that Kress might be involved in a terrorist bombing and denied knowing anything of Kress's recent activities. The Bundeskriminalamt could find no holes in Stromm's story to exploit and in the end they gave up on her.

But one item that came to light during the Bundeskriminalamt sessions stood out—Stromm had admitted that she lived with Kress for several months in 1985. The Bundeskriminalamt hadn't made anything of it in 1988 but now, to Vogel and Hagen, it was a telling admission. Kress, as the Stasi-sponsored terrorist known as Natzweiler, had spent quite a bit of time in East Germany in 1985. Perhaps Stromm knew of Kress's East German trip. Perhaps Stromm had gone with him.

But where was she now?

Hagen and Vogel sent out inquiries through BND and CIA channels. Three weeks later the French Direction de la Surveillance du Territoire—Directorate of Territorial Security—replied with a short message indicating that a woman identified as Ingeborge Stromm, formally of Kiel and Hochenhiem, now resided in a small town near Morlaix on the Brittany coast in northern France. She was a freelance writer who traveled extensively throughout Europe and the Middle East.

"You're going to visit this woman," Severance said at a meeting with Hagen and Vogel in his office. Severance outlined a simple plan that had been used successfully before. "The French have nothing on Stromm. Neither do we. If she is Totenkopf or Hohle or if she knows who they were, she is safe at the moment. But she doesn't know that or at least she can't be sure. So we need to shake her hard. You're going to tell her that you know she was involved with the Stasi and that you want to employ the remaining members of Kress's cell. You're going to threaten to make this information known to the authorities if she doesn't play along. Then we sit back and see what happens. If she knows nothing, she'll go to the police, and the DST will notify us. If she doesn't go to the police, then you keep going back until she tells you something we want to know. She's going to sink or swim, gentlemen. If she swims, we let her go. If she sinks, we'll throw her a rope so she can hang herself."

Vogel dyed his brown hair a shade darker, combed it differently and grew a thin mustache. Hagen cut his hair close to the scalp, affected a pair of large thick glasses, inserted lifts in his shoes to change his gait. When they arrived in the village of Locquénolé, seven kilometers northwest of Morlaix, they were armed with two French-made pistols and the name of one of the Stasi case officers who had overseen the training of Totenkopf, Natzweiler *and Hohle—Kurt Glaub. Glaub's name was useful because Glaub was now dead. He couldn't blow their cover.*

Hagen and Vogel arrived at her house early in the morning to find her on the blanket in the yard, her legs treading the air above her head, like an upside-down swimmer treading water. Sink or swim . . .

Ingeborge Stromm was in her mid-forties now. She was thin and wiry, with black shoulder-length hair. Her face was drawn, her eyes sharp and inquisitive. Hagen introduced himself and Vogel as onetime associates of the late Kurt Glaub. The woman picked up on Hagen's accent, thought he was an Englander. Hagen didn't say one way or another.

"Glaub?" Stromm shrugged, pushed a curling length of hair off her forehead. "What is that to me? I know no one by that name. Who are you?"

"Businessmen. We're interested in engaging your services."

"Are you with a magazine?"

"It's not exactly in that line."

Stromm led them to a brick patio behind her house. A pitcher of ice water and a single glass stood on the patio table, beside a blue package of Gitane cigarettes. Hagen and Vogel sat down. Stromm pushed a cigarette from the pack and lit it, remained standing. A hundred feet away a man in a gray jacket and straw hat was clipping a hedge that ran along the back of the house. He paused to look at the three of them on the patio, then continued with his work.

Hagen did most of the talking. Vogel slumped down in his chair with a disinterested look on his face. The conversation began in French but quickly shifted to German. Hagen mentioned Glaub and he mentioned Heinrich Kress. Then he spoke of Totenkopf, Natzweiler and Hohle. As Hagen described the terrorist cell that Kress was a part of, a smile appeared on Stromm's face and remained there, frozen in place. When Hagen suggested that Stromm had also been a member of that cell, Stromm glanced at the gardener across the yard, as though wondering if it were time to call for help.

"Once again, gentlemen, you have me at a disadvantage," Stromm said. "As I've already said, I didn't know your friend Glaub. And as for

Heinrich, I told the German authorities everything I know years ago. I think I'll have to ask you to leave now."

"You worked with Kress. You could be valuable to us."

"This is all very amusing," Stromm said after a long pause. "Do you mind if I get my tape recorder, so I can get this down just as you have told it to me? And my camera too—surely you won't object to me taking your photograph? And when I'm finished, perhaps I'll call the police. You can make your proposition to them as well."

"That's not advisable."

"And why not?"

"If you go to the authorities, we'll have to tell them what we know about you. And if you choose not to assist us, we will also drop a line to the authorities."

"Do what you think you must, gentlemen." Stromm chewed on her lower lip as she studied the faces of her two visitors, then glanced once again at the gardener. He'd finished clipping the hedge and was now tossing the clippings into a metal trash can. "As for me, I have more important things to do today than listen to your nonsense. You'd better go now. I don't know how it is you've come to me or why and I don't care. But please don't come back. Rest assured, I'll tell the police whatever I like if you continue to bother me."

Hagen asked Vogel for a pen. On a piece of notepad paper he wrote the name and phone number of their hotel in Morlaix and tossed it onto the table.

"We'll be in Morlaix for a few days," Hagen said. "You can contact us there—when you are ready to discuss this further."

Stromm lit another cigarette as she watched Hagen and Vogel walk out to their rented car.

The plan was to stay in Morlaix for two or three days. They had to give Stromm time to think about the proposition and then to act, in whatever way she chose to act. In the meantime, Vogel and Hagen would spend as much time as possible away from the hotel. The false passports and other carefully prepared documentation they'd left in the hotel rooms would tell anyone who searched their rooms that they were who they claimed to be, two men traveling on Russian passports with extensive ties to the Middle East. Their belongings, right down to the labels on the clothing packed in their suitcases, were all chosen to support their cover story. The Russian angle was legitimate—many former Stasi operatives had retreated to Russia after the fall of East Germany. The Stasi had always worked closely with the Soviet KGB and many officers in the new Russian intelligence service had belonged at one time to the Stasi, including the now deceased Kurt Glaub.

They killed time in Morlaix all afternoon. When they checked back at the hotel that evening there were no messages for them. Vogel and Hagen went to their rooms to wash up before dinner. Neither man found any evidence that their rooms had been searched.

That night Vogel and Hagen drove to a country auberge several kilometers outside of Morlaix, on the road to Trégastel. The restaurant was recommended by the innkeeper in Morlaix and the auberge kitchen was as good as they had been led to believe. Vogel and Hagen finished the meal with half a bottle of Normandy Calvados, then settled the check and departed.

The channel fog rolled over the landscape. The air was crisp. Their breath left clouds of vapor as they walked out to the Mercedes. The Calvados was making Hagen feel sluggish and sleepy. Vogel agreed to drive.

"What if Stromm doesn't bite?" Vogel asked as they drove along the narrow country road. The fog was growing thicker and Vogel kept the speed down to seventy kilometers an hour. "Will we try the next name on the list? I hope the next person lives someplace a little more hospitable. The south of France perhaps. Or Italy—I've always wanted to go to Capri. Have you been to Capri, Bodo?"

Hagen was half asleep when the front end of the Mercedes suddenly bucked and the vehicle veered off toward the shoulder of the road. Vogel hit the brakes, pulled the car over. A flat front tire. And they were somewhere out in the forest, far from any petrol station. Vogel swore. Hagen sighed.

They got out of the car. Hagen stretched, took a deep breath of cool air. Vogel walked around to the trunk.

There was no warning. Hagen didn't hear a thing. One second there was only the deep evening silence along the empty country road, and the next second Vogel was screaming.

When Hagen reached him Vogel lay facedown behind the car, half in the roadway and half on the strip of grass at the edge of the road, his right hand under him, clutching his chest. In the glow from the taillights of the Mercedes Hagen saw the blood running out from under Vogel and down the incline of the road toward the tall grass.

Hagen was reaching for the pistol under his jacket when another shot cracked the rear window of the Mercedes like an eggshell . . .

A crash—loud enough to be heard over the pounding music.

A fight had broken out near the bar. Two young men had knocked over a small table covered with empty glasses as they swung their fists at each other in wide drunken arcs. Two bouncers rushed up, pulled the two men apart, hustled them toward the front door.

Hagen felt a hand on his shoulder.

"Hello, Bodo."

Harry Needles stood over him, a highball glass and a long thin cigar in one hand, a smile on his round and well-tanned face.

"How are you, Harry."

"I heard about Ronnie. I'm real sorry."

"Thanks, Harry." Hagen stood up. "Is there someplace we can talk?"

"You mean without shouting?"

"Something like that."

"I think I can manage that."

Hagen followed Harry Needles to the back of the club, then through a door and up a long narrow staircase to the second floor.

"How long has it been, Bodo?"

"Ten years."

"You're starting to look like your old man. You know that?"

"It's come up once or twice."

Harry Needles's office was a large rectangular room with a desk positioned at one end and a long couch upholstered in black leather at the other end. Three of the walls were covered in dark wood-grain paneling. The fourth wall of the office was composed entirely of sheets of one-way glass, through which Hagen could see the entire club laid out one floor below. A glass-topped table surrounded by eight chairs sat in front of the one-way glass and a large and well-stocked bar trolley stood near the desk. The room was surprisingly quiet, the music downstairs audible only as a muffled bass beat. Hagen was grateful for the calm.

Harry Needles stepped up to the bar trolley. "What are you drinking these days?"

Hagen asked for a bourbon and soda. Needles poured it, then freshened his own drink while Hagen stood at the window, studying the view.

Needles brought the drinks over, set them on the table.

"When did you get into town?" Harry Needles said.

"Yesterday. The funeral was yesterday."

Harry Needles shook his head. "It's hard to believe, Bodo. I'm not sure I do believe it. I just saw Ronnie last week. He'd just gotten into town and he came by. Next thing I hear he's dead. I hope they find whoever did it, hang that bastard good. I'd like to be there when they do."

"McGrath is working the case."

Harry Needles nodded, a circumspect look on his face. "McGrath is a good cop."

"I ran into him at the funeral."

"I didn't hear about it or I would've been there."

"Wasn't much to it."

Harry Needles nodded. He seemed to want to say something more about Ronnie and his death and the funeral but he couldn't find the words. He shifted gears, motioned toward the table. "Have a seat, Bodo. Best seat in the house." Needles puffed on his cigar, raised his chin, blew a stream of smoke up toward the ceiling. "What do you think of my place?"

"The restaurant didn't work out?"

"Steak and eggs, tits and ass—it's a living, either way."

Before sitting down Hagen and Needles turned their chairs side-ways to the table so they could keep an eye on the nightclub below, as though the flashing lights and milling crowd and dancers and pounding music were all boiling and building up to a dangerous explosion that neither of them wanted to miss. Harry Needles's hair had gone gray but he looked fit and trim and successful. Harry Needles had always looked successful. It was in the well-preserved tan and the straight white teeth and the pleasant, knowing smile. It was in the crisply pressed white shirt he wore and the sharply creased black slacks and tasseled two-tone loafers. It was in the way he carried himself, with an air of entitle-ment. Harry Needles hadn't always lived well but he knew how to look like he lived well. To some people—like Harry Needles—it was the same thing.

"Tell me about Ronnie," Hagen said. "What was he up to last week?"

Needles sat back. "Nothing much to tell. He showed up here a week ago Sunday. Said he'd just gotten into town. I was surprised to see him—I thought Karl Hagen's boys had left this town for good. I brought him up here and we had a few drinks and talked. It was good to see him. Ronnie had his problems like anybody, but he was a good kid, Bodo."

Hagen took a drink. The bourbon went down warm and solid. "What did he say?"

"Not too much. Just bullshitting. He was happy to be out of the Legion and back home. Didn't seem to have any plans other than drinking and screwing. Nothing wrong with that."

"Where was he staying?"

"I don't think he said." Needles gave Hagen a sharp look. Hagen recalled Jack Gubbs's remark—"Do you always make noises like a cop?" But Hagen wanted answers. He needed answers. And the only way to get answers was to ask questions.

"You see him again, after Sunday?"

"I didn't see him at all. He came by on Tuesday but I wasn't here. Then on Friday I heard on the news about what happened. What was he doing out at Hoover, Bodo? If he was in trouble, I wish he'd told me. I would've helped him out. He knew that. You know that."

"I know, Harry."

"I wish he'd told me."

"Did Ronnie mention a fellow named Gubbs?"

"Jack Gubbs?" Harry Needles looked surprised to hear that name. "You know Gubbs?"

"Sure."

"What's he all about?"

"Who have you been talking to?"

"Marty Ray."

"Marty Ray showed up at the funeral?"

"No, I went to see him today. What about Gubbs?"

Needles flicked cigar ash into a glass ashtray. "Gubbs works for Marty Ray. Worked for him for years. I never liked Gubbs. He's a loose cannon. Then again, Marty Ray's a loose cannon so maybe that's why they get along. What's Ronnie got to do with Gubbs?"

Hagen explained that apparently Ronnie knew Gubbs when Ronnie worked for the Ray brothers, and that Ronnie might have stayed at Gubbs's apartment last week. Hagen didn't mention that he'd talked to Gubbs the day before. He kept his visit to the Sniff out of the conversation as well. Perhaps it was only habit—over the last ten years Hagen had grown used to playing his cards close to the vest.

Harry Needles knew nothing about Ronnie's association with Jack Gubbs. "I know Gubbs because I used to have business with the Rays. The Rays loaned me some of the capital to buy this place. For a while there a lot of money changed hands. Above the table, under the table—business is business. At first I dealt with Jimmy, but after Jimmy died Marty used Gubbs as a go-between. Until a few months ago Marty still owned a percentage of this place. But I paid him off. This place is mine now, top to bottoms."

Harry Needles smiled at his pun, crushed his cigar out in the ashtray. Then, "Let me tell you, Bodo, I didn't like being in debt to Marty. I don't like the man. Don't know too many people who do. He's always been strange but since his brother died he's gotten very strange. But you know how he is. How did you like working for him?"

"Jimmy had the brains. Marty was along for the ride. So tell me, Harry—who whacked Jimmy Ray?"

Harry Needles snorted. "I never asked. You can get yourself into trouble asking questions like that. Who whacked Jimmy Ray—a lot of people would still like to know. Like McGrath. He was on that case. Gave him some torment, I'm sure. I hope he does better . . ." Harry Needles's voice trailed off as he gave Hagen an awkward glance.

Harry nearly choked on his drink when Hagen asked him about the rumor that Ronnie might have been implicated in the Jimmy Ray murder.

"Marty didn't tell you that."

"Sure he did."

"Then he needs his medication adjusted." Harry Needles started to say more, took another drink instead. After a pause he continued. "Marty talks trash. You know that. He's a clown. But he can be a dangerous clown. So be careful. Don't fuck with him too much. Jimmy's not around to keep him on a leash like in the old days. And your old man isn't around to bail you out of trouble."

"He never bailed me out."

"That's not what I remember."

Hagen changed the subject. "Marty also told me Ronnie was hanging around with one of your dancers."

"Marty did a lot of talking."

"You know the girl?"

"Of course. Theresa—Theresa Sanchez. Ronnie met her when he

was downstairs at the bar the night I saw him. Then he came by again on Tuesday to see her and I guess they went out. She isn't a dancer anymore. She's one of my bar managers. Smart woman. Goes to college. She's down there right now."

"I'd like to talk to her, Harry."

"She'll be off work in about a half hour. You can talk to her up here if you want."

Harry Needles pulled the small cigar tin out of his shirt pocket, flipped it open. Offered Hagen a cigar, then took one for himself. Harry lit Hagen's cigar and then his own. "Ronnie did a little work for me too, when I opened this place. Did he ever mention that? I had a hard time finding good people at first, so he'd come by some nights and look after things, work the front door. Help me keep an eye on the bouncers, make sure they weren't ripping me off every time I turned my back."

"Was that before he went to work for the Rays?"

"Same time. He did a little work for them, a little for me. Like I said, the brothers put up some of the money to open this place, so it was all in the family. I liked having Ronnie around. He was having a tough time of it right then—a little too much drinking, a little too much dope. Kind of a lost soul. I tried to keep him busy just to give him something to do so he'd stay out of trouble. I thought he might stick around and come work for me full time, but then he joined the Legion. I was kind of disappointed when he told me."

As they smoked the cigars the conversation shifted to small talk. Hagen was surprised to learn that Harry lived down in Laughlin, Nevada. Hagen could remember when Laughlin was nothing but a wide patch on a long hot desert road. Harry Needles asked Hagen what he was doing these days in Germany. Hagen gave Harry the same story he'd given McGrath—he was a security consultant for a German industrial firm. The only people Hagen had ever told about his work for the CIA were his father, Ronnie and the Sniff. He was sure that his father and the Sniff had kept it under their hats, as he'd asked them to. He wasn't so sure about Ronnie. Not that it mattered much now.

The telephone on the desk rang. Harry Needles got up to answer it. A small pair of binoculars with Zeiss lenses sat in the center of the table and Hagen picked them up and peered through them, studying the scene below. The Japanese tourists Hagen had seen earlier were gone. They had been replaced by three young men in football jerseys who looked almost shamefaced as they stared at a young Latina dancer who lay on the stage, rolling forward and back, her ankles locked behind her neck and her chin resting between her large round breasts.

Harry Needles's phone conversation was brief and monosyllabic. When he hung up the phone he said to Hagen, "Small world."

"How so?"

"Jack Gubbs is downstairs. And he wants to talk to you."

8.

"HELLO, JACK," Needles said, when Gubbs stepped into the office. "Wish I could say it's a pleasure."

"Sorry to drop in on you like this, Harry," Gubbs said. He paused in the doorway, his hand on the doorknob. His bleary red eyes moved between Harry Needles and Hagen, back and forth, as though he wondered which of the two men he might have to physically defend himself against in the next few seconds. He nodded toward Hagen, said to Harry Needles, "I just wanted to talk to your man here for a minute."

"Talk away," Hagen said.

"Maybe we can talk alone."

Needles looked at Hagen. Hagen shrugged. Harry Needles walked to the door, keeping his eyes on Gubbs as Gubbs moved aside to let him pass. Harry Needles said he had a few things to do downstairs. "Back in a flash," he said before closing the office door behind him.

Gubbs noticed the bar trolley, said, "Well, thank you, Harry, don't mind if I do," as he walked over to it. He poured three fingers of vodka into a highball glass, drank some of it down, paused to study the contents of the glass in the light, then poured the rest of it down his throat. He set the glass down hard on the trolley, seemed to smile to himself at a job well done.

"Harry Needles is a fine fellow," Gubbs said.

"He doesn't like you much."

"He doesn't have to anymore."

"Did he like you before?"

Gubbs turned to face Hagen, shrugging his shoulders to adjust the hang of the loose-fitting yellow sport coat he wore over a maroon polo shirt. His pasty face looked like a clay sculpture that someone had pummeled with their fists. "When Marty owned him he liked me just fine. Too bad that Marty sold out. I liked the old days. Harry used to introduce me to the girls." Gubbs shook his head at the memory. He didn't seem to quite believe it himself. "Lot of nice girls in this place."

"How did you know I was here?"

"You're not so hard to find." Gubbs came over to the table, pulled out a chair and sat down. "I talked to Marty. He said you were headed in this direction. Looking for the dancer who was with Ronnie. So I decided to drop by. Gives me a chance to see my girls again."

Hagen didn't believe it. It was more reasonable to conclude that Marty Ray knew where he was because it was Marty Ray who was having him followed.

"So what do you want to tell me?"

"First things first. If I tell you what I know, you're going to get off my back. Understand? Forget you ever met me. I don't know what happened to Ronnie. But whatever it was, it has nothing to do with me. Is that clear?"

Hagen almost laughed. This wasn't the Gubbs he'd talked to yesterday. Someone had pumped Gubbs full of courage and sent him over here like a windup toy. It could only have been Marty Ray. What kind of line was Gubbs going to try to feed him?

"The police are going to find out about you sooner or later," Hagen said. "All I can promise you is that I won't pick up the phone five minutes after you leave here and tell them about you."

"It's not the police I'm worried about."

"Then who is it?"

Gubbs pulled out a pack of cigarettes, lit one with a gold Zippo lighter. Took a long drag, then scratched his forehead with the thumb of his cigarette hand, puzzling something together. "Ronnie was your brother. You want to find out who killed him. I can understand that.

I'm fine with that. Ronnie was a friend of mine. Maybe you don't be-lieve that but he was. But you're stirring up a pot full of shit and if you keep throwing my name around, then maybe someone's going to get the idea that I know something I shouldn't know. And then maybe what happened to your brother happens to me too. All I'm saying is, go on about your business, do what you have to, but leave me out of it. I don't feel like catching a bullet because some asshole keeps drop-ping my name in all the wrong places. People get shot in this town every day, for all kinds of reasons. I don't want to be one of those people."

"If you're not worried about the police, why haven't you talked to them?"

"Maybe I have."

"Have you or haven't you?"

"If I told you I had, would you believe it?"

"Probably not."

"There you are. I'd be wasting my breath. And I like my breath, Hagen. I'd like to keep breathing it. Maybe it's not worth much but it's all I've got."

"What did you come here to tell me?"

Gubbs took another long drag, exhaled cigarette smoke through his nose. "You asked me yesterday if Ronnie was looking for a fence."

"That's right."

"Well, he was."

"That's not news, Gubbs."

"Let me finish. He asked me if I knew a fence and I told him about a guy I know. Not someone I know—someone I've heard of. Working for Marty, I hear things sometimes. You know how it is. So I asked around and got the guy's phone number. I gave it to Ronnie. I didn't hear anything more about it. I didn't know whether Ronnie called him or not and I didn't care. None of my business. Today I called the guy myself. I told him what happened to Ronnie and I told him about you. The guy said he talked to Ronnie last week. He was supposed to talk to him again on Saturday but Ronnie didn't show up. He hadn't heard that Ronnie was dead. I asked him if it was okay if I told you about him. He said he didn't care. He sounded kind of interested in talking to you."

Gubbs puffed on his cigarette. The fingers of his free hand tapped the surface of the table, stopped, started again. Gubbs was a nervous man. Was he always nervous or was he just a poor liar? Hagen was inclined to believe that he was always nervous. But that didn't mean that Gubbs wasn't lying right now.

"What's the guy's name?" Hagen said.

"His first name is Winston. I don't know his last name. Everybody calls him Winnie the Poof."

"What kind of name is that?"

"It's what people call him, that's all. I guess he's some kind of flamer. What do I care? Live and let live. Right, Hagen? Live and let live."

"Did he say why he wanted to talk to me?"

"He's looking for whatever it was that Ronnie wanted to sell him, he didn't tell me what. He wonders if maybe you know where the thing is. Yesterday you asked me about a wooden hand. That's the thing, right?"

Hagen ignored the question. "How do I get in touch with this Poof fellow?"

"He wants you to call him tomorrow." Gubbs set his cigarette on the lip of the ashtray, pulled a leather billfold out. He removed a slip of paper and handed it to Hagen. It was a phone number—written in a crooked, childlike hand.

"Don't cross him, Hagen. He's got juice. He might be a little light in the heels, but he'll walk all over you if you cross him."

"You said you didn't know him."

"I don't. But I know of him. And that's enough."

"What about Sidney Trunk? What do you know about him?"

Gubbs shook his head. "Never heard of him."

"You sure?"

"What do you want me to do, cross my heart and spit on a Bible?"

"Trunk was some kind of fence too. He talked to Ronnie on Monday—which was a neat trick because Ronnie was dead. Then he got even trickier, got himself burned to death in his house out in Boulder last night before I could talk to him. If any of this starts sounding familiar, Gubbs, just speak right up."

"I don't like what you're getting at, Hagen."

"Gubbs, why did Marty send you here to tell me all this?"

Gubbs stubbed his cigarette out in the ashtray with short jabs. Down in the club the deep bass beat of the music pounded on and on, louder now than it had been. Hagen could almost see the synapses in Gubbs's foggy brain pulsing and pounding in time to the beat. Hagen wondered how fast Gubbs's mind was working, and where it was taking him.

Gubbs stood, pointed a shaky finger at Hagen. "You don't listen too well. You wanted some names, I gave you a name. It's the only one I've got and I'm sticking my neck out by giving it to you. Now you can just forget about me. Leave my name out of this mess. We're square now. Right?"

"If you say so."

Gubbs walked out of the office. Slammed the door shut behind him.

Hagen smiled. Winnie the Poof? Well, he'd asked Gubbs for names. And that was certainly a name.

Hagen picked up the binoculars—

Down on the center stage two young women in leather boots, G-strings and feathered tiaras on their heads were going to town. One of the women was on her knees, kneading her bare breasts and bobbing her head in the air while the other one stood over her, gyrating her hips, the sequins of her G-string only inches from the kneeling girl's face. A standing crowd had gathered. Hagen could see the crumpled greenbacks landing on the stage.

Hagen thought of the sex clubs in Berlin. Hagen had interviewed more than one ex-Stasi agent in the smoke-filled reaches of those clubs. The clubs were dark, anonymous and hidden—just the place for a clandestine conversation—and the line between what was make-believe and what was real was often blurred beyond distinction. The women were seldom beautiful but they were willing and creative, and the stage was a hothouse floor that had to be mopped every hour or two to keep the artistes from slipping and falling under the lurid theater lights.

If Harry Needles had ever tried to re-create a Berlin sex club show here in Las Vegas the audience would be stunned into an uncomfortable silence and Harry Needles would quickly find himself in jail. But that was the difference between Las Vegas and Berlin, at least the Berlin that Hagen had been required to live in. The one was strictly show business. The other was murkier, seedier, perhaps a little psychotic.

Like Jack Gubbs.

Gubbs was distasteful. Gubbs was seedy. Gubbs was off balance. But was he telling the truth? Maybe he was. But true or not, someone else had told Gubbs to come here to tell him about Winnie the Poof, Hagen was sure of that. And Marty Ray was the likely choice.

Hagen set the binoculars down, walked over to Harry Needles's desk and picked up the phone. He dialed the number for the Venetian, asked the clerk who answered to connect him with his room phone so that he could check his messages. There was one, from the Sniff. He'd talked to Dallas Martinez. Martinez had agreed to meet Hagen that night, eleven o'clock. At the top of the Stratosphere Tower. The southwest side, facing the Strip.

"He's not thrilled about it, Bodo," the Sniff said on the recording. "But he'll play along—just this once."

Hagen hung up the phone.

When Harry Needles returned he disappeared into a small bathroom adjoining the office, came back out with his shirtsleeves rolled up, wiping his hands on a white hand towel, as though a visit from Jack Gubbs required a good scrub afterward.

Hagen said, "Harry, did Ronnie ask you if you could find him a fence?"

Harry Needles started to laugh. The laugh died out when he saw the expression on Hagen's face. Hagen hadn't been sure earlier that he wanted to tell Harry Needles the whole story. But right now Hagen needed to know if Harry Needles had heard anything about it. Anything at all. Harry Needles knew the Sniff from years ago, when Harry Needles worked for Bodo's father at the Sands, and now Hagen told Harry what the Sniff had said, about Ronnie looking for a fence and asking for a loan. About the photograph of the wooden hand—what Ronnie called the dead man's hand. About Hagen's visit to Gubbs's apartment the day before. Hagen didn't mention the woman from Paris and he didn't mention Sidney Trunk—the story was clear enough without those two angles. When Hagen told Harry what Gubbs had said, about the fence named Winnie the Poof, Harry Needles could only shake his head. Harry had heard the name before, but he wasn't sure where, or when.

A slow ponderous look appeared on Harry Needles's face. "What kind of trouble did Ronnie get into, Bodo?"

"I wish I knew."

Harry Needles turned away. He looked out on the bright flashing lights of his nightclub. Deep lines appeared at the corners of his eyes, as though he'd spotted something down there that could explain to him what Hagen couldn't, if only he could squint hard enough to bring it into sharp focus.

Hagen worked on his drink for a minute before he broke the heavy silence.

"Harry?"

"Yeah, Bodo?"

"Can you get the girl now?"

"I'm very sorry," Theresa Sanchez said to Hagen, her brow knitted together in sympathy, as soon as she entered Harry Needles's office.

"When I heard that your brother died in such a terrible way—" The unfinished remark hung in the air. Theresa Sanchez shook her head slowly.

The woman's condolences sounded genuine but there was a wariness in her eyes as she studied Hagen. She wasn't sure what this was about and wasn't sure she wanted to find out. Harry Needles explained that Hagen wanted to ask her a few questions. "Bodo thinks it might be important." Harry Needles motioned toward the table, gave Hagen a questioning look. Hagen shook his head. He wanted Harry to stay. The woman was nervous. Harry's presence might calm her.

She was a short woman, no more than five foot three. Twenty-five years old, Hagen guessed. Her face was full and dark, with brown eyes and long eyelashes and black hair that was parted in the middle and hung past her shoulders. She wore black slacks and the requisite Venus Lounge polo shirt. She wasn't a naturally thin woman but she had a thin waist that called attention to her full hips and breasts. An attractive woman, and one who spent some time keeping herself attractive.

"So you met Ronnie on Sunday, is that right?" Hagen began when the three of them were seated at the table.

"He was downstairs at the bar," Theresa Sanchez said, soft Spanish inflections in her voice. "Waiting for Harry to come in. Business was kind of slow so I talked to him for a little bit. He said he was an old friend of Harry's and that he worked here at the club when it first opened."

"What else did you talk about?"

Theresa Sanchez looked to Harry Needles for help. He smiled, nodded—go ahead and tell the man. "Just shooting the breeze," she said, hesitant. "He told me he'd just gotten out of the military and that he'd been away from Las Vegas for many years. He'd had a little bit to drink but he was pleasant. He asked me if I wanted to go out for a drink when I finished work. I couldn't go—I had to get home and study. I told him some other time maybe. He said okay. That was all."

"When was the next time you saw him?"

"Tuesday night. He came in about eight o'clock. He sat at the bar and asked me again if I wanted to go out for a drink. I was off at nine so I said okay, and when I finished we drove over to the Bellagio and had a couple of drinks and talked. He told me about the places he'd been to—Africa and France. I'm in the nursing program at UNLV so we talked about that a little bit. After we left Bellagio we drove to Diamond Jim's. He said he used to work there too. We had a couple of drinks there and then I had to go. I had class in the morning—I didn't want to stay out late. We were going to maybe go out again last weekend. . . ." Theresa Sanchez's voice trailed off.

"What happened at Diamond Jim's?"

Sanchez shifted in her chair. "Nothing much. We had one drink at the bar and then he asked me if I wanted to play blackjack. I don't gamble, but I sat with him at the tables and watched while he played blackjack. He said I'd bring him good luck. I'm afraid I didn't."

Theresa Sanchez's gaze fell from Hagen's face, came to rest on the surface of the table. The idea that she hadn't brought Ronnie Hagen luck seemed for her to extend beyond the game of blackjack at Diamond Jim's.

"Did he lose a lot of money at the tables?"

"Not so much. He didn't play for long."

"How much?"

"Maybe a hundred dollars, I'm not sure."

Hagen glanced at Harry Needles. Harry was smiling, throwing encouraging looks at Sanchez, trying to make her feel more comfortable than she obviously felt. A hundred dollars—that was nothing. A hundred dollars was cab fare. But right then one thing struck Hagen as strange—Ronnie saw Harry Needles on Sunday night. He didn't mention needing money, didn't ask to borrow any. On Monday he went to the Sniff, looking for a fence and asking to borrow a thousand dollars minimum, more if the Sniff could spare it. Why hadn't Ronnie gone to Harry Needles for a loan? Harry Needles would've been an easier touch. Harry Needles had always been fond of Ronnie and Ronnie knew that.

Hagen didn't get much else out of Theresa Sanchez. After Diamond Jim's, Ronnie had dropped her off at her apartment. That was the last time she saw him. Sanchez didn't recall Ronnie speaking to anyone at Diamond Jim's—didn't recall much else at all. She shook her head sadly, told Hagen that she wished that she could be of more help, but she simply didn't know anything. Or was it that she just didn't want to tell him all that she knew, Hagen wondered. She was nervous. She was worried. Was it because Harry Needles was here? Hagen wanted to talk to her alone now, see how she acted without Harry Needles sitting next to her.

Hagen saw his chance when Theresa Sanchez got up from the table, asked Harry if she could use his phone to call her roommate for a ride home.

"I'm leaving now too," Hagen said. "I can give you a lift."

"Thank you but no, my roommate will pick me up."

"It's no trouble."

Harry Needles got up from the table, placed his arm around Theresa Sanchez's shoulders, gave her a friendly squeeze. "I'll vouch for Bodo, Theresa. He's a safe driver."

Theresa Sanchez looked from Harry to Hagen, tried to smile.

Theresa Sanchez's apartment was on the east side of town. Hagen took the surface streets—Industrial to Wyoming, Wyoming to Las Vegas Boulevard, then right on Bonanza Road. The woman's manner had changed as soon as they left the club. The politeness and reserve melted away. It was replaced by a hardness and suspicion. Theresa Sanchez was more savvy that she let on. But then a woman probably didn't work as a professional stripper without learning a few things about the world and how it works.

"You used to be a dancer, is that right?" Hagen said.

Theresa Sanchez stared straight ahead. "Did Harry tell you that?"

"Marty Ray told me that."

"Did he?"

"How well do you know Marty?"

"I know who he is. He used to own part of the Venus Lounge. But I don't know him."

"He remembers you."

"What did he say about me?"

"He said he remembers you when you danced."

"I don't dance anymore."

"Do you make more money working behind the bar?"

"I made more money dancing."

"So why did you switch?"

"Mister Hagen, have you ever spent six hours dancing in four-inch heels?"

"Not that I can recall."

"Try it some time. You won't last long."

"I'm sure of that."

Theresa Sanchez kept her hands in her lap, her fingers worrying a small gold ring on her little finger. She slid the ring off, slid it back on.

Hagen tried a lie, just to see where it got him. "Marty Ray also said he saw you and Ronnie at Diamond Jim's last week."

"Maybe he did. But I didn't see him." The woman's answer was quick and firm.

Hagen changed the subject. "Why does Harry Needles make you nervous?"

"Does he?"

"You weren't very comfortable in his office. You seemed bothered by the fact that he was there."

"Harry is my boss. I like him. I don't want him to think badly of me. Having him there listening while I'm being questioned by the police isn't my idea of a good time."

"You think I'm a cop?"

"Aren't you? You ask questions like a cop. You have a gun under your coat. If you're not a cop, what are you?"

Hagen wondered if the Heckler & Koch in the shoulder holster un-

THE RAGGED END OF NOWHERE

der his sport coat stood out more than he thought. Either that, or Theresa Sanchez had sharp eyes and knew what to look for.

Farther out on Bonanza Road Theresa Sanchez busied herself with giving directions. Turn left here, then down one block and turn right. They were near the address now. She opened her handbag and began sifting through the contents. She pulled out a key ring. A rabbit's foot covered in white fur was attached to the ring.

"Mister Hagen, I'm very tired," Theresa Sanchez said as she got out of the car. "I've told you what I know. I wish I could help you more but I can't. I hope you find what you're looking for. Thank you for the ride. Good night."

She closed the car door hard.

Hagen watched her ascend the outside stairway that led to the second-floor walkway of her apartment house. A line of palm trees stood out front. The streetlights threw the shadows of the palm fronds against the side of the building, long fingerlike shadows that seemed to grip the building tightly.

Hagen was certain of one thing—Theresa Sanchez knew a few things about cops.

And she had learned them the hard way.

Hagen drove to the Stratosphere Tower, turned his car over to the valet at the hotel entrance. He had some time to kill before his meeting with Dallas Martinez. He walked around inside the casino, watched the action at the tables, studied the faces in the crowds. The Stratosphere might be the tallest building in Las Vegas—tallest observation tower in the United States, according to a sign on the wall near the entrance—but the action was all low rollers, the kind of grind action that came into town on tour buses and left again at two o'clock in the morning to save on the price of a hotel room. Day-trippers—old folks betting their pension checks, young parents with bad haircuts and souvenir T-shirts, a few wide-eyed young men whooping it up on free casino beer that they spilled on themselves and the card tables while they tossed dollar bills around like someone cared.

After a while Hagen rode the elevator up to the tower's observation deck.

The circular deck was noisy and crowded. A roller coaster flew around the circumference of the roof above the deck and another carnival ride called the Big Shot—some type of multiseated platform that shot riders straight up to the tip of the tower on a burst of compressed air—stood above the roller coaster. Need a strong stomach for that kind of entertainment, Hagen thought. Or several stiff drinks that just might come back up after a few good jolts up into the night sky a thousand feet in the air above Las Vegas.

Hagen worked his way around to the southwest edge of the deck. A crowd of young people dressed for a swank nightclub milled around, pointing out the landmarks on the Strip. The lights of the city looked like a sparkling carpet. The nightclubbers took snapshots of each other and toasted themselves. They slowly dispersed and now Hagen noticed a man standing farther down the deck. An older Latino man, dressed in black—thin black silk shirt that hung loosely from his thick frame, black slacks, black shoes. As the man studied the view of the city before him he pulled a peanut out of his pants pocket. He crushed the shell with deliberation, pulled the nuts out and chewed them slowly, tossed the pieces of shell aside, wiped the palms of his hands together. Then he proceeded on with another peanut plumbed from the depths of his pocket.

The man's face was long and wrinkled. His gray hair was as unkempt as his bushy gray mustache.

"Quite a view, isn't it?" the man said as Hagen approached him. "Vegas looks nice and tidy from up here. Looks like a place where a person might want to live. It's a different story down on the street, but up here it looks kind of peaceful." The man glanced over his shoulder as a metallic rumble filled the air. The roller coaster sped around the tower above them in tracks that looked too narrow, turns that looked too sharp to be anything other than fatal. "The kiddie rides kind of ruin the effect, but I guess you can't have everything."

"Martinez?"

The man nodded. "And you're Hagen." The man popped another peanut into his mouth, wiped his hands together. "I was going to stuff a red carnation in a buttonhole but I didn't have one. Wasn't sure you'd recognize me without some kind of signal. Big spic with a beer gut— they grow on trees around here." Martinez patted his stomach, his eyes focused off into the distance. "And if they're not careful, sometimes they hang from trees. Like Sidney Trunk."

"Was he a big spic with a beer gut?"

"No, and he didn't hang from a tree, but the result was the same."

"Who killed him?"

"Is that all you wanted to ask me?"

"That's one thing."

Martinez shrugged. "I don't know who killed Trunk. Maybe you killed him. What do you think of that? Next stupid question."

"All right. The Sniff gave you a photograph of a wooden hand the other day. Something my brother wanted to sell. You passed on it and gave it to Trunk. Why?"

"Why did I take a pass, or why did I give it to Trunk?"

"Both."

Martinez turned away to spit a piece of peanut skin out. Then, "First thing, I took a pass because it wasn't anything I wanted to deal with. So I gave it to Trunk. Trunk was no friend of mine, but we traveled in the same circles now and then and I tossed him a bone when I had one to toss. The Sniff gave me the picture and a phone number that went with it and I handed it off to Trunk. What he planned to do about it, I don't know. And before we go any further with this, let me tell you one thing, Hagen. If you drag me into a police jam because of what happened to your brother, you're going to have a fight on your hands. Maybe a bigger fight than you can handle. In case the Sniff didn't make that clear."

"He made it clear."

"Just so you understand."

"What I don't understand is why you took a pass on the hand."

"It wasn't my line."

"What is your line?"

"I deal in rare and precious objects."

"The Sniff says you're a fence."

"The Sniff has an odd sense of humor."

"Sure he does."

Martinez stroked his mustache. "The hand—you know what it is?"

"I've got a good idea. I had a conversation with a little French-woman last night. She came to town to talk to my brother about the hand, but she got here too late. She works for some kind of high-end antiques dealer in Paris—a firm called Amarantos. From what I gather, the hand came from a piece of religious statuary—a wooden carving of Jesus that came out of a town in Russia called Vologda. The statue was cut to pieces years ago. She knows someone who wants to put the pieces back together again and is willing to pay for the privilege."

"What was the woman's name?"

"Suzanne Cosette. Know her?"

"Can't say that I do. But Amarantos—I've heard that name. Georges Amarantos."

A pair of young lovers walked slowly past, arm in arm. Martinez fell silent until they moved on. Then, "Amarantos operates in European circles. Didn't know he was branching out into Vegas."

"Is he legit?"

"He buys and sells. Like me." A frown crossed Martinez's face, made his mustache look lopsided and weighty. "But I'll give you this much for free—the woman told you a fish story."

"So give me a story without the fish."

Martinez felt around in his pocket for another peanut. His hand came out empty. He sighed. "The Sniff tells me you know a few things about the French Foreign Legion. So try this on for size—what do you know about the Hand of Danjou?"

The name didn't ring any bells for Hagen. Martinez gave Hagen a crooked smile. "Let me tell you a story, Hagen. A little piece of history. I wouldn't want you to leave here without learning something.

"Fact—in the middle of the nineteenth century, about the time of the Civil War in the United States, the French started fucking around in Mexican politics. Mexico didn't want to play along and the French came up with the harebrained idea of putting an Austrian archduke in charge of the country to help the French control their little brown brethren. His name was Maximilian. The French made him the Emperor of Mexico. The Mexicans didn't appreciate the gesture and they put up a fight. So France sent the Foreign Legion into Mexico to fight back.

"Fact—one of the Legionnaires was an officer named Danjou. He was a captain, commanded a small force of men. One thing that was funny about Captain Danjou—he'd lost his left hand in an explosion before he got to Mexico. In place of his real hand the Legion fitted him with a wooden hand. It was a clever piece of work—the fingers of the hand were made so that they could be moved. Kind of funny when you think of it. Guy sitting around pushing his wooden fingers different ways, just for something to do.

"Fact—the good captain's luck ran bad in Mexico. His troops were surrounded one day by Mexican forces and they were slaughtered. The story goes that they fought like mad dogs right up to the end. But the Mexicans knew how to put down mad dogs. Too bad for the Legion. After the battle was over, the captain's wooden hand was found in the debris. The Legion took it back home with them, locked it up in a crypt. They set about building a myth around it—an object lesson in valor for all the young Legionnaires who might not be as keen to die in battle as Captain Danjou was. To this day the Legion drags the hand out every now and then. They march around with it, salute it, pray to it for all I know. It's become a sort of sacred relic. Some people have even ascribed to it certain occult powers. It's all bullshit, of course—Captain Danjou and his troops died because they were outmanned and outgunned and his hand is nothing but a piece of rotten wood. But in some circles that hand would be a valuable commodity, if it were to somehow disappear from its resting place and become available on the open market. You see what I'm getting at?"

The Hand of Danjou—Hagen didn't recognize the name. But the story Martinez had just told him stirred something in the back of his mind. A vague recollection that flickered at the very edge of his memory. An image of a long line of Legionnaires, standing at attention in dress uniforms. The sun beating down on them. An honor guard of three Legionnaires bearing bright battle flags marching before the assembled soldiers, following a single officer carrying in both hands a small glass case that contained—what? A wooden hand? Hagen wasn't sure. But he was sure that it was his father who had once shown him a photograph of this scene. Many years ago.

"Did my brother tell you all of this?" Hagen said.

Dallas Martinez looked down, pushed the toe of one shoe back and forth against the cement surface of the deck, like he was trying to rub away the patina of dirt to see more clearly what lay below his feet. "He gave me the gist of it. He also told me that the hand was in his possession and that he wanted to sell it for whatever he could get. I might have been interested in working with him—I've got Mexican blood in my veins, in case you haven't picked up on that. Selling this wooden hand that the good captain lost while fighting and killing my forefathers in their own land appeals to my sense of justice, or at least my sense of humor. But when I looked into your brother's story I found one awkward problem. He was full of shit."

"What do you mean?"

"Just what I said. His story was bullshit. I'm not without resources, Hagen. I have a few contacts in Europe myself. I had them check on things. What they told me was this—the Hand of Danjou is sitting in a well-guarded Legion museum in Aubagne, France, right now. Like it has for years. It hasn't gone anywhere. Believe me, if someone stole that hand, everyone would know. It's a national treasure in France. They'd turn the country upside down looking for it. And if they heard that it had run off to Vegas, the whole thing would become a diplomatic hassle. The French would pull strings in Washington and before you knew it there would be so many federal cops running around here looking for that hand, Vegas would look like a doughnut convention. No, Hagen, whatever your brother was hawking, it was pure baloney. One hundred percent all-beef wiener. If he really had a wooden hand in his possession and not just a picture of one, it wasn't the Hand of Danjou."

"If the thing is a phony, why did you give it to Trunk?"

Martinez frowned, scratched himself. "Trunk wasn't bothered greatly by questions of authenticity. He sold what he could sell. Caveat emptor—that was his philosophy. And it's not a bad philosophy. Until someone gets pissed off and comes around looking for their money back because they bought a shaggy-dog story. I told him what I thought of the deal when I gave him the photograph. I gave him fair warning. Trunk wasn't smart but he hadn't lost all his marbles. He'd have known how dangerous it would be to try to sell the hand as the real thing. My guess was that he'd go ahead and try to sell it without claiming that it was real. Even a phony might be worth a few bucks, if it was a good phony. Trunk would've been happy with that kind of profit. I don't deal with that kind of crap—it's small change. Not worth the trouble."

"If the dingus were real, what would it be worth?"

"Whatever the market will bear."

"Take a guess."

Martinez pursed his lips as he thought about it. He didn't have to think about it too long. "Five million. That would be a fair starting price. It could go higher, depending on who was involved." Martinez looked squarely at Hagen now. "But it's not real. My sources in France are good. I trust them."

"So if this thing is a fake, why does Amarantos want it?"

"Good question. And one that I can't answer. But this Russian Jesus nonsense is a smoke screen."

"Let's say that Amarantos thinks the hand is real."

"Not likely."

"Let's just say it is likely. Would he be trying to buy it so he could turn around and sell it, knowing that it was stolen and that a police hassle came with it?"

"Hagen, in this business 'stolen' is kind of a nebulous concept. Amarantos deals in things he knows he can sell. If the hand were real and Amarantos was trying to buy it, then I would say that he's already lined up a buyer who wants the thing bad enough to pay the freight and then keep it under wraps for good. And that's not an impediment. There are people in this world who'll buy anything if they can get a good price. They might not give a shit about what the hand is. They'd buy it and use it as currency. Like a box full of greenbacks they picked up for pennies on the dollar. Where do you think all the stolen paintings go that you hear about—the Vermeers and Picassos and Renoirs? Currency—nothing but black currency. There's a black economy operating in the world that most people never hear of, but it's as real as any economy and it has its own kinds of currency. But that wooden hand your brother was pushing—it's not real. That's what I came here to tell you, Hagen. And that's all I can tell you."

Hagen asked the question he'd been waiting to ask. "Any idea who Trunk was trying to sell the hand to?"

Martinez winced. Shook his head slowly. Like he'd known the question was coming, had seen it coming from far off, and now that it was here it pained him.

"None whatsoever," Martinez said.

"But you could find out."

"I could find out a lot of things if I had a mind to."

"I'll make it worth your while."

"I doubt it."

"I thought you said you had a sense of justice."

"I have sense, period. Right now my good sense tells me to stay away from you. Don't lean on me, Hagen. I've told you what I can tell you. I owed the Sniff a favor and now it's paid. Leave it at that. And remember, you don't know me. We didn't talk. Whatever I just told you, I never told you."

"Name your price, Martinez. Just ask around for me."

"Adios, Hagen."

Martinez turned and walked away, his hands thrust deeply into his pockets as though searching for one last peanut. He disappeared into a crowd of people standing near the elevators. A chorus of screams filled the night and Hagen looked up to see the carnival ride shooting straight up into the sky.

The Hand of Danjou . . .

Five million dollars, Martinez had said. *A fair starting price*. It was a story that made more sense than Cosette's tale. But if Martinez was right and the hand was a fake, what had Ronnie been up to? Had he known the hand was a fake? Or had someone sold Ronnie a bill of goods?

What kind of deadly game had Ronnie been playing?

Hagen had the valet bring his car around. He checked his watch—ten minutes past midnight. Hagen drove away from the Stratosphere on Las Vegas Boulevard, heading south. Checked his rearview mirror. He'd noticed a black Chrysler pull out behind him as he left the Stratosphere. On the boulevard the Chrysler dropped back and stayed with him.

His watchers were back.

A mile down the boulevard Hagen turned left and cut eastward on side streets until he reached the High Numbers Club. He parked out front. The electric sign hanging above the front door of the bar was lit up in red and green. Next door a loud wedding party mingled in the parking lot of the wedding chapel. Drunken whoops of joy and well-wishing drifted down the street.

Business was much better at the High Numbers Club now than it had been the afternoon before. The bar was crowded and a brassy swing arrangement floated out of the jukebox—Frank Sinatra singing about Chicago and how it was his kind of town. Hagen maneuvered through the crowd on his way to the back of the barroom. He hoped what he was looking for was still in use.

It was. At the back of the bar, a few feet farther along from the doors to the two restrooms, was a third door marked Exit. Hagen opened the door, stepped outside into the alley behind the bar.

The door closed behind him, cutting off the light.

Hagen walked quickly down the alley, past rows of trash bins and piles of bagged trash. He came out at the cross street and turned left. Walked toward the street corner. When he reached the corner he stopped. Looked back down the street in the direction of the front door of the High Numbers Club. On the opposite side of the street from the club the black Chrysler was parked near a small all-night grocery store. In front of the store four young black men were standing around shooting the breeze and listening to loud thumping rap music on a portable radio. Farther down the street a man stood in the shadows of a dark storefront, smoking a cigarette. The Chrysler was pulled up to the curb in front of him. The driver's side window of the Chrysler was rolled down. Hagen could just make out the silhouette of a man sitting behind the wheel, the dark figure backlit by the lights of a gas station farther along the street.

How well did his watchers know him by sight?

One way to find out.

Hagen crossed the street. Hands in his pockets. Eyes on the ground. He reached the opposite corner and stepped into the pool of light from the grocery store. The four black men were in front of him now, taking up most of the sidewalk. They quit talking, looked Hagen over as he approached. One of them, a teenager wearing a pair of elephant-leg blue jeans, stepped aside and gave Hagen room to pass.

The smoking man was now thirty feet ahead of him. Hagen stepped out of the light from the grocery store and walked on. Keeping his head down. Just a man mulling over something as he walked.

Twenty feet.

The smoking man flicked his cigarette onto the sidewalk and straightened up.

Ten feet.

He watched Hagen approach.

Five feet.

The man finally recognized him, started to say something, started to move—

Then Hagen was on him. Grabbing the front of his brown shirt. Throwing him up against the side of the black Chrysler.

The front of the shirt tore.

The man hit the car hard.

Hagen pulled out his pistol and moved in, fast and close. Grabbed the man's throat with his free hand to hold him against the car while he pressed the pistol barrel against the side of the man's head.

The man shouted, or tried to. He was a young man with closely cropped blond hair. Hagen heard his choked cry and understood him. It took a further second before it registered in Hagen's mind that the man had cried out in German.

"Who are you?" Hagen said in German.

The young man stared at him. Eyes wide, his hands half raised.

Suddenly the driver of the Chrysler appeared on the other side of the car. He held a pistol in both hands. One hand gripping the butt of the automatic, finger on the trigger, the other hand cradling the butt. The underside of the cradling hand rested on the roof of the car. The barrel of the automatic was pointed directly at Hagen's forehead.

"All right, mate," the driver said. "Let go of my friend there and step back."

The driver spoke in English. And with a British accent.

Hagen had expected to find two local thugs sent by Marty Ray. What he'd found instead was an Englishman and a German. They weren't Marty Ray's style at all.

Hagen said, "Who do you work for?"

"Don't work for anyone," the Englishman said.

"Marty Ray?"

"Don't know who you mean."

"Suzanne Cosette?"

"You're off your beam."

"Then why are you following me?"

The Englishman smiled. He was a young man with a square face and dark curly hair. He held the automatic rock-steady. "No one's following you, mate. Just out for a night on the town. Nothing the matter with that, is there? Now let go of the Boche and step back and we'll be on our way."

The German sputtered, began to spew a few choice obscenities at Hagen in German, then thought better of it and shut up.

The Englishman nodded toward the storefront. "It might interest you to know that one of those fine young gentlemen with the radio just stepped inside that store there. I suspect he's calling a policeman. Would you like to talk to a policeman? It won't bother me much. I've got four witnesses who'll say that you accosted us with a pistol. What've you got?"

"Tell your boss I want to talk to him."

"Let go of my friend."

"And tell him that if he keeps sending stooges around to follow me, I'm going to start busting heads."

"Whatever you say, mate."

"Put your piece away. Then I'll let him go."

Slowly, still smiling, the Englishman pulled the automatic off the roof of the car, dropped it to his side.

Hagen let go of the German and stepped back, keeping his pistol raised. The German straightened up, massaged his throat with one hand as he opened the car door with the other. He got into the car slowly. The Englishman climbed in behind the wheel and started the engine. The German spit out the open window at Hagen, then raised his middle finger. *"Tchuss, arschficker."*

The black Chrysler pulled away from the curb, sped off down the street.

Hagen glanced to his left as he slid his pistol back into the shoulder holster. One of the young black men had indeed disappeared, but the other three were still there, staring at him in silence. One of them was leaning against the front window of the store coolly, arms folded, ankles crossed. The other two lay flat on their stomachs on the sidewalk, just in case bullets began to fly.

9.

DARKNESS . . .

The pistol felt cold in his hands. Warm blood ran down his arm.

He heard a voice. From somewhere in the trees.

"Bodo . . ."

It was Vogel's voice.

Vogel was hurt. Vogel was in pain.

"Bodo . . ."

The voice seemed to come from every direction at once.

Hagen knew that Vogel was dying. But Hagen couldn't move. He was frozen in place, no different than the trees that surrounded him in the darkness. Hagen knew he'd never get to Vogel in time.

"Bodo . . ."

The voice again, but weaker now. And different. It wasn't Vogel's voice, was it? Hagen listened for the voice again. All he could hear was the susurrus of the wind in the tree branches above him. All he could hear was the sound of his own heart pumping the blood that was running down his arm.

When the voice did come again it was only a whisper.

"Bodo . . ."

Ronnie? It was Ronnie's voice. How could that be?

Hagen tried to call to his brother but the words died in his throat. Where was Ronnie? Somehow Hagen moved his foot, took a step forward. It seemed to take all his strength. But he was moving. He was coming. If Ronnie could only hang on for a short while Hagen would find him.

Hagen took another step. The ground was wet and his foot sunk into the dirt. Blood dripped from his fingers. The earth was moist with his own blood. Was he moving in the right direction? He didn't know. He waited to hear Ronnie's voice again.

Suddenly a great screaming tore through the silence. Bullets kicked up the dirt at Hagen's feet. Hagen dived behind the nearest tree and lay on the ground. The bullets kept coming, ripping and tearing and clawing at the ground only inches from Hagen's head.

The gunfire ceased.

The voice returned. Ronnie's voice.

"Bodo . . ."

Somewhere in the darkness, Ronnie was dying . . .

Hagen woke up.

He wasn't sure where he was. He sat up quickly, looked around the room. He saw the room and the things in it through a haze. Then the haze cleared and he remembered.

The dream lingered in his mind.

He'd had it before. Many times. In it he always heard Vogel's voice, calling to him, plaintive and pleading, crying out for Hagen to come help him. But this time it was different. It wasn't Vogel's voice. It was Ronnie's voice he heard in his dream.

His brother's voice, calling to him for help in the darkness.

It was half past nine in the morning. Hagen got up, pulled the curtains open, turned up the air-conditioning. He shaved and showered. Put on a pair of gray slacks and a black polo shirt. He called room service for a pot of coffee. Asked if they could deliver it hot this time.

Hagen sat down on the couch and studied Ronnie's two closed suitcases. He wondered now if it had been the Englishman and the German who had tossed his room the night before last. His watchers. Two Europeans—did they work for Suzanne Cosette? On the drive back to the Venetian last night—this morning—Hagen had stopped at a drugstore and purchased a flashlight and batteries. When he returned to the hotel garage he searched the engine compartment of the Buick, felt around inside the wheel wells and behind the bumpers, got down on the ground in a push-up position and looked under the front, rear and both sides of the car. Then he checked the interior—the underside of the dashboard, the glove compartment, the floor of the car under the front seats, the trunk. He was looking for some indication that a homing beacon or a global positioning unit had been attached to the car. Hagen knew it was probably wasted effort—GPS units were so small these days they could be hidden just about anywhere. But he gave it a shot. And found nothing.

An absurd thought crossed Hagen's mind. Perhaps the two watchers had other reasons for following Hagen, reasons that were entirely removed from what happened to Ronnie. Might the Englishman and the German be working for someone in Germany? Hagen had made a few enemies there, and elsewhere in Europe. Probably more than he knew. Were his watchers here to settle an old score? Indeed, an absurd thought—but Hagen wasn't prepared to rule it out entirely. At this point he couldn't afford to rule anything out.

A soft knock at the door. The coffee had arrived.

But when Hagen answered the door it wasn't room service.

A tall young man wearing a black suit, a white shirt and a black bow tie stood in the corridor. A wisp of curly blond hair fell out from under the billed black chauffeur's cap he wore at a jaunty angle. His hands were covered with black leather driving gloves. His muscular physique showed clearly through his well-tailored suit.

He smiled at Hagen.

"Good morning, Mister Hagen," he said as he handed Hagen a business card.

It was a white business card with a name on it—WINSTON W. WILSON. Underneath the name, in small serif script was an address. While Hagen examined the card he noticed the strong, heady smell of flowers. It seemed to fill the hallway. A scent of lilacs? Hagen looked at the chauffeur. The chauffeur smiled his bright white smile.

"Mister Wilson wonders if you are available to speak with him this morning," the chauffeur said. His voice was soft and pleasant. "If so, I'm prepared to take you to him."

"How about if I drive there myself?"

"If you prefer. Can you make it in an hour?"

"I think so."

The chauffeur gave Hagen directions to the Wilson residence, then wished him a good morning and departed. The cloud of flowery perfume departed with him. Hagen saw that Gubbs had been right. Winnie the Poof was interested in talking to Hagen. So interested that he'd contacted Hagen before Hagen had a chance to contact him. Well, that was all right. Hagen held the business card to his nose. Yes, definitely lilacs.

As Hagen drove along the Summerlin Parkway he watched a late-model sport utility vehicle—dark blue, possibly a Ford—in his rearview mirror. He wasn't sure how long it had been behind him. Might've been there since he left the hotel.

He slowed down, waited to see whether the SUV followed suit.

Suddenly a yellow taxi cut in front of Hagen, missing his front bumper by inches. Hagen hit the brakes. The taxi slowed down. Hagen honked his horn. The taxi driver gave his machine a burst of gas and the taxi lurched forward and slid into the far right lane, exhaust pipe trailing thick black smoke. Hagen sped up to get past him. When Hagen searched his rearview mirror again the SUV was nowhere to be seen.

The address on Winnie the Poof's calling card belonged to a residence hidden away behind a high stone wall on the west side of Las Vegas. Hagen pulled up to the wrought-iron front gates and pressed the button on the intercom. A voice buzzed over the small speaker. Hagen gave his name and a moment later the gates swung open, then closed behind him as he drove up the circular driveway.

The house was a low ranch-style structure with two large picture windows that looked out on the driveway and a circular flower garden

in the center of the wide green lawn. Tall green and yellow cacti growing up out of a bed of jagged red rocks lined the walkway leading up to
the double front doors. The chauffeur stepped out of the house and met
Hagen at the car. Only he wasn't a chauffeur now. He'd replaced the
black coat and chauffeur's cap with a white sport coat. He looked like
an oversized houseboy.

"I'll have to frisk you," the chauffeur said. "Mister Wilson would
prefer that his guests not arrive with weapons."

"Sounds like a good policy."

"It's the prudent view."

The chauffeur patted him down thoroughly and professionally. The
heavy scent of lilacs once again wafted up to Hagen's nose.

"Perhaps you can leave the firearm in your car," the chauffeur said,
giving him a benign smile.

"Perhaps I can."

Hagen removed the Heckler & Koch from under his sport coat and
tucked it into the glove compartment.

He followed the chauffeur into the house.

The sunken living room was decorated with wood paneling and
wood-finished furniture. Where a fireplace might have been in most
homes was a water fountain made of flat white stones. Water streamed
across the rocks above, fell from the edges, landed on the rocks below,
filling the entire room with the soft contemplative sounds of a trickling
mountain stream. Very relaxing, Hagen thought. And very extrava-
gant for Las Vegas, where water was at a premium. Between the large
green lawn and the flower garden and this indoor waterfall, Winnie
the Poof was operating some kind of oasis out here on the edge of the
desert.

Hagen followed the chauffeur through a pair of sliding-glass doors
and out onto a patio. Behind the house there was more water, in the
form of a long kidney-shaped swimming pool. In the distance the
brown peaks of the Spring Mountains looked parched and forbidding.

Winnie the Poof lay on a chaise longue beside the pool.

He was a small thin man, possibly sixty years old, short gray hair receding well back onto his narrow head. He wore nothing but a pair of thin baby blue swimming trunks and a pair of sunglasses with dark green lenses. His chest and legs were shaved hairless and his rough, well-tanned skin was covered with a lotion that made it glisten in the sunlight like patent leather. The frames of his sunglasses were made of pink plastic, the two eyepieces shaped like valentine hearts.

"Good morning, Mister Hagen. I'm so glad you could drop by. I'm sure you're a busy man. But who isn't these days?" Winnie the Poof pulled the sunglasses down on his nose, studied Hagen. His eyes were bloodshot, with deep lines at the corners and dark patches underneath. He pushed the sunglasses back up on his nose, picked up a tall Bloody Mary in a fluted glass from the low table next to him, took a sip. A buff-colored file folder lay on the table.

"You'll have to excuse me if I say that you don't look too busy right at the moment," Hagen said, taking a seat on the other side of the table. The chauffeur stood a few steps behind Winnie, waiting for instructions.

"The life of the mind, Mister Hagen. The life of the mind." Winnie the Poof's voice was deep and melodious. The voice seemed too big for the small wrinkled body. "I find that I do my best thinking lying beside this swimming pool covered from head to toe in this stinking lotion. My dermatologist tells me that it will bring back the soft smooth skin of my youth but so far it hasn't done a thing except give me a rash on my backside."

"Maybe you should stay out of the sun."

"In Las Vegas? Not very workable. Would you like a cocktail, Mister Hagen?"

"Just coffee, thanks. I don't drink much before noon."

"Merely a question of practice."

Winnie the Poof snapped his fingers and the chauffeur disappeared back into the house. A white Chihuahua dog appeared from under the chaise longue and began sniffing around Hagen's legs. A second Chihuahua, identical to the first, appeared from somewhere behind Hagen and jockeyed for position with the other dog at Hagen's feet. "Troy, come away from Mister Hagen's leg." Both dogs retreated, skittering back under the table to hide under the chaise longue. When the chauffeur returned with a cup of coffee on a silver tray a third Chihuahua dog trotted along with him and also gave Hagen's leg a cursory inspection. "Troy, that's enough," Winnie the Poof said to the new dog. "Come here." The new dog joined the other two on the other side of the table.

"I thought the other one was called Troy," Hagen said as the chauffeur set the coffee and a small container of cream down on the table. A spoon and two cubes of sugar rested on the lip of the saucer, the cubes wrapped together in bright green and gold paper.

"They're all named Troy, Mister Hagen."

Hagen nodded toward the chauffeur, who had moved off to set his tray down on a table near the patio doors. "Is his name Troy too?"

"His name is Dagmar."

"I knew a woman in Heidelberg once named Dagmar."

"I don't think it was my Dagmar. Although you never know. He does like to dress up. Actually his real name is Henry, but I much prefer Dagmar. Henry is such a lunch-bucket sort of name, don't you agree?"

"Haven't given it much thought."

Winnie the Poof took another sip of his drink. "But don't get the wrong idea about Dagmar, Mister Hagen. He may have a fetching name but he's no nancy. He speaks four languages and he can tear you limb from limb in every one of them."

"I'm glad to hear he's so articulate. What about the other two boys?"

"Which two might those be?"

"The Englishman and the German you've had following me."

Hagen watched the man's reaction. Winnie the Poof merely shrugged off the remark. "I'm sure I don't know what you're talking about, Mister Hagen. I know a lot of boys, but I've told none of them to follow you. An Englishman and a German, you say. How international."

The chauffeur returned and resumed his position standing a few paces behind his boss. While Hagen stirred cream into his coffee, Winnie the Poof set his Bloody Mary down and picked up the file folder. Inside was a photograph and a single sheet of yellow paper covered with handwritten notes. Winnie the Poof tossed the photograph across the table with a flick of his wrist.

The photograph came to rest against Hagen's saucer.

It was a color photograph—and one that Hagen had seen before. The dark wooden hand shining under a coat of polish, the curled fingers, the brown shipping paper underneath, the patch of flashbulb glare up in the corner of the photo. *Dead man's hand*—the thought hit Hagen with force. The photograph was a copy of the photo that Suzanne Cosette had shown him in the atrium of the Mirage Hotel. And no doubt the same photograph that Ronnie had given the Sniff to pass on. How many copies of this picture were floating around Las Vegas?

"What is it?" Hagen said, poker-faced, setting the photograph down. He'd let Winnie the Poof tell him. Might be interesting to find out what the Poof's take on this was.

"Some kind of a relic," Winnie the Poof said. "An early prosthetic device. Slightly more than a hundred years old, or so I'm told. Whoever used that particular device had his work cut out for him. The joints of the fingers do in fact move but I doubt they were of much use to the owner, whoever that might have been. No, mostly a cosmetic appliance, I should think. Have you seen it before?"

"Can't say that I have."

"That's too bad."

"Why?"

"Because I'm looking for it. I was hoping that perhaps you knew where I could find it." Winnie straightened up in the chaise longue, leaned forward, both hands flat on the table. His fingernails were filed and covered in clear polish. "Your brother came to me last week, Mister Hagen. He gave me that photograph and told me that he had this item in his possession. He wondered if perhaps I knew someone who might be interested in buying it. I told him I'd see what I could do. Your brother was going to bring the article here last Saturday so that I could inspect it firsthand, but—" Winnie the Poof frowned.

Hagen finished the thought. "But he was murdered."

"Yes."

"Now you think I have it."

"Or you know where it is."

"Where was it stolen from?"

"If it's stolen, I'm not aware of it."

"If it's not stolen, why did Ronnie need a fence to sell it?"

"You're laboring under a misconception, Mister Hagen. A fence is a dirty little man who sells cheap jewelry rifled from grandmother's jewelry box. I'm not a fence. I simply know a lot of people. Some of them want to sell things. Some of them want to buy things. I bring them together."

Hagen almost laughed. Winnie the Poof—another prickly fence with too much pride. Like Dallas Martinez.

"This hand—what's it worth?" Hagen said.

"I don't think it has a lot of intrinsic value. But I do happen to know a collector who has expressed a minor interest in the piece."

"That's not an answer."

"It's as much of an answer as I'm going to give you." Winnie the Poof sat back in the chaise longue with his drink in his hand. "If you have this appliance or if you know where it is, Mister Hagen, I'm prepared to pay you a reasonable sum if you'll make it available to me."

"How much?"

"Five thousand dollars."

"That's not so much."

There was a pause. The thin hairless man shrugged his shoulders again. "I might be able to go as high as ten thousand, under the right circumstances. I don't know if it's worth that kind of expense but I'm willing to be accommodating if I can afford to be."

Hagen said, "How much were you going to pay Gubbs?"

"Jack Gubbs?"

"He put my brother in touch with you. There must've been something in it for him."

"A gratuity."

"Five thousand?"

"I shouldn't think that much."

"Who else knew my brother was selling this artifact?"

"I wouldn't know."

"But Gubbs knew."

"That would all depend on what your brother told him. I haven't told him anything. Jack Gubbs is not a person I confide in."

"What about Suzanne Cosette? Or Georges Amarantos? Do you confide in them?"

"Should I know them?"

"You tell me."

"I believe I just did. I've never heard of either of them."

"How about Sidney Trunk—what was his stake in this?"

"Trunk?" Winnie the Poof shook his head. "Now you've really lost me, Mister Hagen. I don't know what you've heard but you've acquired some funny ideas. Sidney Trunk was of no account to me. I was sorry to hear that he passed over but not too sorry. And if you've heard that Trunk was interested in brokering the sale of this hand, you must remember one important thing—Sidney Trunk is dead. He isn't brokering anything anymore. There's no money to be shaken out of that tree."

Winnie the Poof raised his drink in the air and studied it, frowning, as though he'd just found a long crack in the glass. He snapped his fingers. "Dagmar, bring me a bottle of Tabasco sauce. This Mary isn't kicking as hard as she ought to."

Dagmar disappeared into the house.

"You've got him well trained," Hagen said.

"You'd be surprised."

"I probably would be."

Hagen looked out on the shimmering water in the pool. He sipped his coffee. "What did you tell my brother it was worth?"

Winnie the Poof laughed softly to himself. "Well, there we are again—this question of *value*. All I told your brother was that I was interested in seeing this item firsthand. I didn't put a price on it. Our negotiations hadn't gone that far. I have no idea what your brother believed it to be worth."

"But you're willing to pay me ten thousand for it."

"A blind investment on my part."

"That's difficult to believe."

"The difficulty is yours." The valentine heart sunglasses stared at Hagen. Hagen could see beads of sweat on Winnie the Poof's forehead. "I understand your predicament, Mister Hagen. Your brother was murdered. You want to know who murdered him. I won't take it personally if you think that perhaps I know something about it. But as it happens, I know nothing about it. Your brother had something to sell that I'm interested in and that's the extent of my association with your brother. I sympathize with your plight and I wish you the best of luck, but in the meantime I'm still interested in this artifact, and I agreed to speak with you on the basis of that continued interest. So let me encapsulate this discussion for you in case you've lost the thread of it somewhere along the way. If you have this artifact, I'm prepared to pay you ten thousand dollars if you'll turn it over to me. If you don't have it but you know where it is, I'll pay you five thousand dollars for that information once I've verified its accuracy. So what do you say, Mister Hagen? Can we do business?"

Hagen picked up the photograph again, studied the image of the prosthetic hand—dark, wooden, and somehow exotic. The lifeless fingers seemed to be reaching for something, grasping at something. The hand of the Vologda Jesus or the Hand of Danjou or a complete fake all the way around—it didn't matter what it was called or how phony it was. Too many people wanted it. Maybe badly enough to kill Ronnie for it.

Dagmar returned with a bottle of Tabasco sauce and a leafy stalk of celery. While Winnie the Poof held his glass up, Dagmar shook several drops of Tabasco into the drink, then stirred it with the celery. Winnie the Poof took a sip, swirled the tomato drink around in his mouth like a fine wine, smacked his lips together and smiled. Dagmar smiled back, then moved off. The whole scene had the feel of an inside joke—two grown men playacting an elaborate master-and-servant routine for Hagen's benefit.

Hagen set his coffee cup down. "I don't know that I can help you, Wilson. It might be harder than you think for me to put my hands on this thing."

Winnie the Poof pulled his valentine heart sunglasses down on his nose again. The bloodshot eyes studied Hagen. "So you do know where it is?"

"I may."

"And you can get it?"

"There may be complications."

"Such as?"

"Such as, I'll let you know when I come up against them. But one or two complications might bring the price up. And before we can do business, I want to know who the buyer is."

"I can't help you there."

"I don't believe that."

"Believe what you like."

"Then maybe I'll turn the hand over to the police. They might be interested in a piece of stolen property."

"You'll be ten thousand dollars poorer."

"I can live with that."

Winnie the Poof made a sour face. Pushed his sunglasses up. "Do what you have to do, Mister Hagen. I'm merely a businessman offering you a business proposition. If you're not interested—fine. If you are interested, we can talk further when you have the artifact in your hands."

"I'll have the artifact soon. But first, you're going to tell me who the buyer is."

Winnie the Poof removed the celery stalk from his drink. He leaned his head back and let the thick red liquid drip off the stalk into his mouth, then bit the end of the stalk, dropped the remainder back into his drink.

"Let me look into things," Winnie the Poof said when he finished chewing the bite of celery. "Perhaps an arrangement can be worked out."

"I need to know now."

Winnie the Poof shook his head. "Impossible."

"Tonight then. Look into it. I'll call you."

A long pause. "Call me tomorrow. You have my card?"

Hagen said that he did.

"Until tomorrow then," Winnie the Poof said, impatient now to get rid of Hagen before Hagen made any other awkward demands. "Ciao, Mister Hagen."

Hagen stood up. Winnie the Poof snapped his fingers and Dagmar escorted Hagen back through the house and out the front door, the three Chihuahuas named Troy nipping at his heels.

Hagen stopped at a gas station to fill up the Buick's tank. He pushed the gas nozzle in, watched the numbers clicking by on the face of the gas pump, thinking of Winnie the Poof and his nameless buyer and the photograph of the wooden hand that he'd seen twice now. One thing was certain—Ronnie's personal belongings didn't include an antique wooden hand. Either the hand was taken from him, or he'd sold it, or he'd hidden it away, or he'd never had it at all.

But now Hagen saw a fifth possibility.

Ronnie had spent five years in the Foreign Legion, in Europe and Africa. And yet when he returned home to Las Vegas he carried only two suitcases with a few changes of clothes, a shaving kit, and not much else. There should have been more. A man would generally acquire many things over the course of five years. Hagen had assumed from the outset that Ronnie had probably shipped some of his belongings to Las Vegas rather than trying to bring them with him on the plane—that's what Hagen had done when he'd gotten out of the military. It occurred to Hagen now that maybe the wooden hand had been shipped along with them. That might explain why Ronnie had passed out photographs of the wooden hand rather than showing around the genuine article. He didn't have the genuine article—not yet. He'd been waiting for it to be delivered to him. And shipping the hand back to Vegas from France rather than carrying it with him wouldn't be an unreasonable precaution to take. Shop around photographs of the hand and see what kind of deal he could make. Then sit back and wait for the hand to arrive, turn it over to the highest bidder when it did. It would keep the hand safe and out of the way—no one could take the hand from him by force if he didn't have it with him.

But if Ronnie had shipped some of his belongings home before he left France, where were they? Maybe they hadn't arrived yet. Or maybe they had arrived and were sitting around right now in a shipping company warehouse, waiting to be picked up. Or maybe Ronnie had wanted them delivered somewhere. He wouldn't have had the address of the apartment he rented, Hagen was sure. But he might've had Gubbs's address. Gubbs said that he hadn't been in contact with Ronnie, but at the moment Hagen saw no good reason to believe anything Gubbs said. Hagen believed one thing though. If Ronnie had shipped his belongings to Gubbs's address, he would've told Gubbs to expect the delivery.

Perhaps they had already been delivered.

And the wooden hand with them.

Gubbs—everything came back to Jack Gubbs. Gubbs knew Ronnie

and Ronnie had stayed with him. Gubbs worked for Marty Ray. Gubbs threw business to Winnie the Poof. Gubbs hung around Harry Needles's club. Gubbs stood at the crossroads like a baneful jittery scarecrow, pointing off in all directions at once. And all directions led right back to Gubbs.

Hagen checked his watch. Twelve fifteen.

It was time to visit Jack Gubbs again.

Hagen drove over to Rainbow Road, followed it to the cross street that led to Gubbs's place. The street in front of the apartment complex was quiet. Hagen parked and sat in the car for a moment, enjoying one last breath of cool air-conditioning. What was it the Sniff used to say on days like this? *Hot enough to fry an egg on the roof.* Ronnie had always liked that one. Who the hell wanted to fry an egg on the roof? A kid, laughing at the weirdness of his elders.

Hagen walked onto the well-manicured grounds. The apartment buildings seemed deserted—not a soul in sight. Hagen climbed the stairs to Gubbs's apartment. The curtains were closed but a radio inside was playing rock-and-roll music.

Hagen knocked on the door and waited. No answer. Hagen knocked again, harder this time.

Still no answer.

Hagen tried the doorknob.

It turned.

Hagen slipped inside the apartment, closing the door quietly behind him.

He looked around the dark living room. Dust motes floated in a rectangle of sunlight that crept onto the living-room carpet from the kitchen. Hagen half expected to find Gubbs lying on the couch in a drunken stupor but Gubbs wasn't there. The rock song on the radio reached a crescendo. A high arching guitar riff flew past Hagen's shoulder. Then a second one, softer, full of electric trills, floated lazily up to the ceiling.

Hagen found Gubbs in the bedroom.

Gubbs lay on his back on the bed. Fully clothed. His arms out-stretched. His head rested on one pillow and a second pillow lay nearby, large burn marks in the center. The pillow under his head was stained dark red but the blue-and-black hole in Gubbs's forehead, just above the bridge of his nose, was small and round and mostly bloodless. Gubbs's eyes stared opaquely at the ceiling. On the radio in the living room the rock song ended and a disc jockey talked of the weather—"Hot and getting hotter . . ."

10.

HOUSEFLIES HOPPED and fidgeted across Gubbs's face and the mess on the pillow.

Gubbs had been dead for hours.

Someone had covered Gubbs's face with the second pillow, pushed the barrel of a pistol down into it, and fired. The pillow muffled the sound of the gunshot. Gubbs's face was covered with bruises and abrasions. Gubbs had put up a fight before he was shot.

Hagen stepped back from the bed. Took a deep breath. He knew he should get out of there. Right now. But he told himself to wait. If he wanted to take a look around Gubbs's apartment, this was the only chance he'd get.

Hagen opened the top drawer of the chest of drawers, found a pair of white cotton socks. He pulled the socks over his hands, wiped the knob of the drawer, then began searching the chest of drawers in earnest. When he finished he moved to the closet, pulling everything off the shelves, looking inside boxes, empty suitcases, a nylon gym bag. He wasn't sure what he was looking for. He didn't expect to find the wooden hand. If it had been here it was almost certainly gone now. But he might find something else—something that might give Hagen an idea where the hand was now and who had taken it. Something that might tell Hagen who killed Ronnie.

After searching the bedroom Hagen moved into the living room. He kept glancing at his watch, knew that he was pushing his luck every second he stayed in the apartment. Suddenly he heard feet running on the walkway outside. He stopped dead still, not even breathing. The running feet belonged to children, three or four of them. They passed by the apartment and moved on down the walkway. Hagen resumed his work. The music on the radio sounded exuberant and macabre—a buoyant pop music melody for the listening enjoyment of the corpse lying in the bedroom.

Hagen picked through the trash on the coffee table. Underneath a section of newspaper he found a personal address book. Six inches by four, with a black plastic cover. He opened it and paged through it as best he could, his sock-covered fingers bending the pages as he pushed them back. Names and telephone numbers. Most of them belonging to women.

Hagen set the address book aside and moved on, but after ten more minutes of searching through the detritus of Jack Gubbs's pitiful existence he found nothing else that interested him. Hagen pulled back the curtain and looked down into the courtyard. Empty—blessedly empty. He pulled the socks off his hands, picked up the address book and stepped outside. He wiped the doorknob with one of the socks before closing the door and stuffing the socks into his trouser pockets.

Driving back to the Strip Hagen stopped at a convenience store, disposed of the two socks in the trash can out front, and went inside to buy a pack of cigarettes. Hagen didn't smoke much anymore but it seemed like a good time to pick up the habit again. Nothing like a fresh corpse to put the kibosh on healthy resolutions. Hagen wondered how long it would be before the body was discovered and reported to the police. It might be days. By then every housefly in Las Vegas would have taken up residence on Jack Gubbs's cold bloated face.

Back in his hotel room at the Venetian Hagen flipped through the pages of Gubbs's address book.

Studying the names.

Marty Ray's name was there, of course, followed by several phone numbers. And there was an entry for Winnie P. But most of the phone numbers belonged to women. Many women. Dozens of women.

Theresa Sanchez was one of them.

So Gubbs knew Theresa Sanchez well enough to keep her name and phone number in his address book. What did that mean? Gubbs had said that he knew a lot of the girls who worked at the Venus Lounge, so maybe it meant nothing. But it made Hagen wonder. Sanchez had been worried about something last night when Hagen tried to talk to her. Might it have had something to do with Jack Gubbs? She must have seen Gubbs when he arrived at the club last night. What had he told her? What was she afraid of?

Once again he saw Gubbs at the center of this—whatever *this* was.

But Gubbs was dead now.

Like Ronnie. Like Sidney Trunk.

Hagen leafed through the phone book once more, didn't find what he was looking for. An entry for Sidney Trunk.

Hagen set the book down, picked up the phone, ordered a double bourbon and soda from room service. It wasn't until right then that he noticed the message light flashing on the phone. There were two messages. The first one came in a couple of hours ago. It was from Peach, reminding him that they had a lunch date. Hagen played the second one. It was Suzanne Cosette. She wanted him to call her as soon as possible. It was Friday and she wanted an update on his progress.

His *progress*—that was funny. Since he'd talked to her two men had died. Two men who knew something about this goddamned hand. If she wanted to call that progress, she was welcome to it. But maybe she knew what the body count was already. She and her friends—whoever they were.

When the drink came Hagen drank half of it down right off. Then he picked up the phone and dialed.

Cosette answered on the first ring.

"So good to hear from you, Mister Hagen. I was afraid I might not."

"I haven't forgotten about you, Suzanne."

"What is the status of our business matter?"

Hagen kept his voice steady. It took some effort. He was on edge—way out on the edge. "Tell your boss I can get the hand. I don't have it but I know where it is. But I want some information before we make any kind of a deal. First, I want to know who your buyer is. I want the name and I want some background. Second, I want to talk to Amarantos. Give me a number where I can reach him or have him call me, I don't care. But I want to talk to him. Third thing, I want to know what the hand is really worth to you."

There was a long pause on the other end of the line. Then, "I'm not sure I understand."

"There's not much to understand. You want the hand and I want information. This story about the Russian Jesus—it's bullshit. This hand was supposedly stolen from the French Foreign Legion, isn't that right? It's supposed to be the Hand of Danjou. Except that maybe it's not real. I want to know whether it's real or not and I want to know what kind of price your people have put on it."

Another pause. Hagen thought he could hear Cosette taking a deep breath, as though trying to regain her composure. Then, "The Hand of Danjou—I'm not familiar with such a thing. Let me suggest this, Mister Hagen. Let's talk about this in person. I'm finding this phone conversation to be a little disturbing. Let's talk face-to-face and we can work out these differences."

"There's no point in meeting unless you can tell me what I want to know. And one other thing—tell the boys you've got following me to back off. I almost shot one of them last night. Next time I might not be in such a good mood."

"You're not making sense, Mister Hagen."

"The Englishman and the German—tell them to disappear."

"You are making a mistake. No Englishmen and no Germans work with me and I have asked no one to follow you. Let me do this—let me call Mister Amarantos right now. It may take some time to reach him but I will keep trying. Perhaps he can put to rest these concerns that you have. Then we can meet. And please don't do anything precipitous with the hand until we can work this matter out. Does this sound satisfactory, Mister Hagen?"

"Work on it, Suzanne. Don't bother calling me back until you've got what I want."

Hagen hung up the phone. He wasn't sure what he'd just stirred up and he didn't care. He was going to keep stirring and keep stirring until he found some answers that made sense.

Hagen stood at the window, drank down the last of the bourbon and soda and smoked a cigarette. Outside the traffic was thick along the Strip but Hagen didn't notice. What he saw was Gubbs's corpse in the dark apartment. Gubbs had been afraid that whoever killed Ronnie might come after him too. Now Gubbs was dead. Dead in a dusty apartment. He'd rolled the dice one last time and lost. He was out of the game for good. Were they the same dice that Ronnie had rolled?

Hagen crushed his cigarette out in the ashtray. He picked up Ronnie's two Delsey suitcases, set them on the couch, and went to work searching them one more time. This time he'd be thorough. If there was something here to find—a shipping receipt, a key to a storage locker or a safety-deposit box, a piece of paper with a name or a phone number on it—he'd find it this time. Hagen searched all the zippered compartments, pulled out all the clothing, checked the pockets of shirts and pants. He sliced open the lining of the suitcases, looking for something hidden underneath. He pulled out the can of shaving cream from the leather toiletries bag and inspected it carefully, looking for a way to unscrew the top or bottom. The can hid nothing—it was an entirely ordinary can of shaving cream. The handle of the razor didn't unscrew to reveal a hidden compartment either. He tore out the inside soles of a pair of tennis shoes. He cut the stitching out of a brown leather belt and pulled the belt apart. Finally he gave up. There was nothing here. The suitcases were exactly what they appeared to be—two anonymous suitcases containing clothing and a toiletries bag.

Had whoever killed Gubbs taken the wooden hand? It was a reasonable conclusion. But if Gubbs had the hand all along, why didn't he sell it to Winnie the Poof? Perhaps Gubbs didn't have the hand, but someone thought he did—and that was why he was killed.

Hagen decided he could use another bourbon and soda. He called down to room service and ordered one, then sat back on the couch. Hands clasped behind his head. Staring at the ceiling. What would *he* have done? If he'd arrived in town with something valuable, something that he wanted to keep in a safe place, something that he knew certain people might want to take from him forcibly, how would he have proceeded? He might have done any number of things. But there was one obvious answer that presented itself. He would have gone to the one person he trusted in town—the Sniff—and left that item with him until Hagen needed it.

But Ronnie hadn't been as close to the Sniff as Hagen was.

He'd been much closer to Harry Needles.

And that was where Ronnie had gone his first night in town—to Harry Needles's place.

But if Ronnie had left something valuable with Harry Needles, why hadn't Harry mentioned it to Hagen? Easy enough. If Harry Needles knew that it was valuable up front, he might want to keep it for himself and sell it. Ronnie was dead. Harry Needles had no obligation to turn it over to anyone else. After all, it was stolen property—presumably. And if no one else knew that Harry had it, Harry wasn't taking a risk by keeping it.

Hagen wasn't convinced that his reasoning was correct, but he had no other direction to go in. He'd go back to the Venus Lounge and have another talk with Harry Needles.

And while he was there maybe he could talk with Theresa Sanchez again.

He stepped into the bathroom, took off the holstered automatic, hung the rig on the hook behind the bathroom door, ran cold water into the sink. He cupped the cool water in his hands and pressed it against his face, ran it through his hair. The cool water helped to revive him. The second bourbon and soda would help even more.

When he heard the knock Hagen walked to the door, drying his face with a heavy bath towel.

It wasn't room service.

Standing in the hallway were two men. One of them heavyset and middle-aged, wearing a blue blazer. The other one thinner and younger, with a beard and an olive green suit. Without a word the heavyset man stepped forward, tried to push his way into the room. Hagen threw a punch at him that clipped the man's jaw and sent him stumbling backward. The second man rushed forward and pushed Hagen back into the room. Hagen slugged him. The man doubled over, both hands on his stomach, mouth open but no sound coming out. Behind him the heavyset man was pulling a nickel-plated revolver out from under his coat. He braced his legs. Raised the revolver. Pointed it at Hagen.

He said one word. *"Police."*

Hagen slowly raised his hands.

The bearded man found his breath and straightened up. He walked up to Hagen and slugged him in the stomach in return. "See how you like it, asshole," the man said as Hagen doubled over, gasping. Then for good measure, the man's knee came up and hit Hagen in the forehead and Hagen fell backwards onto the floor.

They were detectives.

Las Vegas Metro.

The heavyset detective flashed his gold Metro badge while the bearded detective pulled Hagen's arms behind his back, slapped cold steel handcuffs on his wrists, none too gently. What was he under arrest for, Hagen wanted to know. He wasn't under arrest, the heavyset detective said, rubbing his jaw with his hand. The detectives only wanted to talk to him. Down at the station. The handcuffs were simply to keep his hands were they ought to be. But of course, if Hagen would feel more comfortable under arrest, the detectives would be happy to oblige. Assaulting a police officer might do for a start.

"You didn't identify yourselves when I answered the door," Hagen said.

"Didn't we?" the bearded detective said. "That's not what I remember. What do you remember, Bill?"

"I'm sure we did, Arnie."

"I'm sure we did too."

"You have any identification?" the heavyset detective said. His face was egg-shaped, like his body. His nose was wide and flat.

Hagen nodded at his coat, draped over the chair beside the bed. The heavyset detective removed the passport from the inside pocket, studied the photograph, then slid the passport into his own coat pocket.

"We'd like to talk to you about a friend of yours," the heavyset detective said. "Jack Gubbs. You know him, don't you?"

"I've met him."

"That's good," the bearded detective said. "Isn't that good, Bill?"

"That's good," the heavyset detective said.

"He's no friend of mine," Hagen said.

"We've heard that," the bearded detective said.

"What kind of trouble is he in?"

The heavyset detective—"That's what we want to talk about."

"I want to talk to McGrath."

"Who's McGrath?"

"You know who he is."

"You'll have to settle for us."

"He works out of the southwest station. Call him."

"We're going to the downtown station. We don't need to call anybody."

"Then I want a lawyer."

The heavyset detective shrugged. "Sure. Call a lawyer. You call a lawyer, we'll have to charge you with assaulting a police officer. You still want a lawyer?"

They left the hotel room, a detective on either side of Hagen, their arms locked under his. Hagen's thoughts raced around sharp corners. Hagen had found Gubbs's body two hours ago. Now he was being picked up for questioning by the police. That was fast work. Had someone seen him at the apartment house? Someone who knew who he was? Hagen wondered if his luck had gone cold. Stone-cold. Like Jack Gubbs.

At the downtown station the two detectives led Hagen into a small room with white walls and a single narrow window covered by venetian blinds. A table and four gray metal chairs sat in the center of the room. The sun shining through the half-open blinds cast long parallel shadows across the table.

The bearded detective removed the handcuffs, twisting them hard one way and then another as he did so, the metal edges of the cuffs digging into Hagen's wrists. Then the bearded detective left the room and the heavyset detective motioned Hagen toward one of the metal folding chairs.

Hagen sat down. The detective remained standing as he examined Hagen's passport. The meager strands of hair that the detective combed over the top of his shiny scalp looked solid and crusty, as though he dipped them in model airplane glue every morning to keep them in place.

"What do you do for a living, Mister Hagen?"

"Unemployed."

"Unemployed what?"

"Unemployed nothing."

"My name's Coyne, by the way."

"Who's your partner?"

The bearded detective's name was Mansfield and presently he returned, carrying a yellow legal-sized notepad, two ballpoint pens, and a police file. Both detectives took off their coats and rolled up their shirtsleeves before sitting down at the table. The heavyset detective carried his revolver in a worn leather shoulder holster. The bearded one carried an automatic in a side holster fitted into the waistband of his pants. Hagen's Heckler & Koch was still hanging in his shoulder holster from the hook on the bathroom door of the hotel room. That was a lucky break for him. These two detectives would have been quite happy to confiscate his pistol if they'd found it on him.

Coyne handed Hagen's passport to Mansfield. Mansfield looked the passport over closely, wrote something on the legal pad. Then Mansfield set the passport on the table and slid the police file across the table to Coyne. Coyne opened it, flipped through the pages.

"Ronald Hagen was your brother?" Coyne said, looking up from the file.

"That's right." The file in front of Coyne looked like the same investigation file that McGrath had shown Hagen after Ronnie's funeral.

"Your brother is deceased?"

"Look, you two can save yourself a lot of time by calling McGrath. McGrath knows me. He showed me that file you're reading two days ago."

The two detectives weren't interested in Hagen's conversation with McGrath.

Coyne did most of the talking. Mansfield made notes on his yellow pad when he wasn't giving Hagen a menacing stare. Mansfield's beard was neatly trimmed but his short brown hair was pushed back off his forehead in every which direction. He looked too young to be a detective. Must've had a relative high up in the department, Hagen thought.

It was several minutes before they got around to the subject of Jack Gubbs.

Coyne said, "Have you seen Gubbs since you got into town?"

"I saw him the day before yesterday."

"When?"

"In the evening. I went to his apartment."

Mansfield looked up sharply from his notepad. "What time was that?"

"Maybe six o'clock."

"Maybe?"

"I'm not sure."

"You have a watch?"

"I have a watch. I don't stare at it all day."

Coyne said, "Why did you go see Gubbs?"

"He was a friend of my brother's. My brother stayed with Gubbs for a couple of nights when he got into town last week."

"Is that what Gubbs told you?"

"That's what he told me."

Mansfield tapped his ballpoint pen on the notepad. "Which two nights?"

"Monday and Tuesday."

Coyne said, "What else did Gubbs tell you?"

"Not much. My brother rented his own place last Wednesday and moved out of Gubbs's apartment. Gubbs didn't see him much while he was staying at the apartment and he didn't see my brother at all after he moved out."

"Is that the only time you've seen Gubbs?"

"I saw him again last night, at a strip club called the Venus Lounge. I ran into him there while I was visiting a friend."

"What kind of friends do you have at the Venus Lounge?"

"The usual kind."

Mansfield said, "Answer the question."

Coyne gave Hagen a patient smile. "There's all kinds of friends."

"An old family friend. Harry Needles. He owns the place."

"Gubbs just happened to be there?"

"He showed up while I was there. He knows Harry Needles too."

Mansfield said, "What time was that?"

Hagen told him. Mansfield jotted it down on the notepad.

Coyne said, "What did you and Gubbs talk about last night?"

"Nothing much. Shooting the breeze. Like I said, I just ran into him there." Hagen wasn't going to mention Winnie the Poof. And he wasn't going to mention the wooden hand. It was a risk, not telling the detectives the whole truth, but if they were going to trap him in a lie they'd have to know the truth already. Hagen didn't believe they knew the truth or much of it. No, these two were on a fishing expedition. Hagen decided to roll with this and trust his wits. He wasn't under arrest. He hadn't been read his rights.

Coyne said, "When did you see Gubbs next?"

"I haven't seen him since."

"Bullshit," Mansfield said.

A puzzled look crossed Coyne's face. "You saw him today, didn't you, Mister Hagen? You saw him this morning."

"I haven't seen him today. What's he done?"

Mansfield slammed his fist down on the table and shot up from his chair, his face turning red with anger. Coyne raised his hand for calm and Mansfield sat back down. Were these two detectives trying to work a good cop, bad cop routine? The thought made Hagen smile.

Coyne said in quiet voice, "Why don't you tell us what you did this morning and this afternoon, up to the time we visited you at your hotel room."

Hagen told the two detectives he'd taken a drive out to Hoover Dam to see the place where his brother was murdered. Then he drove back to town, bought something to eat, returned to the hotel. The lie about driving out to Hoover Dam was a safe lie. There was no one who could deny the truth of it except Winnie the Poof.

Unless Hagen had been followed that morning.

Coyne asked more questions and Mansfield wrote down Hagen's answers on the pad of paper, sometimes pausing to underline certain passages, circle something, draw an arrow pointing back to something else, write a question mark in the margin. Mansfield kept throwing angry looks at Coyne, as though incensed at just about everything Hagen was telling them, but Coyne never raised his voice, never pushed too hard on Hagen's story.

When Hagen finished giving him the details of his morning's activities Coyne went back to the beginning, to the point where Hagen arrived in Las Vegas. Hagen told them the truth about his visits to McGrath and the Sniff, Marty Ray and Harry Needles and Gubbs, about meeting Theresa Sanchez and driving her home after work. It was only the details that he left out, details that these two detectives couldn't possibly know—the Sniff telling him that Ronnie was looking for a fence, the rumor that Ronnie was involved in Jimmy Ray's murder five years ago, the dead man's hand. Hagen didn't mention Suzanne Cosette and Dallas Martinez, or the Englishman and the German who'd followed him, might still be following him. Mansfield tried once or twice to trip Hagen up in his own story, but Mansfield didn't have any luck.

After they had gone through the story twice, Coyne folded his arms across his chest and sat back in his chair. "Bodo, we're not getting to the crucial point."

"Tell me what the crucial point is. If I've got anything to say about it, I'll let you know. I'm always happy to discuss crucial points with officers of the law."

"You're scared, Bodo," Coyne said. "And if you're not, you should be. We know that after you saw Gubbs at the Venus Lounge last night, you saw him again, early this morning, at his apartment. Which brings us to the crucial point—you shot Jack Gubbs. You killed him. Because you believe he murdered your brother."

"Gubbs is dead?"

"You know he is."

"I have no recollection of that crucial point."

"It's a fact, nonetheless."

"If it's a fact, it's one I can't help you with."

Coyne's expression was benevolent now. "Maybe you didn't mean to shoot him. Maybe it was an accident. We understand that, Bodo. The law isn't blind to that. But it'll be better for you if you tell us now. Manslaughter will get you eight years, maybe less. Murder one—that's a harder nut to crack."

Hagen shook his head, smiled. "You two have had your fun. I think I'll talk to McGrath now. Maybe he can make some sense out of this. You two aren't making any sense."

Mansfield slammed his pen down on the table and stood up again, his eyes boring into Hagen's.

"You've been lying to us from the start," Mansfield said. He kicked his chair back, then stepped around the side of the table, speaking through clenched teeth and keeping his eyes on Hagen, coming up on Hagen like a growling junkyard dog. Mansfield was trying hard—too hard. Coyne sat back with a bemused expression on his face, watching his partner, then turning to look at Hagen, like a man waiting for a contest to begin. And that's what this was, Hagen knew. A contest. A game.

Hagen sat there, waited.

Mansfield leaned down, one hand flat on the table, his face so close that Hagen could feel his hot breath. "Your shit is most definitely weak, Hagen. You're twisting in the wind. You were at Gubbs's place this morning. Start filling in the blanks." Mansfield grabbed the front of Hagen's shirt, pressed his fist hard into Hagen's throat. "What do you want—manslaughter or murder one?"

Hagen's answer wasn't long in coming.

Hagen reached up, grabbed the young detective by the hair on the back of his head and slammed his face down onto the surface of the table. Then Hagen was out of his chair and on his feet. Before Mansfield could react Hagen pulled him away from the table and threw the detective against the wall. Mansfield hit the wall hard, stumbled to one side. A thin trail of blood ran out of one nostril and down into the young detective's beard.

When Hagen turned around Coyne was standing. His legs braced, his police revolver pointed at Hagen.

"You shouldn't have done that," Coyne said. "You really shouldn't have done that."

Mansfield spat and cursed while he slapped the handcuffs on Hagen's wrists once again.

The two detectives dragged Hagen out of the interrogation room. They pushed him down a long white hallway, Mansfield pressing Hagen's arms up behind his back so hard that the muscles in Hagen's shoulders felt like they were stretched to the tearing point. They led Hagen to a small holding cell and threw him inside. While Coyne stood guard outside Mansfield punched Hagen in the face. The force of the blow sent Hagen reeling. He tried to stay on his feet but with his hands locked together behind him he lost his balance and fell to the floor. Mansfield gave him a solid kick to the small of the back before slamming the door of the holding cell closed behind him.

Hagen lay on his side on the cold linoleum floor, his legs pulled up. The pain shooting through his back made his head swim. He tried not to move. Even breathing was difficult. He took slow shallow breaths and waited. After a few minutes he was able to move, climb to his feet.

The holding cell was not much larger than a good-sized closet. The walls were white. The white door was made of metal. There was a small observation window in the door. Stark white light shone down on him through a sheet of opaque plastic in the ceiling.

A wooden bench rested against the wall.

Hagen sat down on the bench.

The holding cell. The heavy silence within it. The pain shooting through his body as he sat there—

It all seemed quite familiar.

II.

COLD DARKNESS. Cold fog. A cold and deserted forest road ten kilometers outside of Morlaix . . .

Hagen lay flat in the wet grass along the edge of the road, his body pulled in close to the right side of the car, his pistol in his hand. He couldn't see anything. Couldn't hear anything except the occasional ticking of the warm car in the cold night air and Vogel moaning in pain as he lay on the ground behind the car.

The shooter was a professional. Must've been using a rifle fitted with a nightscope. And there had been no gunshot that Hagen had noticed. Which meant he was using a silencer. The rifle had to be a high-powered one—a sniper rifle—if he expected to shoot with any degree of accuracy through a silencer.

And because visibility was reduced by the fog he had to be close by.

Very close.

But where?

The shooter had been waiting for them. The shooter knew where Hagen and Vogel had gone, knew which road they'd be taking on their way back to Morlaix. As the Mercedes traveled down the narrow lane in the fog the shooter had taken out the front left tire. Then he shot Vogel as Vogel stepped around to open the trunk. The third shot hit the rear window.

The shooter was somewhere behind them—for the moment.

A very precarious moment.

Slowly Hagen crawled past the rear tire, pushing himself along a few inches at a time. He heard Vogel's pain-racked breathing. He heard his own pulse, pounding in his ears. He had to get to Vogel. He had to pull Vogel out of the line of fire.

"Bodo . . ."

Vogel's voice was weak. Vogel tried to say something else but his voice was choked off by a liquid sound somewhere deep in his throat.

Hagen crept forward. When he reached the back of the car he paused, listening. Another liquid cough from Vogel. No other sounds out there. Hagen moved forward the last few inches, his head low, his chest flat on the ground.

In the red glow of the taillights Hagen could see that Vogel hadn't moved. He still lay prostrate behind the car, the lower half of his body lying in the grass along the edge of the country road, the upper half of his body on the concrete surface of the road itself. His hand was tucked under him, holding his chest. His head was turned to one side.

There was a sharp popping sound. Somewhere down the road. The rear taillight of the Mercedes shattered above Hagen's head. Plastic flying in every direction, a dull metallic sound as the bullet tore into the back of the car. Hagen dropped his head, scrambled back around to the side of the car.

Then another sound.

Footsteps on concrete. Somewhere down the road behind the car. Very soft and faint. But not far off. Soft-soled shoes running on the road . . .

No time to think. He had to move. Now. He picked himself up and ran in a crouch toward the trees along the road. Only fifteen feet away but it seemed like miles. Hagen's left foot came into contact with a rock or an exposed tree root and he stumbled forward, somehow kept his balance. Then another sharp popping sound from behind him on the road and suddenly Hagen was falling through the air.

He landed facedown in the grass at the edge of the tree line. He tried to pick himself up and move that last few feet into the protective cover of the tall trees but his right arm didn't do what he wanted it to and he fell forward again. His right arm was numb, all the way up to his shoulder. He'd been hit. It was a dull realization, seemed to be of little consequence. He had to get into the trees. That was the only important thing. Gripping the pistol in his left hand he raised himself on his bent left arm, placed his weight on it.

On one elbow and his knees he pushed himself the last yard into the trees, then struggled to his feet and stumbled forward. He felt suddenly dizzy. His legs didn't want to hold him up. He ran forward, hunched over. Ran deeper into the trees, until he encountered a tree trunk in his path. He fell against it, then turned himself around so that he faced the direction from which he thought he'd come. His back against the tree trunk for support, his heels dug into the ground to keep him upright. He felt a great warmth down his right side. His own blood against his skin. The air was cold and there wasn't enough of it—he was gulping air as fast as he could.

Ahead of him, through the trees, he could see a dim light. The headlights of the Mercedes. He raised the pistol and pointed it in the direction of the light. The shooter would be coming from that direction. If Hagen was lucky he might see the shooter's silhouette as he moved into the trees with the light behind him. Hagen waited. He knew the pistol was shaking in his left hand but he couldn't do anything about it. One shot, he told himself. One shot was all he needed. As his eyes adjusted to the darkness he noticed that the trees around him all stood in neat rows, like pieces on a chessboard. He smelled the sweet scent of the pine trees and the heavier scent of freshly turned earth.

The light. He kept his eyes on the light. But then the light went out. The shooter had reached the car and switched off the headlights. Hagen stared into the darkness where the light had been. Without being aware of it he'd slid down the tree trunk. He found himself sitting on the ground at the base of the tree, his legs out before him, the pistol pointed uselessly out into the darkness.

"Bodo . . ."

It was Vogel. He was screaming Hagen's name. Then a gunshot echoed through the trees. Not a silenced rifle shot but the report of a pistol, clear and loud and rolling through the tree branches above him. Hagen knew what it meant instantly. Vogel was dead. The shooter had reached the car and de-livered a coup de grâce *with a handgun and now Vogel lay dead on the concrete surface of the road with Hagen's name dying out in his throat.*

Now the shooter would come after Hagen, and Hagen wouldn't be able to even save himself. Hagen would die here too. It all seemed so logical.

Hagen waited.

Another light appeared. Through the trees, off to the left. The light moved. Hagen's dizziness had increased. His eyes swum in his head as he watched this new light. It was the shooter. The shooter was the light and the light was the shooter. The light would come toward him and wash over him and then he'd be dead too in a sudden rush of hot bright light. Hagen wasn't even sure if he still held the pistol in his hand anymore. But what did it matter? There was no way to shoot the light.

But this new light had a sound too. A loud groaning sound. Growing louder. Then a high screech as the light slowed down and stopped moving. From somewhere deep in the blackness that Hagen was falling into a thought rose to the surface. Hagen caught it and clung to it. A vehicle. The light was a vehicle. Coming along the road. Coming upon the dark Mercedes and Vogel's body behind it. Stopping. Hagen heard the rattle of a diesel engine idling. With the last of his strength he raised the pistol in the air and fired. Then again and again. In his mind he saw the bullets rising up into the sky, exploding in great bursts of red fluorescence like distress flares from a ship far out to sea.

Then he saw nothing else.

Nothing until—a room. A white room. White sheets. Heavy white bandages up his arm and around his chest. A nurse in a crisp white uniform with a small gold watch dangling from a gold chain attached to her breast pocket. She stood over Hagen, her hand on his wrist. Then she called to someone who sat in the corner of the white room. The figure stood up. A doctor? No. A man in a blue uniform. A policeman.

A gendarme . . .

Later when the drugs wore off and his head cleared they took him to another room in the hospital. A much smaller room, painted a clean sterile white like the first room but with no bed, no nurse, no doctor. The door was shut but Hagen knew there was a gendarme on the other side of it, standing guard. They'd placed him in a wheelchair and left him in here. Waiting. He knew what for. Vogel was dead and a gendarme captain was on his way to the hospital to question Hagen about the events out on the road between

Morlaix and Trégastel. The gendarme captain would know nothing about William Severance and the shredded Stasi records and the puzzlers in Berlin. He would know nothing of a former Stasi agent named Heinrich Kress or two other agents known only as Totenkopf and Hohle. He would know nothing of Ingeborge Stromm. He would know nothing of the cooperation of the French DST with the BND and Severance's CIA team in Berlin. And Hagen couldn't tell him. Couldn't tell him a thing.

Hagen sat there in the wheelchair, waiting for the white door to open and the questions to begin . . .

"Hello, Bodo."

"Hello, McGrath."

McGrath stood in the doorway of the holding cell, grim-faced and tired. Rolled up in his hand was a typed report of four or five pages.

McGrath removed the handcuffs from Hagen's wrists, then led Hagen down the hallway and into the same room that Coyne and Mansfield had questioned him in earlier. Hagen sat down at the table. The parallel shadows running across the table from the half-closed venetian blinds were longer and darker now.

McGrath closed the door slowly, dropped the report onto the table and sat down across from Hagen. Hagen saw his own name at the top of the first page of the report, followed by Coyne's and Mansfield's names. The report was a typed copy of the notes that Mansfield had taken earlier.

"Jack Gubbs is dead," McGrath said.

"That's what I hear."

"Did you kill him?"

"No."

McGrath rubbed his eyes with his long thin fingers. His narrow face was a mass of dry wrinkles, a contour map of a hard life, right there for everyone to see. "Maybe you didn't, Bodo. But if you did, I'm going to find out. It'll be better all around if you tell me yourself. You make me work for it, things might not be so easy for you."

"That's what your friends said too."

"Mansfield and Coyne?"

"The ones you sent to put the screws to me."

"I asked them to pick you up and have a talk with you. I would've done it myself but I've been over at Gubbs's place with the forensic people and the coroner. A gunshot to the head is a messy business."

"Is that how he died?"

"That's how he died."

"What makes you think I had anything to do with it?"

"You talked to him day before yesterday. You seemed to think he knew something about what happened to Ronnie. It occurs to me that you might've arrived at the conclusion that Gubbs killed Ronnie himself. And that would be one good reason for you to kill Gubbs."

"Who told you I spoke to Gubbs?"

"Gubbs told me."

"I didn't realize he was a friend of yours."

"He wasn't. Not a bit. Jack Gubbs had a lot of bad habits. He wasn't much into clean living and going to church. But he knew a lot of people and he traveled in interesting circles and over the years I helped him out when he needed it and when I could, and in his gratitude he helped me out. Jack Gubbs was an informant, Bodo. I've had him on a leash for years. He worked for me, I guess you could say. Now he's dead. That bothers me somehow. I want to know who and I want to know why."

Hagen understood the words coming out of McGrath's mouth but he had a hard time believing what they signified. Jack Gubbs—a police informant? Hagen cleared his throat. "If Gubbs was an informant, why didn't you know that Ronnie stayed at his apartment last week?"

"I knew. Gubbs told me."

"It's not in the file I read."

"There's probably quite a few things that I know that aren't in those files. I keep that kind of information under my hat. Too many people read those files and too many people talk. Even inside the department. An informant's no good when everyone knows he's an informant. An informant's no good when he's dead either."

"Like Ronnie and Jimmy Ray? Is that something that didn't make it into a file? The Jimmy Ray murder was your case, McGrath. Some people have the idea that you think Ronnie was involved."

A patient smile appeared on McGrath's face. "Some people being who?"

"Marty Ray, for one."

"I wouldn't believe everything Marty Ray told me."

"What part should I believe?"

McGrath looked away, laughed quietly to himself, as though he'd just realized that he was the butt of a mildly amusing joke. "You do get around, don't you, Bodo." McGrath reached into his shirt pocket, removed a pack of cigarettes, slid one out and lit it. He looked around for an ashtray, didn't see one. He got up and walked over to the trash can by the door, pulled an empty soda can out and brought it over to the table, flicked cigarette ash into the can. "I didn't tell Marty Ray anything about Ronnie. Not five years ago and not since. When Jimmy Ray was killed I asked Marty questions about Ronnie, but I asked him questions about a lot of people. That's my job, Bodo—I'm a cop. You remember what that is, right? If Marty Ray thinks your brother was involved in Jimmy Ray getting whacked, he didn't get it from me. But I'll tell you one thing. When I heard that Ronnie was back in town I dug out those old files and went over them again. Ronnie and I were going to have a talk."

"So you do think he was involved."

"I didn't say that. I said I wanted to have a talk. I never got the chance to ask him the questions I wanted to ask him five years ago. Ronnie left town right after Jimmy Ray was killed. He joined the Legion. Next thing I knew, he was on the other side of the world. Good place to be when things get sticky at home."

Ronnie wasn't involved in Jimmy Ray's murder but McGrath wanted to talk to him about it all the same? What was McGrath holding back? What was it that McGrath didn't want to tell him?

Hagen said, "Did you talk to Ronnie last week?"

"Didn't get the chance. Hell, I didn't even know he was back in town until the day before he was murdered, when Gubbs told me. Gubbs told me something else that was interesting—he told me that Ronnie had been to see Harry Needles and he also told me that Ronnie was looking for a fence. Now what do you suppose Ronnie wanted to sell to a fence? Any ideas, Bodo? I told Gubbs to find out what he could about whatever nasty little pie Ronnie had his fingers in. I wanted to know if Harry was involved too. Didn't work out, I'm sorry to say."

Harry Needles? A couple of hours ago Hagen had come to believe that Harry Needles might be involved in this. Now McGrath was suggesting the same thing. "How does Harry work into this?"

McGrath asked Hagen how much he knew about the events surrounding the murder of Jimmy Ray five years ago. Hagen told McGrath what he'd heard—Jimmy Ray was murdered at his home and a couple hundred thousand dollars that he'd kept in a safe was stolen. And the money was skim money, if Hagen knew the Ray brothers as well as he thought he did.

McGrath nodded. "That's most of it. I'll tell you the rest. Don't want you running around with only half the story. One of the people who knew about the money Jimmy Ray had in the house the night he was killed was Harry Needles. Back then, Jimmy and Marty were backing Harry in that strip club he runs, and Harry Needles was there in Jimmy Ray's office when Jimmy and Marty Ray and the rest of them were cooking the books and counting up the leftover cash. Some of that money came from Harry's strip joint, I'm sure. Then Jimmy Ray takes the lion's share of the skim money and goes home and puts it in his safe and he gets himself killed and the money takes a hike. That's no coincidence—whoever killed Jimmy knew the money was there or knew someone who knew. So I talked to Marty Ray. I talked to an accountant who was there that night and a couple of Marty Ray's boys who were there too. And I talked to Harry Needles. I didn't get far with any of them. But I always wondered about Harry. Nothing solid—just a feeling that he might know more than he'd told me.

"A few weeks later Ronnie leaves town and disappears. It looks— well, let's just say that it looks interesting. Ronnie worked for the Ray brothers then too. He wasn't around the night they were divvying up money in the office, but he worked there. He might've heard something. And you know and I know that Harry Needles and Ronnie were pals. So Ronnie disappearing like that, it made me wonder. Then he comes home and, first thing, he gets himself killed. That makes me wonder too. Who in Las Vegas wants to keep him quiet? You see what I'm getting at?"

"My brother wasn't a murderer."

McGrath shrugged. "Given the right circumstances anyone can commit a murder. Even you, Bodo."

"I didn't kill Gubbs."

"I truly hope not." McGrath took one last drag, then dropped the butt of his cigarette into the soda can. Hagen heard the sizzle as the hot ash landed in the liquid at the bottom of the can. "I know what kind of work you do overseas. Your old man told me after you left town. He was proud of you. Maybe you believe that and maybe you don't, but he was. But don't get the idea that what you do for the government over there gives you any kind of special protection here in Las Vegas. In this town you're just another citizen. You don't have anybody's per- mission to start poking your nose where it doesn't belong. If I find out that you are, I will surely cut that nose off. Do we understand each other?"

"Sure, McGrath."

McGrath riffled the pages of the typed report. "Is there anything you want to add to this? Is this a true and full account of what you've been up to for the last forty-eight hours?"

"To the best of my recollection."

"I gave you my card the other day, didn't I? Wrote my home number on it?"

"Yes."

"Bodo, if it turns out that maybe your memory has played tricks on you regarding your whereabouts since Wednesday"—McGrath held the report up—"I want you to give me a call so we can set the record straight. Or if you come across some information that I'd be interested in—call me. If you're poking around somewhere you shouldn't be, I want to hear it from you first. If I hear it elsewhere, it's not going to increase my good opinion of you."

"Fair enough, McGrath. Are we finished here?"

McGrath glanced ceilingward as he rolled the report into a tight cylinder. "I suspect so," he said, distracted. "But stay in town, Bodo. I'll tell you when you can leave. I've got a little work to do"—McGrath paused, slammed the rolled-up report down on the table, then swept a dead fly off the edge and onto the floor—"before I'm done with you. And if you decide to change your address, let me know first thing."

Hagen walked out of the police station. At a coffee shop down the street he used a pay phone to call a cab. While he waited outside he noticed red drops of blood on the sidewalk near where he was standing. The drops of blood traveled across the concrete in a crazy swaying pattern, then clustered again at a trash can beside the curb.

Then nothing—the trail of blood ended there. Either the bleeder climbed into a car or he disappeared into the trash can. Hagen studied the progress of the dripping blood, saw in those wild patterns on the concrete the trajectory of his own efforts to find Ronnie's murderer. Hagen had been careening through Las Vegas for two days on a crazy, bloody path. Hagen knew he was taking a chance by not telling McGrath the whole truth about his activities, but he'd take that chance. He'd give McGrath the whole story when the time came, when he knew who killed Ronnie. Hand it to McGrath on a platter. A done deal. Right now there were too many loose ends to tell McGrath everything. McGrath or some other cop might use those loose ends to hang him.

The cab arrived. The driver was a black man with a Caribbean accent, his head covered with cornrows of hair.

"The Venetian."

On the ride back to the hotel Hagen wondered why McGrath had said nothing about Gubbs sending Ronnie to see Winnie the Poof. Was that a piece of information McGrath was keeping to himself? Or was it that he didn't know about Ronnie's visit? Winnie the Poof had planned to throw some money Gubbs's way as a finder's fee—that might have been reason enough for Gubbs to keep it from McGrath. But maybe Gubbs expected more. Maybe Gubbs thought he'd get all the money. Because he'd planned to take possession of the hand himself. Last night at the Venus Lounge Gubbs had suggested that he didn't know about the hand when he sent Ronnie to the Poof, but that didn't mean anything.

Hagen kept running the same names over and over in his mind, the flesh-and-blood names. Trying to put them together in new combinations, trying to make them add up to something. There was still a big hole somewhere. But when Hagen thought again of who Ronnie might have trusted—not just who knew him but who he might have confided in—the hole became smaller. There was only one man—Harry Needles. Ronnie trusted Harry Needles in a way that he would never have trusted the Sniff or Marty Ray or Gubbs. Even McGrath knew that. He knew that Harry Needles and Ronnie were close.

Harry Needles—he'd always needed money, was always looking for a new angle to get his hands on some. He liked to go for broke and broke was what he usually ended up with, at least in the past. But Harry Needles didn't seem like a likely candidate for killing Jimmy Ray. Harry Needles killed Jimmy Ray or had him killed, then continued doing business with Marty Ray for five years while Marty was busy looking under every rock in town for Jimmy Ray's murderer?

No, it didn't wash. McGrath said that Harry was there in the office the night Jimmy Ray took the skim money home with him. Which made Harry an obvious suspect—a little too obvious. Harry Needles wasn't always smart but he was smart enough not to shit in his own backyard.

But Hagen would ask Harry Needles about it, all the same.

When Hagen next saw him. Which would be soon.

Hagen half expected to find his hotel room tossed by McGrath's detectives but he found everything as he had left it. His coat still draped over the chair. His pistol in its shoulder holster still hanging from the hook on the bathroom door.

The only change was that the message light on his telephone was blinking again.

Hagen picked up the phone and played the message back. It was from the Sniff.

Hagen dialed the Sniff's phone number.

"Bodo, I've got news."

"What've you got, Sniff?"

"Dallas Martinez called me about an hour ago. He slid me a little information and told me to pass it on. He thought you might be interested. I think so too."

"Let's hear it."

"Martinez's got friends in all kinds of places. One of them just told him that Sidney Trunk put out some feelers a few days ago with a couple of big-time fences in Los Angeles. Trunk was trying to sell some kind of historical artifact that he called the Hand of Danjou—I guess you know what that is. Martinez doesn't know if Trunk found a buyer or not, but he heard the asking price was high."

"How high?"

"Thirteen million, Bodo."

"Thirteen million?"

"That's what the man said."

"What does Martinez make of it?"

"He says the hand is a fake. He thinks Trunk was planning on putting over a world-class con job and then disappearing with the big money. That's the only way Martinez could slice it. There's quite a buzz going in L.A. Apparently this little item is a hot ticket, even at that price. No one is sure whether Trunk actually had the thing or whether he was just taking the idea out for a walk. But Martinez said you'd want to know that there's a fellow named Amarantos who has a couple of people in L.A. who are jumping through their own assholes trying to get a line on the dingus. That's what Martinez heard. He says you don't owe him anything for the information—he just wants you to stay the hell away from him for the rest of your natural-born days. At the rate you're going, I'm not so sure that's going to be a long time. A wooden hand that's going for thirteen million clams, that's high-profile product. People disappear for that kind of money. People wind up taking a dirt nap out in the desert for thirteen million."

"Like Ronnie."

"Like you too, if you don't watch yourself."

Hagen told the Sniff about Gubbs's murder. He didn't go into details, just that Gubbs was dead and McGrath had questioned Hagen about it. And that Gubbs had been a snitch for McGrath for years. That piece of news didn't make the Sniff feel any better about Hagen's future prospects. "Bodo, listen to me. I put together Ronnie's funeral. I don't want to put together yours."

Dusk was approaching when Hagen stepped out of the front doors of the hotel and handed his claim ticket to the uniformed valet. His sport coat felt heavy in the heat but he needed it to hide the shoulder holster. While Hagen waited for his car to be brought around a man in a white dinner jacket and a woman in a black evening gown appeared beside him in the valet queue. The man had just won a few dollars at roulette and he was explaining his winning strategy with great bluster. But the woman had other ideas. The woman noticed Hagen listening to their conversation and she asked him, "Do you know any-thing about roulette?"

"A bit."

"Which do you think is better, always playing the same numbers over and over or playing numbers that haven't come up in a while?"

"It doesn't matter. The roulette wheel doesn't have a memory. You can play the same numbers or you can play different numbers—it doesn't make any difference. That's why they call it a game of chance."

The couple didn't appreciate Hagen's take on roulette and turned away. They both wanted to believe that their personal touch with the numbers on the roulette wheel could somehow influence their win-nings for the better, but what they saw as a strategy was only supersti-tion. It was a common mistake, and one that kept the casinos in the black and the players in the red.

Roulette was strictly chump action.

But a wooden hand worth thirteen million dollars—that was action that required skill and cunning. That was action that required a strat-egy. People died for that kind of action, like the Sniff said.

Three men already had.

But Harry Needles wasn't dead—yet. Maybe it was time to remind Harry Needles of his mortality too. Hagen was going to walk into Harry Needles's place, pin him up against the wall, and tell him that he just might be the next dead man if he didn't tell Hagen everything he knew about Ronnie and this dead man's hand.

"Hello, Bodo."

Hagen turned.

Maxine Peach stood there on the sidewalk. Her hands clasped in front of her. Looking up at him, a little hesitant, like she wasn't sure what to expect. Pink capri pants, leather sandals, a small white purse on a long strap hanging from the shoulder of her loose white blouse. She looked like a schoolgirl on a summer outing. A well-developed schoolgirl, with mischief on her mind.

"Peach, what are you doing here?"

"Well, since you're so obviously not interested in lunch, I thought I'd drop by and see if dinner was more your speed. What do you say? Let me settle my debt, Bodo." Peach stepped forward and kissed him. A quick, friendly kiss. A kiss with no baggage behind it.

Peach turning up—right here, right now. Hagen wasn't happy about this. This was no time for mooning and soft chatter with Peach. There were things he needed to get done. Things that shouldn't wait. But he also realized that he hadn't eaten all day. And he couldn't just leave Peach standing on the sidewalk. "I'm sorry, Peach. I've got some things I have to do tonight. How about a quick sandwich somewhere?"

"I hope my debt is worth more than a sandwich."

"All right. A sandwich and coffee."

Peach made a comical face. "I'll take what I can get, but I'm not usually this easy."

"I'll buy. We'll save your debt for a night when I can savor it fully."

"My debt deserves nothing less." Peach reached up, lightly touched the side of his face. "You've got a bad bruise there."

"I walked square into the bathroom door this morning. Must've been half asleep."

"You shouldn't do that."

"I'm full of bad habits."

A quick sandwich then, it wouldn't take long. Then he'd make some excuses and stuff her into a cab or drop her at her car. And get back to business. The valet drove up with Hagen's car and jumped out, ran around to the other side and held the door open for Peach while she got in. Hagen climbed in behind the wheel. He was fastening his seat belt and asking Peach where a good place was for a sandwich when a short man in a glen plaid double-breasted suit emerged from the valet parking queue and climbed into the backseat, behind Hagen. For half a second Hagen thought he was a hotel guest who was climbing into the wrong car. The short man leaned forward, put one hand on Hagen's shoulder, like he was giving Hagen directions. With his other hand he reached through the console space between the two front seats, pressed the barrel of a revolver into Hagen's side.

A second man climbed into the backseat, behind Peach.

"Drive out of here," the short man said. "Slowly."

"Bodo?" Peach said, wide-eyed. Turning in her seat to look at the short man.

"Turn around," the short man said to Peach.

At the first stoplight on Las Vegas Boulevard the short man relieved Hagen of his pistol and handed it to the second man, who took it without a word.

12.

HAGEN DID AS HE WAS TOLD. He drove along Las Vegas Boulevard, then got onto Interstate 15 heading south. Peach sat in silence, her arms folded tight, as if she were suddenly very cold. Her eyes moved nervously from Hagen to the road ahead and back. Not daring to say a word. Not daring to turn her head enough to look over her shoulder.

The short man was slumped down in the backseat, his left shoulder resting against the car door. Hagen couldn't see his hands in the rearview mirror but he didn't need to see them to know that the revolver was either pointed at the back of Hagen's seat or the back of his head.

Hagen knew one thing—these two goons weren't detectives.

The short man was middle-aged, with dark brown hair that lay flat on his head. His ears stood out from the side of his head like the handles of a soup tureen. Small face, sharp nose, eyes that were dark and blank. A rat's face. The man sitting behind Peach was younger than the short man. Round face, round jawline. A pair of sunglasses with rectangular green lenses hiding his eyes. He wore a black suit with a green shirt and no tie. Hagen watched him in the rearview mirror. The young man's mouth was thin and bloodless.

"You look pretty stupid in those sunglasses," Hagen said in German. He wondered if the young man or Rat Face would respond in the same language. They didn't. The young man's forehead wrinkled into a frown but that was all.

"Take this exit," Rat Face said when they reached a turn off near McCarran Airport.

"Where are we going?" Hagen said.

"Shut up," Rat Face said. He raised the revolver and pressed the tip of the barrel against the back of Hagen's neck. Just long enough for Hagen to get the message.

They were on Highway 215 now. Heading southeast toward Henderson. A band of orange was just now appearing on the horizon as the sun began to set over the desert. When they reached Henderson Rat Face told Hagen to exit the highway. They drove along surface streets until they reached the south side of town. In the rearview mirror Hagen saw Rat Face looking around, unsure where exactly they were at. Then Rat Face spotted something that he recognized and soon they were pulling into a deserted parking lot in front of a long white warehouse. At the front of the building was a narrow window, a small access door, and a large sliding garage door for vehicles.

"Pull up to the door and honk the horn."

When Hagen applied the horn a face appeared in the narrow window, then disappeared again quickly, an indistinct blur from inside a dark room. A moment later the garage door rose. Hagen drove forward into the warehouse. The garage door descended behind them, shutting out the sunlight.

"Get out of the car."

Hagen turned the engine off. Rat Face asked for the car keys and Hagen handed them back. Then Hagen and the two men climbed out. Rat Face told Peach to stay seated in the car. The look in Peach's eyes seemed to plead with Hagen to do something. But there was nothing Hagen could do. Not right then.

"Don't worry, Peach," Hagen said. Trying to sound calm. "I'll get this straightened out and then we'll be on our way."

"You must be an optimist," Rat Face said.

The interior of the warehouse was cool and dimly lit. Large wooden shipping crates stacked in rows ten and fifteen feet high stretched back into the long building. A smell of wood and engine oil filled the air. Rat Face kept his revolver pointed at Hagen. The young man in the black suit had stepped back and was leaning against the wall, keeping an eye on Peach in the car, a large automatic pistol in his hand and the butt end of Hagen's Heckler & Koch hanging out of the waistband of his pants. He'd taken his sunglasses off and now he looked even younger than before. A kid with a menacing stare and a big gun.

After a moment an office door opened off to Hagen's right and a third man stepped out. He was tall and bald-headed and wore a blue suit. He was the man named Cleveland that Hagen had encountered the day before at Marty Ray's office.

So it was Marty Ray who wanted to talk to him. Did Marty Ray think Hagen had whacked Jack Gubbs too?

Or was this about something else?

Cleveland motioned to Hagen and Hagen followed him down an aisle between stacks of shipping crates, Rat Face staying a few steps behind Hagen. Somewhere near the center of the building they reached a solid wall of shipping crates and turned to the left, down a narrower aisle lined with metal shelves. Fifty or so feet farther on they came out in a wide clear area lined on three sides by still more metal shelves full of white boxes of various sizes. To the left, behind three file cabinets and two metal storage lockers, the aisle connected to another walkway that ran along one wall of the building.

In the middle of the clearing sat a wooden desk. A shipping clerk probably sat there during the day but this evening it was Marty Ray who sat behind the desk. A newspaper laid out in front of him. A half full highball glass in his hand.

"Hello, Sauerkraut. About time you got here."

"If you wanted to talk to me, Marty, you could've called me and asked me to stop by. Most people would've done it that way. It usually works." Hagen nodded in the direction of Rat Face. "Saves money on the hired help too. Not that you spent much money on that one."

"Maybe I don't want people to know I associate with you."

"You've never complained about my company before."

"Maybe I never will. Because you won't be around."

"That's tough talk."

"These are tough times."

"Let Peach go home, Marty."

"Peach?" Marty Ray's eyebrows crept up a fraction of an inch. Cleveland leaned down and spoke quietly to his boss. Then Marty Ray said to Hagen, "Peach—she used to work for me, right? That girl you used to see, back when? You don't waste any time picking up where you left off, do you, Sauerkraut."

"Let her go, Marty. She's not involved in this."

"Maybe she is, maybe she isn't. Maybe I'll talk to her too. But I want to talk to you first."

Cleveland set a metal folding chair down on the floor several feet in front of the desk, told Hagen to sit. When Hagen was seated Rat Face moved off to the right, cocked an elbow up on one of the metal shelves and struck a casual pose, the pistol at his side. Cleveland propped a leg up on the edge of the desk and folded his arms. Marty Ray pushed the newspaper aside. Strands of his dyed black hair, so well coiffed into a pompadour yesterday, now hung down over his forehead in a ragged pattern, and his eyes were heavy, either from lack of sleep or too much liquor. Marty Ray lifted his highball glass. "I'd offer you a drink, Sauer-kraut, but the bar is closed."

"I'll get by."

"I hope you will. Because there's something I want to know about. Couple of things. If you fill me in like I want, then we can all go home and forget about this. We'll all be good friends again. But if you don't want to tell me then we're going to sit here all night until you change your mind. And you will change your mind. But if you hold out too long, you might not be in good shape to walk out of here. You might have some aches and pains."

"I'll see what I can do."

"You'll do more than that."

Marty Ray pushed his chair back and stood up. He placed both hands squarely on the surface of the desk, leaned forward. "I told you not to fuck with my people, Sauerkraut. And I know you understood me when I told you. You still speak English, I've seen you do it. But then you go and take down Jack Gubbs. After I told you to lay off. Now what's that about? Can you help me come to an understanding about that? Because right now it weighs heavily on my mind."

"I didn't kill Gubbs, Marty."

"Please do explain that to me."

"What's to explain? I didn't kill him, that's all."

"You don't look real surprised to hear he's dead."

"I know he's dead. I just got finished talking to McGrath. He had the same idea that you do. He was wrong. So are you."

Marty Ray's eyes narrowed. "What's McGrath got to say about it?"

"He heard that I went to Gubbs's place the other night. He knows I've been asking around about Ronnie. He figured it like you do—I decided that Gubbs killed Ronnie and so I killed Gubbs. He asked me some questions. I answered them. He was happy with the answers."

"I'm not happy, Sauerkraut."

"All right. You're not happy."

"Gubbs had something you want, I know that. And I know it might be worth some large, this thing he had. It might even be something he took from your brother. You think he did. So you go to see Gubbs and you kill him and now you have the thing. And I want it. And you're going to give it to me."

"You've been talking to Winnie the Poof."

"Doesn't matter who I talk to. I talk to a lot of people. I talk to fucking God every morning. When I talked to him this morning he told me to kick your ass. So I'm kicking. If you don't give me what I want, you'll be talking to God too. Face-to-face. Just you and God, floating up there in the clouds. Like two little birdies."

"I talk to people too, Marty. I talked to Gubbs last night. He told me Ronnie was looking for a fence when he got into town. He also told me that he sent Ronnie to Winnie the Poof. So I talked to Wilson. He told me about this thing that Ronnie was trying to sell. He thought I might know where it was. I told him that I might, just to string him along. I think Ronnie was killed because of this thing he was trying to sell and I wanted to keep Wilson on the hook until I knew more. But I don't have the thing. Never did."

Marty Ray straightened up, pushed his hands into the pockets of his white slacks. He looked down his nose at Hagen. "Why would Gubbs tell you all that?"

"Someone put him up to it. Maybe you. What's it worth to you, Marty—this wooden hand?"

"Sauerkraut, my sainted brother Jimmy was murdered. Your brother was in on it, that's what I think. But I can't talk to your brother about that now. Your brother took a powder big-time. But he left that thing he had behind and I want it. It won't bring Jimmy back but it's better than nothing. It's like a little insurance policy—your brother dies and he leaves me some money. To compensate me for the loss of poor Jimmy. But I need the goods so I can cash in. You've got the goods. Maybe you don't think you do but I'm going to help you remember."

Marty Ray nodded to Cleveland. Cleveland pushed himself off the desk, stepped over to one of the metal storage lockers. He opened the locker and bent down, pulled out a coil of thick rope and set it on the floor. He started looking for something else in the bottom of the cabinet.

"I always liked you, Sauerkraut," Marty Ray said. "We go back a ways. But good times don't count for shit. This is business."

Hagen heard Rat Face moving around behind him to his right— hard-soled shoes scratching against a dirty cement floor. Then suddenly there was another sound, from somewhere on the other side of the warehouse. It sounded like an empty cardboard box hitting the floor.

Cleveland stood up, eyes alert and focused on a point somewhere above the metal shelves to Hagen's left. Cleveland looked like a hunting dog picking up a scent on the wind. Marty Ray didn't seem to have noticed the sound. His eyes were fixed on Hagen.

Cleveland motioned to Rat Face and pointed in the direction the sound had come from. Hagen heard Rat Face moving around behind him.

Then the lights went out.

"What the hell?" Marty Ray shouted in the darkness.

For half a second Hagen thought that Rat Face had turned off the lights. But that didn't add up.

There was someone else in here.

Someone who wanted the warehouse dark.

Hagen didn't waste time wondering who it was.

Hagen dived out of the chair. Hit the floor. Scrambled to his feet.

A gunshot cut through the darkness. Loud and very close to Hagen. There were sounds of a struggle coming from over by the metal cabinets, where Cleveland had stood when the lights went out. Something hit one of the metal cabinets hard. The cabinet toppled over and landed on the floor with a loud crash.

Cleveland cried out in pain.

It sounded like several men were fighting now with Cleveland, Marty Ray and Rat Face. They had come in from the aisleway behind the metal cabinets. One of these men was shouting and cursing at the top of his lungs—in German.

Hagen rushed forward into the darkness toward the aisle that led out into the center of the warehouse. He ran into a metal shelf, stumbled. He stood still for a second, trying to get his bearings, then pushed on, a blind man trapped in a maze. He kept his right hand out, his fingers touching the shelves. Suddenly the shelves ended and his fingers hung out into empty space. He'd reached a connecting aisle. He turned right. Crouching down he began moving as quickly as he dared down the dark aisle toward the front of the warehouse.

Another gunshot echoed through the building.

Behind him a man was shouting in German for the lights to be turned on. "*Lichter! Lichter!*"

Then a second man called for the lights. In broken French.

Hagen had almost reached the front of the building when a shaft of light appeared ahead of him. Hagen saw Peach, framed in a rectangle of light as she rushed through the doorway. The access door closed behind her and darkness returned. Hagen moved forward and then stopped again.

He heard footsteps. From somewhere off to the left. Approaching the aisle where Hagen now stood.

One set of footsteps. One man. Walking slowly in the darkness.

Hagen crouched down low beside a stack of shipping crates as the footsteps came closer.

The man entered the aisle. Kept walking.

The man was very close. Only a few feet away and a little to the right of Hagen. Hagen could hear the man breathing. He sounded winded. Hagen straightened up slowly. Silently. Then with all the strength he could muster he rushed forward, holding his forearms level with his chest and elbows out, to give him as wide a point of impact as possible.

He hit the man squarely. The man fell backward against a stack of shipping crates. Hagen reached out, found an arm and grabbed hold of it. He slugged the man twice in the stomach with his free hand. Hagen heard something solid hit the concrete floor and slide away.

The man moaned and collapsed onto the floor.

Then the lights came back on.

Hagen saw that he stood at the end of an aisle. Off to the left was his car, the garage door still closed behind it. The passenger side door of the car hung open. Directly ahead of him was the access door that Peach had escaped through. Hagen turned. Behind him the man he'd tackled was on his hands and knees on the floor, shaking his head, his breath coming in pained gasps. The man looked up and saw Hagen.

It was the Englishman Hagen had run into outside of the High Numbers Club the night before. The Englishman who'd been tailing

Hagen with his German friend. He looked dirty and unshaven, was still wearing the same shirt he'd worn last night. Hagen noticed one thing he hadn't seen last night when the Englishman had trained a pistol on him from the other side of the car—a dagger with an ornate hilt and a grinning skull for a handle, tattooed on the inside of the man's left forearm. A death's-head dagger.

A *totenkopf* dagger . . .

Then Hagen saw the pistol the man had dropped lying on the floor a few feet away. The man saw it at the same moment and started to scramble toward it on his hands and knees.

Hagen reached it first and picked it up.

The man rose to his knees. Hagen pointed the pistol at him. The man slowly raised his hands.

"You don't want to shoot me, mate," the Englishman said, his voice weak. "You've got enough trouble as it is."

Hagen had questions for this fellow. A lot of questions. Questions that he wanted to put to this man forcefully. But there was no time for questions. If Hagen wanted out of there, he had to go now.

Hagen turned and ran.

He reached the warehouse access door. Kicked the crash bar to open it, kept running.

He half expected to hear a gunshot behind him, following him out the door.

Outside the sky was full of the last glimmerings of dusk. Two new Chevrolet sedans stood parked along the street in front of the warehouse. Cars that belonged to the Englishman and his friends, no doubt. Hagen kept his eyes on the two cars, kept the pistol ready as he ran across the street. The two cars were empty. The Englishmen and his friends hadn't left a lookout behind.

Hagen ran to the street corner. He paused there, looking left and then right. He spotted Peach running down the sidewalk to his right and he took off after her. Finally caught up with her halfway down the block. He took hold of her arm and the two of them ran together. They came upon an alley that would hide them from the headlights of the cars passing on the street and they ducked into it.

Halfway down the alley Hagen and Peach stopped running. They leaned up against a brick wall, catching their breath. Through an open window a few yards away came the sound of machinery whirring and pounding, squeaking and shuddering. Sounded like a printing press but the sign on the back door said it was a *tortilleria*. Hagen's thoughts spun with the pounding of the machinery.

A German. An Englishman. And the man Hagen heard at the warehouse speaking in broken French. It could only mean one thing, Hagen was sure.

Ronnie had brought some of his friends from the Legion home with him.

Or they had followed him home.

"Peach, are you okay?" Hagen said.

Peach nodded, laid her arm across Hagen's shoulders. Leaning on him. Still trying to catch her breath. After a moment she said, "What kind of trouble are you in, Bodo?"

"I'm not quite sure," Hagen said. Not wanting to explain. There was no time. "But we've got to get you out of here."

"You're not quite sure?" Peach said. Her voice jittery. "I heard gunshots. Does that make it clearer for you? Men were shooting at you, Bodo. I would think you might have a clue as to why."

"They were shooting at someone. I don't think it was you or me. How did you get out of there?"

"Some men came into the warehouse. They had guns. They grabbed the man who was watching the car and took him over to the office and did something in there. Then some more of them came inside and walked off toward where you went. That's all I know. Except that the lights went out and I heard gunshots. I got out of the car and found the door and ran. And now you tell me you're not quite sure what happened. Does this happen to you a lot, Bodo? Just for no reason at all? Because I'm not really enjoying this. In case that's also not quite clear to you."

"I'm sorry, Peach. I'll tell you all about it later. Right now I've got some things to do. And you're going home."

Hagen realized he still carried the Englishman's automatic in his hand. Probably shouldn't be running through the streets of Henderson with a loaded pistol in plain sight. It was a small automatic, an old Beretta model. The clip held 9-millimeter short cartridges, with one round chambered. Hagen slapped the magazine back in and slid the Beretta into his shoulder holster. It wasn't a good fit but it would do.

Just then Hagen noticed the headlights of a car turning into the alley. He grabbed Peach and stepped back into the shadows of a recessed doorway, pulled the Beretta back out. Hagen peered around the corner of the wall. Over the top of a trash bin he saw the car enter the alley and stop.

Then it proceeded forward again. Slowly.

"Stay back," Hagen said. "Don't say a thing."

"Like you need to tell me that."

Hagen pushed Peach farther back into the darkness of the doorway. Then he peered around the corner of the wall again. The car moved closer. Hagen tightened his grip on the pistol. Whoever was driving was looking for something. Maybe it was someone with business at the *tortilleria* but Hagen didn't think so. He couldn't afford to. Things were going to look awfully funny if Hagen was wrong but he didn't care if things looked funny. It would look even funnier if Hagen had come this far only to be shot in an alley behind a tortilla factory.

The front of the car rolled into Hagen's line of sight. A big late-model Lincoln. Hagen took a deep breath and waited. The white paint and heavy wax on the hood of the car reflected the light from a bulb burning over a back door a few yards farther down the alley.

Hagen wasn't sure what he was going to do until the car was right there beside him and he saw that the driver's window was rolled down.

He didn't stop to think—didn't have time. He jumped out of the shadows. Holding the Beretta in both hands he leveled the automatic at the driver of the car. The barrel of the pistol was only a few inches from the open window.

The driver's head whipped around—two dark eyes opened wide in surprise and fear.

Hagen shouted, "Stop the car."

The car kept rolling and for a second Hagen thought the driver was going to step on the accelerator, gun the engine, shoot forward down the alley. Then the car lurched to a stop as the driver's foot came down heavy on the brakes. In the half-light of dusk Hagen couldn't see the man's face well. Hagen kept the automatic pointed at the man's head.

"Get out."

Hagen stepped back to give the man room to climb out of the car. The man stared at Hagen, didn't move.

"Do what he says," came a voice from the passenger side of the car. A woman's voice. Until right then Hagen hadn't realized that there was a passenger in the car. But he recognized the voice, knew who the passenger was.

Suzanne Cosette.

"Listen to your boss," Hagen said to the man behind the wheel. "Get the hell out of the car."

The man cleared his throat. His voice wavered as he spoke. "I've got to put the transmission in park."

"Do it slow. Then get out. Both of you. Keep your hands where I can see them. I don't want to make a mistake and shoot someone."

The man behind the wheel kept his eyes on Hagen as he reached over with his right hand for the shift lever on the console. He pushed the lever forward and it clicked into place. The idling of the engine changed in tone.

The man pushed the door open and got out. He stood beside the car with both hands near his face, palms out and fingers splayed, as though he was more worried about Hagen hitting him in the face than shooting him. On the other side of the car Cosette was moving slowly, climbing out of the car, standing up with both hands raised shoulder-high. She stared at Hagen over the top of the car.

Hagen recognized the driver. He was the swarthy young man that Hagen had seen at the atrium bar at the Mirage casino two nights ago. The one who'd been watching Hagen when Hagen arrived to talk to Cosette. Which meant that he was probably the man who had searched Hagen's room. But did any of that matter now? Right then Hagen didn't care who had searched his room.

Hagen motioned for the man to step around behind the car. The man did as he was told, his back sliding along the side of the car as he moved, keeping himself turned toward Hagen. His eyes focused on the barrel of the pistol in Hagen's hand.

"Suzanne, walk around to the back of the car," Hagen said.

"Mister Hagen, let me explain what is——"

"Move. Keep your hands in the air."

Cosette's high heels made sharp deliberate noises on the concrete surface of the alley as she moved back to join her partner, who stood now in the middle of the alley, several feet behind the car. Hagen took up a position beside the rear of the car. Kept the automatic raised.

"Throw your pistol on the ground," Hagen said to the swarthy man.

"I don't have one—I swear." The man's voice was thin and choked. His accent was heavily French. The glow from the red taillights made his dark face look even darker—a smoky Levantine complexion with narrow eyes that didn't stop moving. Hagen decided the man wasn't lying—the yellow silk shirt and tan slacks he wore didn't leave much room to hide a weapon. And Cosette was wearing only a white blouse and a black skirt. She didn't have any place to hide a pistol unless she'd hidden it up her skirt. Hagen doubted that she was that resourceful.

"We don't have guns, Mister Hagen," Cosette said now. "That's not what this is about. I saw what happened to you at the hotel. Those men—they weren't friends of yours. I was just on my way to see you and I saw them take you away. So I followed. I thought you might be in trouble and I was right about that. I thought maybe I could help you. I still think I can help you."

"What kind of help were you going to give me? Or was it your Legionnaire friends who were going to help me? The Hand of Danjou— do you still not recall that name, Suzanne? It's a wooden hand and it didn't come from a Russian statue. Some people say it's a fake. I'm beginning to wonder."

"That's not true, Mister Hagen. I've told you who I work for and what I want. I can put you in touch with Mister Amarantos right now. He can answer the questions you have. Let us go someplace where I can make the phone call. Let's settle this misunderstanding. It will be profitable for you. More profitable than perhaps I have led you to believe."

"Who killed Jack Gubbs, Suzanne?"

"I don't know what you're talking about."

Hagen nodded to the swarthy man. "I say you killed him. You went to his place looking for the hand, just like you tossed my hotel room the other night. But Gubbs got in the way and you killed him. Right? Or did you two try to work out some kind of deal with Gubbs first, but he wouldn't play on your terms so you had to get him out of the way."

"I've killed no one," the swarthy man said.

"Are you with the Legion too?"

"My friend, you're speaking in riddles." The man glanced at Cosette before he went on. "My name is Yves Gilleron. I also work for Mister Amarantos. If you will agree to speak to him right now then he will vouch for both of us. We know nothing about Legionnaires or your dead man."

A truck horn sounded on the busy street at the end of the alley behind Cosette and her partner. Hagen could see the crisscross of the evening headlights. Somewhere out on the streets, within a few block radius of where Hagen stood now in the alley, the men who'd broken into the warehouse were out looking for him. And Marty Ray and his men might be looking too—if they were still in any condition to look for anything. Hagen motioned toward the far end of the alley with the automatic. "Tell Amarantos he's going to have to wait. But you can do one thing for me right now. Turn around and start walking."

"What do you plan to do with us?" Cosette said. The nervous edge in her voice was sharper now.

"I don't plan on doing anything with you," Hagen said. "But I do have plans for your car. And since you're going to be doing some walking tonight, you might as well get started."

Hagen motioned with the barrel of the automatic for the two to get moving. Cosette and her partner looked at each other, then turned slowly, began walking down the alley, still holding their arms out and their hands up. Their footsteps were slow and hesitant. They moved like two people who expected at any second to hear a loud noise behind them—the sound of the other shoe dropping. But the only noise in the alley was the pounding of the tortilla machine pouring out of the open window. Hagen wondered if either of them truly believed he might shoot them in the back as they walked away. Then he wondered why he cared what they believed.

Cosette and her partner had almost reached the end of the alley when Hagen holstered the Beretta and motioned to Peach. Peach emerged from the shadows of the doorway and got into the passenger seat of the Lincoln. Hagen got in behind the wheel. Moved the gearshift lever to the drive position. Stepped on the accelerator, hard. They sped off down the alley toward the dark quiet street at the other end.

"You're a real fun date, Bodo."

"That's what the girls all tell me, Peach."

13.

LEGIONNAIRES—HOW MANY OF THEM were out there? Must've been at least four or five at the warehouse. Maybe more. They'd been following Hagen since he'd left the cemetery after Ronnie's funeral. If they were looking for this artifact—this wooden hand—they'd had any number of chances to corner Hagen and question him about it. But they hadn't. They'd held back. Waiting. Following him. Until tonight. Why did they wait? To see where Hagen led them?

And where had he led them?

To Gubbs, for one. And Gubbs was dead now. Was Marty Ray dead, lying in a pool of blood back at the warehouse? Or Winnie the Poof? Or Harry Needles? Hagen had led the Legionnaires to all of them.

And Ronnie—had they killed him too?

Martinez said the hand was a fake. Martinez had to be wrong. Three dead men said so. Somehow Ronnie had gotten hold of the real thing. And the real thing had killed him.

Hagen dropped Peach off at a taxi stand outside of a small Henderson casino. Exacted a promise from her not to call the police. Told her to go home and stay there, he had things under control and he'd be in touch later. When he'd taken care of some business. Peach didn't argue. Then Hagen drove out to the highway and headed north. In the distance the lights of Las Vegas burned bright—a city of jewels.

Hagen had started out twice today to go see Harry Needles. McGrath's detectives got in his way the first time. The second time it was Marty Ray and his boys. He'd make it this time though. He had to get to Harry before the Legionnaires did.

If they hadn't already gotten to him.

Hagen hoped that Harry Needles was still alive.

As Hagen drove on something tugged at his memory. He found himself thinking of his father. The Waffen-SS soldier. The Legionnaire. And of the photograph his father had once shown him. Rows of Legionnaires standing at attention under the hot sun, saluting as an honor guard of stone-faced soldiers passed in front of them, the soldier in the lead carrying a glass reliquary with something inside.

The wooden hand—Hagen was sure of it.

The Hand of Danjou . . .

Suddenly Hagen understood in a way that he hadn't before what the wooden hand truly was and what it meant. And why a small band of Legionnaires wanted it so badly.

Badly enough to kill for it.

Hagen parked the Lincoln in a far corner of the parking lot outside of the Venus Lounge. Using a thin cotton sweater he found lying on the backseat he wiped down the steering wheel and the gearshift lever and anything else he or Peach might've touched—for what it was worth. He found a small black leather purse wedged between the passenger seat and the console. He opened it. It was Cosette's pocketbook—the same one she'd had with her the other night at the Mirage.

There wasn't much inside. A hundred dollars or so in cash. Two credit cards. A small lipstick. Business cards like the one she'd given Hagen. Nothing that told him anything he didn't already know. He wiped the surface of the purse down and put it back where he'd found it. He got out of the car with the sweater in his hand and wiped down the outside door handle.

Hagen tossed the cotton sweater into a trash can near the front door of the Venus Lounge.

Inside the club Hagen pushed through the crowd, elbowed his way up to the bar. The colored stage lights flashed and the mirror balls on the ceiling sparkled. The faces of the people in the crowd changed from red to blue to green with the changing lights. He shouted over the pounding music at a bartender, said he wanted to see Harry Needles. The bartender gave Hagen a dead pan and moved off quickly.

A moment later Theresa Sanchez appeared behind the bar.

Sanchez—whose name he'd found in Gubbs's address book. She looked harried and disheveled, strands of her black hair hanging loose from the bun at the back of her head. She gave Hagen a sour look but she dutifully picked up the house phone and called upstairs when he asked to speak to Harry. When she hung up the phone she pointed toward the door at the back of the club, then went on about her business.

Hagen walked over to the door and stood there with his hand on the handle. The tiny light on the electronic lock turned green. Hagen opened the door.

The back room was cool and empty.

Hagen ascended the stairs and walked down the hallway. The door to Harry Needles's office was open a crack.

Hagen pushed on the door and stepped inside.

"Hello, Harry."

Harry Needles stood at the table beside the wall of one-way glass, a long thin cigar in one hand. Harry Needles's usual smiling nonchalance was gone. His face was sullen and there was a wary look in his eyes. Behind him, through the glass, the lights of the club seemed to burst and explode in the air above the roiling crowd.

"Gubbs is dead," Harry Needles said.

Hagen closed the door behind him. "I've heard."

"He got whacked."

"I heard that too."

"Fix yourself a drink."

"Thanks."

"Word on the street is that maybe you had something to do with it."

Hagen didn't answer. He walked over to the liquor trolley that stood beside Harry Needles's desk. Tossed a few ice cubes into a glass. Poured three fingers of scotch out of a cut glass decanter over the ice. Took a long drink. The scotch flowed down his throat and through his body like a soothing voice that calmed his nerves and cleared his head.

Hagen carried his drink over to where Harry Needles stood.

"What else do you hear, Harry?"

"Isn't that enough?"

"Marty Ray tell you?"

Harry Needles stepped back, tapped the ash of his cigar into the ashtray on the table. "Doesn't matter who told me. Gubbs is dead. People think you killed him. That's what matters."

"You think I killed Gubbs?"

"I don't know. Maybe you did." Harry Needles gave Hagen a sharp look. "Gubbs had friends, Bodo. You might not think so, but he did. Some of those friends just might want a word with you."

Hagen set his drink down on the table. "And I'd like to have a word with them."

Harry Needles didn't see the punch coming. One second he was raising his cigar to his mouth and glancing out the window, the next second Hagen's fist hit him squarely under the chin in a fast uppercut.

Harry Needles flew backward. Landed on his back on the carpet. For a second Hagen thought he had knocked Harry out cold. Then Harry opened his eyes and shook his head. A trickle of blood appeared out of the corner of his mouth.

Hagen picked up Harry's burning cigar, placed it in the ashtray on the table. "Don't want to burn the carpet, do we, Harry."

Harry Needles pulled himself up, propped himself on one elbow. He winced in pain as he ran his hand along his jaw.

"I know about the hand," Hagen said. "Ronnie left it with you. He trusted you, Harry. When he got into town he came right here to see you, and he asked you to keep something for him, isn't that right? What did he tell you, Harry? I'm betting that he didn't tell you about the hand, what it was. He trusted you but not that much. So you didn't know what it was at first. But you found out. Maybe Gubbs told you. Maybe you and Gubbs were in on it together. That's why you had Gubbs come here last night and tell me about Winnie the Poof. You were trying to send me off in the wrong direction. Meanwhile, you and Gubbs were going to sell this hand elsewhere. That's the way it was, isn't it, Harry? That's the way it played out. Can you talk, Harry? It's time for you to start talking."

Harry Needles slowly got to his feet. He stumbled over to the table and leaned against it, dazed and unsteady, working his jaw from one side to the other. He picked up the ashtray and raised it to his mouth and spit blood into it, set the ashtray down.

"You're wrong, Bodo." Harry's voice was a whisper. "So take your bullshit somewhere else. While you still can. In five seconds I'm going to pick up that phone. I've got twelve men downstairs who will be happy to tell you all the reasons why you're wrong. You won't like it much."

"You're not listening to me, Harry."

Hagen stepped forward and punched Harry Needles in the face. Harry's arms treaded air as he flew backward and landed hard on his side on the carpet. He moaned and tried to sit up. His head seemed to wobble on his shoulders. Blood was flowing out of his mouth, much more than the trickle it had been a moment before. A trail of blood ran down his chin and onto the front of his shirt. Harry raised his cupped hand to his mouth and spit some of the blood out. A piece of tooth landed in the palm of his hand. He wiped his hand on his shirt. He started to get up.

Hagen grabbed Harry Needles under his shoulders and pulled him to his feet, then threw him against the table. Hagen pulled the Englishman's Beretta from his shoulder holster. Pressed the barrel of it between Harry Needles's eyebrows. Harry Needles stared wide-eyed at Hagen.

"Now that I have your attention, Harry, you're going to tell me who killed Ronnie. Maybe I did kill Gubbs. And if I killed Gubbs there's no reason why I shouldn't kill you. They can only hang me once. So let's get on with it."

Harry Needles started to choke on the blood in his mouth. Hagen let him turn his head and spit. After a moment Harry Needles found his voice.

"I don't know who killed Ronnie—I swear I don't."

"So what have you and Gubbs been up to?"

Harry Needles's breath came in gasps. "It's like you said. When Ronnie got into town, he asked if he could leave some of his luggage with me. He didn't want to drag it around. He just said it was some of his stuff. Couple of suitcases. I didn't know what was in them." Harry Needles swallowed hard. "After he was killed, Gubbs came to see me. He told me that Ronnie had something that was worth big money. Maybe a million. Maybe more. He wanted to know if I knew where this thing was. Some kind of wooden hand. He said he knew where he could sell it. He'd split it with me if I could find the hand."

"What did you tell him?"

"It sounded crazy at first. I told Gubbs I didn't know what he was talking about. But I started thinking. Ronnie was dead, the hand wasn't any good to him. I didn't see why I shouldn't sell it. So I called Gubbs back yesterday morning. I told him I might know where it was. But I wasn't going to give it to him. I told him to set up a sale, then we'd talk again. I told him I'd turn over the hand when the cash was on the table."

"How did Gubbs know you had it?"

"He didn't. He was guessing. He knew Ronnie had been here so he thought it might be here too."

"Who was he going to sell it to?"

"I don't know."

"Winnie the Poof?"

"No. He was looking for an out-of-town fence. He couldn't sell it to Winnie. Winnie already knew about the hand. I guess Ronnie went to see him. After Ronnie was killed Winnie asked Gubbs about it. That's when Gubbs knew that the hand was worth something. But Gubbs didn't want to sell it to Winnie. Winnie would think that Gubbs killed

Ronnie for it. Gubbs was going take the action out of town—some people up in Reno. He said he could sell it up there."

"Did Gubbs kill Ronnie?"

"I wouldn't have done business with him if I thought he killed Ronnie."

Hagen slammed his fist into the side of Harry's face. The impact sent Harry Needles sliding toward the end of the table. Hagen pushed him the rest of the way off. Harry Needles landed on the floor.

Hagen kicked Harry to get him moving. "Get up."

Harry got up on his hands and knees. Moaning and spitting. Shaking his head, like a dog trying to shake off a collar. Hagen knelt down on one knee, grabbed Harry Needles by the hair and pulled his head back. Pressed the barrel of the automatic against Harry's ear.

"Think harder, Harry. Did Gubbs kill Ronnie?"

"That's not the way it was." Harry Needles spit more blood out. Bloody saliva hung from his chin.

"Then you killed Ronnie. Isn't that right, Harry? Gubbs told you about the hand and you killed Ronnie."

"No." Harry Needles shook his head. His voice rose in pitch. *"No."* He said it again and again, his voice becoming a sharp cry. Harry Needles sounded like a man trying to crawl out from under the black end of a delirium.

But Hagen believed him.

Hagen stood up, slipped the pistol back into the shoulder holster.

"Where's the hand now?"

"My place."

"In Laughlin?"

"Yeah."

Hagen walked into the bathroom that adjoined the office, pulled a hand towel off a towel rack, came back out. Harry Needles was crawling the few feet to the couch on his hands and knees. Harry Needles sat down on the floor with his back against the couch, wiping his bloody mouth with the back of his hand, gingerly feeling his cheeks and jaw with the tips of his fingers.

Hagen dropped the towel into his lap.

"Clean yourself up, Harry."

Harry Needles's Cadillac Allante was parked outside the back door of the Venus Lounge. That was helpful. It saved them a walk through the club, where awkward questions might be raised—a bouncer wondering why his boss was holding a bloody towel to his swollen mouth, with more blood down his shirtfront. And if the Legionnaires were watching the club, they'd be out front, but maybe not in back.

Harry Needles and Hagen departed unobserved. Or so Hagen hoped.

They drove out of Las Vegas on Highway 95. Soon they were out in the rugged landscape of the Mojave Desert, heading south. The desert sky was clear and full of stars and the road to Laughlin was narrow and dark. Harry Needles was silent, one hand on the wheel and the other holding the towel to his mouth. Hagen kept the Beretta out but he didn't need it.

Harry Needles had no fight left in him.

The Cadillac sped through the night. In the headlights a patch of broken glass on the road ahead looked like sparkling diamonds. Hagen thought of another night. Not so long ago. Another dark road . . .

"Bodo . . ."

It was Vogel, crying for help in the night.

Then Hagen heard the pistol shot out on the road.

Then blackness. Later Hagen wouldn't at first remember raising his pistol and firing several rounds into the air.

A truck driver delivering produce to Morlaix came across the Mercedes on the side of the dark country road. He stopped and ran to the motionless body lying behind the car. Vogel was dead. The bullet fired into the back of

Vogel's head as he lay on the ground had taken off much of Vogel's fore-head.

The truck driver was scrambling back into the cab of his truck when he heard several gunshots off in the trees beside the road. He removed a small pistol that he carried with him from under the seat of his truck, then radioed to his dispatcher in Caen. While the company dispatcher called the gendarmerie *in Morlaix, the truck driver drove forty yards down the road, then turned around and sat there, headlights on and engine idling, the pistol in his sweat-covered hands, the Mercedes just barely visible in the fog down the road.*

Twenty minutes later the gendarmes from Morlaix arrived. First one car, then two more, then another four or five. The gendarmes mounted an extensive search, bullhorns and portable crime scene lights crisscrossing in the night and fog. They found Hagen lying unconscious against a tree, his pistol on the ground next to him. The ambulance arrived—

Hagen woke up, his mind hazy from drugs. Thick white bandages on his arm and shoulder and around his chest. A nurse. A doctor. Gendarmes. Then the wheelchair and the move down the hallway to the small empty white room, with a gendarme in the hallway outside the door, standing guard.

Hagen waited. The pain in his arm and shoulder grew as the drugs wore off. The captain of the gendarmes arrived, strutting like a rooster. Questions, one after another. But Hagen said little. Call the Directorate of Territorial Security, Hagen said. I want to speak with someone from the DST. The captain balked. DST indeed. You'll speak to me or no one. But the captain gave in finally and made the call. An hour later a small man with wire-framed glasses stepped into the white room, showed Hagen his credentials.

Monsieur Girard of the DST . . .

Several days later Hagen sat in William Severance's office in Berlin. The gray sky outside the window matched the ashen color of Severance's face. Severance had one question—what the hell happened out there? The DST wants an explanation, Bodo. Langley wants you to disappear. The BND lost a man and wants your ass.

Hagen couldn't explain. Ingeborge Stromm must have told someone about

Hagen and Vogel and their visit to her home and that person had taken mat-ters into their own hands. There was no other answer. But who had Stromm contacted? Totenkopf? Hohle? Or had Hagen and Vogel inadvertently kicked some other hornet's nest?

A copy of a report from the DST, routed through the French foreign min-istry, lay on Severance's desk. The report had gone to the German foreign ministry and the U.S. Department of State. The DST had looked into the Stromm story. The same night that Hagen and Vogel were ambushed on the road to Morlaix, Ingeborge Stromm was found dead in a hotel room in Saint-Malo, two hundred kilometers from her home near Morlaix. The re-port said that she'd placed the barrel of a revolver in her mouth and pulled the trigger, but Hagen didn't believe it. Stromm had told someone about Hagen and Vogel. That person had decided that it was time to get rid of her as well as them. Whatever Ingeborge Stromm knew about Heinrich Kress's association with the East German Stasi, she took it with her to the grave.

The report went on at length about the Stromm story, picking it apart, casting suspicion on Hagen and Vogel. The message was clear—the DST believed that the Stromm story was at least partly a fabrication to cover up some other BND or CIA operation on French soil. The French foreign min-istry demanded an official explanation.

I can't help you, Bodo, Severance said. They want your head on a platter and mine too.

Two pasty-faced men from Langley arrived in Berlin and questioned Ha-gen at great length about the Brittany operation and the death of BND agent Johannes Vogel. Then the BND men took over. When the questions ended Hagen knew where he stood—or, as the case was, where he didn't stand. Hagen was going to take the fall. Langley needed a scapegoat to placate the French and Hagen was their man. Hagen's days with the CIA were numbered in single digits.

Hagen beat them to the punch and submitted his resignation.

Stasi agents Totenkopf and Hohle—just two code names on an old Stasi document. But they had won. Hagen had lost.

And Johannes Vogel was dead.

Hagen sat alone in his Berlin apartment. He didn't know what to do with himself, so he did nothing. At odd moments—walking along the street at dusk, staring out the window, sitting in a gasthaus with another drink in his hands—the image of Vogel lying in the road, bleeding, dying, washed over him and he felt the fear all over again. He should have stayed at the car with Vogel. He could've saved him. He shouldn't have run. He was Vogel's only chance but he'd left Vogel there to die. Hagen lived through those few minutes again and again and each time he left Vogel behind to die. A thousand times.

Then the dreams began. Hagen wandering in the dark forest. Vogel calling out to him—

"Bodo . . ."

Six months later—a phone call from the States. The Sniff on the other end—"Bodo, Ronnie is dead." Now the voice Hagen heard in his dreams was Ronnie's voice.

"Bodo . . ."

It was too late to save Vogel. It was too late to save Ronnie. But there was one thing Hagen could do. He'd find Ronnie's killer. He'd find Ronnie's killer if it cost Hagen his own life.

He wouldn't run this time . . .

A sign along the edge of the highway indicated that they were passing through the town of Searchlight. It wasn't much of a town—a few roadhouse casinos, a cluster of mobile homes and an abandoned gas station with the name JACK'S TRADING POST painted on the side. Hagen checked his watch. How far had they driven? Fifty miles?

Another fifty to go then.

They'd be in Laughlin by midnight.

The headlights of oncoming cars wavered in the distance, then suddenly sped past. Behind them, following Harry Needles and Hagen along the desert highway, were more headlights, keeping their distance, as though giving Harry Needles and Hagen room to run.

"You believe me, don't you, Bodo?" Harry Needles said all of a sudden. Harry spoke without moving his mouth too much. The words came out thick and awkward.

Hagen looked over at Harry. Harry's mouth had stopped bleeding quite some time ago. The bloody hand towel now lay on the console between the front seats. Harry held the steering wheel in both hands, his chin down, his eyes staring straight ahead. In the lights from the dashboard Harry's face took on a greenish hue.

"About what?"

"About Ronnie. I don't know who killed him. I don't know anything about it."

"You could've told me about the hand yesterday, Harry, but you didn't. When you heard I was downstairs waiting to see you, you called Gubbs and told him to drop by and tell me about Winnie the Poof. You wanted to keep me busy while you and Gubbs sold the hand. So why should I believe you now?"

"I got scared. I didn't think you'd understand. I thought if I told you about the hand, you'd add it up all wrong. You'd think I had something to do with Ronnie's death. Sometimes people get scared. Haven't you ever been scared, Bodo?"

"Sure, I've been scared."

"I got scared."

"You still scared, Harry?"

"Yes, I am."

"That's good. You should be scared, for a lot of reasons. One reason is, McGrath thinks you killed Jimmy Ray. Or at least that you had something to do with it."

Harry Needles glanced at Hagen, as though uncertain whether Hagen was serious. Then his eyes returned to the road ahead. "McGrath is out of his mind."

"He says you were there in the office that night. You knew about the cash Jimmy Ray took with him to his house. McGrath thinks you told someone about it. And whoever you told went to the house and whacked Jimmy Ray and took the money. Of course, you might have killed him yourself but I don't believe that. You don't have the guts for that, do you, Harry?"

"If I'd been in on it, I'd be dead now."

"Maybe."

"No, not maybe. Absolutely."

"So who killed him?"

"Who cares?"

"McGrath, for one. Marty Ray, for another."

"Jimmy Ray's been dead for five years. And he's a lot easier to deal with dead than he was alive. I don't give a fuck who killed him. It's ancient history."

"Maybe it's not so ancient. But let's change the subject. Tell me about Theresa Sanchez."

"Why?"

"She was a friend of Gubbs's. Maybe a close friend. And she saw Ronnie a couple of days before he was killed. Maybe she knows something. Maybe she's scared to talk about what she knows. Like you are, Harry."

"I wouldn't call her a friend of Gubbs."

"What would you call her?"

Harry Needles started to speak but the pain in his mouth cut the words off. He grimaced, then started again. "Back when Marty owned a piece of the Venus, he used to send Gubbs around to take a look at the girls. If Gubbs saw one that he thought Marty would like, he'd send her over to see Marty. If Marty liked the girl and wanted to see her again, he'd get in touch with her through Gubbs and Gubbs would set it up."

"And the girls made a little money for being nice to Marty."

"I didn't follow it that closely."

"Doesn't sound like you needed to. Seems clear enough. Let me see if I've got this straight—Jack Gubbs was pimping your dancers to Marty Ray. Does that capture the essence of it?"

"I wouldn't put it like that."

"And Theresa Sanchez was one of those girls. Does she still see Marty?"

"I don't know."

"That's quite a business you run, Harry."

"Theresa is a smart woman. I can depend on her. Which is more than I can say for a lot of people. What she does or who she sees in her personal life is her own business."

"How did she wind up with Ronnie?"

"She told you."

"She told me one story. I'm wondering if there's another."

"Ask her again."

Hagen didn't think he needed to. He could see it already. Ronnie, just out of the Legion and back in Las Vegas, looking for a party. Gubbs, with a black address book full of telephone numbers. A few phone calls. A little sweet-talk about money. And suddenly Ronnie has a hot date for the night. Maybe it happened that way. Maybe it happened the way Theresa Sanchez had said. But Hagen wondered what Ronnie might have told Theresa Sanchez. And what Theresa Sanchez might have told Jack Gubbs or Marty Ray. Once again Hagen saw how small Ronnie's circle of friends—or enemies—was. Everyone knew everyone else, everyone talked to each other. But there was a wild card now. A band of Legionnaires that had come to Las Vegas for their own reasons. Or had one of Ronnie's acquaintances been talking to them too?

Ten miles past the desert town of Cal-Nev-Ari Harry Needles turned off 95 and onto Highway 163, heading due east toward Lake Mohave and Davis Dam. The highway wound through dark hills, then descended toward the Colorado River and the cluster of bright lights that was Laughlin. When they reached town Harry Needles drove along the main drag, Casino Drive, where a long line of tall hotel casinos glowed brightly along the west bank of the river. Hagen was surprised. The last time he'd been to Laughlin it was nothing more than a stain on the roadway. Now Laughlin looked like Las Vegas in miniature. Another town on the edge of nowhere, grown tall and fat on the money of people who carried their dreams in their wallets.

14.

IT WAS A SMALL BUNDLE. Just an old blue sweatshirt, rolled up and tied off with fraying brown twine.

It didn't weigh much. Didn't look like much.

Hagen stood at the table in the kitchen of Harry Needles's house, working at the knot in the twine. Harry Needles sat on the other side of the wooden table, a glass of scotch in one hand, a handful of ice wrapped in a dish towel in the other. He alternated between sips of the scotch and pressing the ice against his mouth to help take the swelling down. The scotch didn't go down easy—eighty proof liquor doesn't mix well with torn gums and broken teeth.

Hagen kept the Englishman's pistol on the table next to him but he wasn't worried about Harry Needles.

Harry Needles only wanted out.

The house was part of a development at the south end of Laughlin— a ranch-style structure with white stucco walls and a red tile roof, built on a couple of acres of dry desert land at the end of a secluded cul-de-sac. Floodlights shone across the front of the house and the three-car garage that stood at the end of a driveway lined with palm trees, cacti and ornamental rocks. When they arrived at the house Hagen followed Harry Needles down a hallway and into a large den. From a wall safe behind a bookcase Harry Needles removed the blue sweatshirt bundle. From a closet on the other side of the room he pulled out a large tan suitcase and a leather valise. Green airport tags were tied to the handles of both bags.

Harry Needles and Hagen carried the two pieces of luggage and the bundle into the kitchen where the light was better and where Harry Needles could pour them both a drink.

Hagen untied the twine and pulled it away from the bundle.

"What is it?" Harry said.

"You haven't looked at it?"

"I looked at it. It's a wooden hand. Why is it important?"

Hagen took a long drink. He set his glass down and began unrolling the sweatshirt. "It's important because a lot of men have died for it. Thousands of men, from around the world. Do you believe that, Harry?"

"I don't know what to believe."

The sweatshirt fell away to reveal the wooden hand.

The hand was nine or ten inches long from fingertips to the end of the black wrist piece. The dark wood was covered with gouges and scratches. The articulated fingers were slightly curled, as though the hand had been taken from its owner just as it was reaching out to grasp something.

Hagen studied the hand under the light, turning it one way and then another. Wooden fingers moved on ancient wooden joints. The middle finger was broken off at the second joint—the hand had been kicked around a bit. The band of black metal around the wrist had once held in place some type of leather sheath that must have fitted over the stump of the forearm—a few small pieces of leather were still visible along the underside of the wristband where it was fastened to the wood. The edges of the leather looked rough and freshly cut, as though the sheath had been removed from the prosthetic hand only recently.

The hand looked even less remarkable now than it had in the photographs.

But it was unmistakably the same wooden hand.

The dead man's hand.

Thirteen million dollars, the Sniff had said.

Hagen set the hand down, took another drink from his glass. He unzipped the battered valise that sat on the table, poked around among Ronnie's belongings. The bag contained clothes, a few paperback books—one in English and two in French, an old pair of leather sandals stained with sweat, several loose centime coins, an envelope with a single color photograph—Ronnie in his Legionnaire's dusty green fatigues, compact FAMAS assault rifle hanging across his chest from a strap around his neck, standing on top of a French-made armored personnel carrier painted in a brown-and-tan camouflage pattern. Ronnie looked cocky, large sunglasses hiding his eyes, sarcastic grin on his face, giving a thumbs-up sign. A long white beach in the background, a palm tree off to the left. Must've been when Ronnie was stationed in the Comoro Islands. Off the coast of Africa.

Hagen slid the photograph back into the envelope.

Toward the bottom of the valise Hagen found a green beret. A well-ironed black tassel hung from the back. The beret was battered, with several holes in the green cloth where it met the thin black leather sweatband. A round gold insignia was pinned to the side—a grenade with seven flames rising from it, the first and the seventh curled downward, the other five flames standing straight.

The insignia of the French Foreign Legion.

Hagen dropped the beret back into the valise. He picked up the wooden hand and wrapped it back up in the blue sweatshirt.

"What are you going to do with it?" Harry Needles said.

"I'm going to give it to the people who want it," Hagen said. "Before they kill me and take it anyway. But first they're going to tell me a few things."

Hagen tied off the bundle with the twine, then tucked the bundle into the valise, zipped the bag closed.

Hagen didn't know where to find the Legionnaires but he didn't think it mattered. All he had to do was return to Las Vegas and stand still for ten minutes. They'd swarm all over him. But the wooden hand would be his safe conduct pass. They wouldn't kill him as long as he had the wooden hand in reserve. Before Hagen gave it to them, they'd have to tell him who killed Ronnie. That was his price. Hagen was sure that they knew.

But first he had to get back to Las Vegas.

"I need your car, Harry."

"All right."

Harry Needles stood up, pulled his key ring out of his pocket. He tossed the keys onto the table.

Hagen couldn't take Harry Needles with him. He'd have to leave him here. Hagen didn't like that but he didn't have much choice. He'd have his hands full when he got back to Las Vegas, he couldn't keep an eye on Harry too. But even if Harry did pick up the phone as soon as Hagen left, called someone—Marty Ray, Winnie the Poof, maybe someone Hagen hadn't heard of—and told them that Hagen had the wooden hand, what good would it do him? Hagen was going back to Las Vegas to talk to the Legionnaires. The Legionnaires would certainly keep him safe from anyone else—at least until they got the hand.

It might be wise though to take a different route back to Las Vegas. Harry Needles and anyone he might talk to would assume that Hagen would return to town the same way they'd come out—on Highway 95. A lot could happen on Highway 95 between Laughlin and Las Vegas. It might be prudent to take the longer route back—Highway 68 out to Kingman, then Highway 93 north to Hoover Dam. It would mean an extra half hour or so, but if anyone was looking for him, they wouldn't think to find him on that road.

"Sit down, Harry."

Harry Needles sat back down in his chair. He gave Hagen a wary look. Hagen picked up the Beretta. Hagen saw a bead of sweat rolling down the side of Harry's face as Hagen holstered the automatic.

"I'm going to leave you here," Hagen said.

Harry Needles nodded slowly.

"You're going to sit here and be quiet. Don't pick up the phone. Don't call anyone. If you interfere with what I have to do tonight, I'm going to come back here looking for you."

Harry Needles raised his hands. A show of surrender. "Bodo, I made a mistake. I know that. I took something that didn't belong to me. But it's yours now. Take the hand and do what you want, but let's just forget where you got it. Is that a deal, Bodo?"

Hagen smiled. "Jack Gubbs told me much the same thing last night. This morning he woke up with a bullet in his head." Hagen picked up Harry's car keys and dropped them into his pocket. "And Harry, if I find out that you had something to do with Ronnie's death, or even that you know who killed him, I'll kill you. You believe that, don't you? You believe that I'd kill you?"

Harry Needles stared at Hagen, nodded his head again. He believed it.

Hagen picked up the suitcase and the leather valise and left the house. As he walked past the large picture window at the front of the house he looked inside, saw Harry Needles walking out of the kitchen and into the living room, one hand holding the ice to his face, the other hand flat on his forehead, as though checking for signs of a fever. It crossed Hagen's mind that Harry Needles might grab a gun and run outside to stop Hagen and take back the wooden hand, but Hagen didn't believe that Harry had the courage to do it, even if he wanted to. Still, Hagen walked a little faster, waiting to hear the first creak of the front door as it opened behind him. It would be the last thing that Harry Needles ever did.

But Hagen heard nothing except the soft insect sounds of the desert and the sound of his own footsteps on the concrete walk. Several small palm trees stood along the edge of the driveway, long fronds hanging motionless in the still night air. When he reached the driveway he looked toward the street. Nothing stirred. No cars parked out there. Only the lights of distant houses.

The car was parked in front of the garage. A floodlight lit the face of the white garage door and small garden lights illuminated the cacti and palm trees on either side of the driveway. Hagen opened the driver's side door, pulled the front seat forward and tossed the suitcase and the valise in the back. He was pushing the seat back again when he heard a noise behind him.

Hagen turned, his hand sliding under his sport coat for the Beretta.

"Don't move." The voice was quiet and firm.

Hagen pulled his empty hand out slowly. Raised both hands, shoulder-high.

A man stepped around the back of the car. A tall young man. Shaved head, broad shoulders. His blue jeans and black T-shirt looked ordinary but the pistol in his hand was far from commonplace. In the light from the garden lights Hagen could see it well enough—a Glock automatic. Looked like one of the full-sized models that carried a 10-millimeter or .357 cartridge. A nasty piece of weaponry. And it was pointed directly at Hagen's chest. Good thing he wasn't quicker, Hagen thought. Good thing he hadn't gotten his pistol out. He'd most certainly be dead now.

Hagen was sure the man was another Legionnaire.

"Reach inside your coat slow-like and remove the pistol with your thumb and index finger. Drop it on the ground." The Legionnaire spoke in English, with a slight British accent. He might have been an Englishman but Hagen didn't think so. British Canadian perhaps?

Hagen did as he was told.

"Kick it toward me."

The pistol skittered across the few feet of concrete between Hagen and the Legionnaire. Keeping his eyes on Hagen and with the barrel of the Glock still pointed at Hagen's chest the Legionnaire bent down, picked up the pistol. He tucked it into the waist of his pants, the butt of the automatic resting against the black case of a cellular telephone that hung from the Legionnaire's belt.

"Where's the hand?" the Legionnaire said.

Hagen nodded toward the car. "In the valise."

"Let's see it."

Hagen felt the sweat on the palms of his hands as he reached in, grabbed the handle of the valise, pulled it out of the car. His luck had run out. The Legion had found him before he could find the Legion. The wooden hand, the only bargaining chip he had, was gone. Had they followed Hagen and Harry Needles here from Las Vegas? Or had they been here already, watching and waiting?

Hagen set the leather valise down on the ground. Unzipped it. Removed the blue bundle.

"Unwrap it."

Hagen untied the twine and let it fall to the ground. He pulled the wooden hand from the sweatshirt and held it up. The Legionnaire studied it for a moment.

"All right, wrap it back up and put it in the bag."

Hagen rolled the hand up in the sweatshirt. When the bundle was once again in the valise the Legionnaire told Hagen to pick up the bag. The Legionnaire had a phone call to make. Some of his friends would arrive soon. They'd decide what to do with Hagen then. In the meantime, they'd wait inside the house.

"Who else is here?" the Legionnaire said.

"A friend of mine."

"Just one?"

"Just one that I know of."

The Legionnaire glanced toward the house. The front of the house was half hidden behind the palm trees along the driveway. The Legionnaire waved the barrel of the Glock at the bag. Hagen picked it up and they started back to the house, the Legionnaire two steps behind him.

"When you open the door, push it all the way open," the Legionnaire said, his voice a rough whisper. "Tell your friend you've changed your mind. You're going to stay here. Make sure the door is wide open."

As they walked along the front of the house Hagen glanced to the right, looked through the front window into the living room. Harry Needles wasn't there.

When they reached the front door Hagen opened it, gave it a push.

The door swung open wide.

Hagen stepped inside.

Hagen called out, "Harry, I'm going to have to stay here for a while."

There was no response. No sound at all. The living room was empty.

Hagen stepped farther into the house, still carrying the bag. Behind him the Legionnaire stood in the doorway. Hagen started across the living room toward the kitchen. Hagen could see one end of the kitchen table but the rest of the kitchen was hidden from view by a dividing wall. Off to his left was the hallway that led back into the house. Several doors stood open. The rooms beyond were dark.

"Harry?" Hagen called out again.

Where the hell was Harry?

The Legionnaire came up behind Hagen. Grabbed the back of Hagen's sport coat, pulled him to the left. Pushed him forward into the hallway, letting go of his coat now. Careful to keep Hagen between himself and the hallway.

Down the hallway a shadow that fell across the surface of an open door moved.

A small and fleeting movement. A matter of an inch or two.

Then Harry appeared.

And Hagen dived for the floor.

The first pistol shot tore through the house. Almost immediately there was a larger sound that seemed to rip through the house like a thunderclap—once, twice, and then a third time.

The gunfire lasted only a second. Hagen lay facedown on the carpet. He waited for the sound of further shots but there were none. His ears were ringing. The smell of burned gunpowder hung heavy in the air. He heard the Legionnaire behind him—a sharp cry of pain followed by the hiss of air sucked through clenched teeth.

The Legionnaire kicked the sole of Hagen's shoe.

"Get up." The words almost a gasp.

Hagen got to his feet. The Legionnaire stood hunched over against the wall, holding his hand to his right side, just below his rib cage. Blood poured out from between his fingers. In the hallway Harry Needles lay on his side, his back to the wall, legs crumpled up underneath him. One limp arm was thrown up over his face at an odd angle—the arm of a rag doll. A small revolver lay nearby. Dark red stains on Harry Needles's shirt bloomed like exotic flowers while the thick carpet soaked up the blood underneath him.

Harry Needles was dead, Hagen was sure.

The Legionnaire straightened up, waved the Glock around. For a moment the look on his face was one of disbelief as the blood poured from his side. Hagen waited for the Legionnaire's legs to buckle and the rest of him to follow his legs down to the floor. Waited for the Glock to fall from his hand. But the Legionnaire pulled himself together. After a moment he pushed himself away from the wall and stood there, unsteady at first but then steadier. His breathing was rough but his voice was clear when he spoke.

"Let's go."

Hagen carried the valise when they left Harry Needles's place. The Legionnaire trailed behind him, stumbling once or twice. He held a bath towel taken from the house to his side, kept the Glock pointed at Hagen's back.

They crossed the rock garden at the edge of Harry Needles's property, then cut across a patch of bare desert before coming out alongside a nearby house. They skirted the edge of a large lawn, keeping in the shadows, then walked quickly down the street to where an Oldsmobile sedan was parked. Hagen wondered if the police were already on their way to Harry Needles's place. Someone in the neighborhood must've heard the gunfire. Someone must've called the police.

Hagen drove. On the way out of town he searched the road ahead and the rearview mirror for a police patrol car while the Legionnaire watched him closely. No patrol car appeared. The only flashing blue lights came from the facades of the casinos along Casino Drive.

Just another festive night in Laughlin—except Harry Needles was dead. Why? Harry must've been watching from the front window, seen the Legionnaire and Hagen out in the driveway. He couldn't have seen them very well through the palm trees, but he'd seen enough. So he got a gun. And when he saw Hagen and the Legionnaire approaching the house, he stepped into the dark room off the hallway and waited. Was that how it played out? Or was the gun intended for Hagen? Had Harry been on his way outside to stop Hagen when Hagen returned to the house with the Legionnaire behind him? Only Harry knew. And Harry was dead. Hagen wanted to think that Harry had tried to help him, but it made just as much sense the other way.

The police would make their own sense out of it. When they found Harry they'd also find the suitcase with Ronnie's belongings in it, and Hagen's fingerprints all over the house and Harry Needles's car. When they looked into it further, they'd find that Hagen had shown up at the Venus Lounge earlier looking for Harry, and that Harry had disappeared from the club at just about that time. Circumstantial evidence, to be sure—but people have been hung on circumstantial evidence. And when the story of the wooden hand came out, as it certainly would, it would look like a tidy motive for murder.

Hagen knew he was behind the eight ball now.

As soon as they were out of Laughlin, driving west toward Highway 95, the Legionnaire pulled out his cellular phone. He rested the phone on his thigh and punched in a number, keeping Hagen covered with the pistol in his other hand. The Beretta the Legionnaire took from Hagen lay on the floor of the car at the Legionnaire's feet.

When the call went through the Legionnaire spoke into the phone in French. "Fournier? Tate here. . . . I'm heading back to Vegas. . . . I've got the hand but I took some fire. . . . I saw a chance and I took it. . . . I'll live. . . . Too late now. . . . He's there? . . . Give me the number. . . . All right. . . . Where are you right now? . . . I don't know. I'll call you back. . . ."

The Legionnaire pressed the buttons for a second number.

"This is Tate. Let me speak to Colonel Zahn. . . ."

Pause.

"Hello, sir. . . . Yes. . . . In Laughlin. . . . I've got the hand but we had a dust up. I took a hit. . . . Needles. He's dead. . . . Didn't have much choice, sir. . . . Yes, sir. . . . Nothing serious. . . . Hagen's here with me. . . . No, sir. . . . Fournier and Sutherland are north of here. I'll meet them. They can help out. . . . About an hour, sir. . . . Yes, sir. . . ."

The Legionnaire disconnected, then called the first number again. The Legionnaire—Tate—wanted to meet up with the others. The Legionnaire on the other end apparently wanted to keep driving south until they came upon each other along the highway, but Legionnaire Tate didn't like that idea. They might miss each other in the darkness. Better for the others to stop somewhere on the northbound side of the highway and wait. The Legionnaire on the other end of the phone made another suggestion, and Tate agreed. The others could wait for Tate and Hagen there.

Legionnaire Tate closed the cell phone, tucked it back into the pouch on his belt. The pouch was spotted with blood. He repositioned the towel against his side, grimacing. He moved the Glock to his other hand.

It was settled, Legionnaire Tate told Hagen. "There's a turnout on the northbound road, about ten miles north of Searchlight. We'll meet some friends there. How far are we from Searchlight right now?"

They were still driving west. They hadn't even reached Highway 95 yet. "Thirty miles. Maybe more."

"Drive faster."

Hagen sped up. They were cruising at eighty miles an hour. The winding highway was deserted. Not a single pair of headlights in front of them or behind them. So quiet. So empty. They might have been driving across the surface of the moon. Alone with a killer, on the dark side of the moon.

"Who's Colonel Zahn?"

"He's in charge."

"I want to talk to him."

"That's up to Colonel Zahn."

"What did my brother do?"

"Don't you know?"

"I know a little."

"Legionnaire Hagen took something that didn't belong to him. That's all there is to know."

"Did you know my brother?"

"I knew him."

"When?"

"In Mayotte. Then later, in Aubagne—I saw him once or twice there. But I kept away from him in Aubagne."

"Why was that?"

"Your brother was a fuckup. He couldn't do anything right. He couldn't even desert when he tried to. In the Legion there's only one crime worse than deserting and that's failure."

"Tell me about him. Tell me what happened."

Legionnaire Tate tried to shift his position in the seat. He grimaced as the pain shot through him. He glanced down at the blood-soaked towel. "Do you think the rental agency will charge extra to clean up all this blood?" Tate tried to laugh but his laughter subsided into a hoarse choking sound. But when the Legionnaire found his voice again he told Hagen what he knew about Hagen's brother the Legionnaire.

15.

MAYOTTE—THE LAST FRENCH outpost in the Comoro Islands. Four hundred square miles of dense tropical vegetation, broken now and then by small native villages of wattle and daub or coconut-frond huts. Situated in the Indian Ocean, halfway between the island of Madagascar and Mozambique on the southeastern coast of Africa.

Ronnie was fresh out of initial training at the Legion's training center in Castelnaudary when he was assigned to the Détachment de Légion Étrangère de Mayotte. The unit was based in Dzaoudzi on Petite Terre, the small island to the east of the main island—Grand Terre. Tate had been there a few months when Ronnie arrived.

"Mayotte was tough," Tate said. "We spent most of our time clearing jungle to make roads. I don't know why, there was no place to drive to. But the sergeant major said clear the jungle for a road, so we went out into the jungle and swung machetes until our hands bled to build his fucking road. And when that was done, another road. And another. All of them going nowhere."

At first Ronnie was an exemplary Legionnaire. "He was good. His shit was together. All the officers and noncoms liked him. They held him up as an example of what a Legionnaire should be. The rest of us resented that. When your brother told us the stories about his father who had served at Dien Bien Phu with the Legion, that's when we saw what was what. He was getting soft treatment because his old man was at fucking Dien Bien Phu. We decided he needed to be taken down a notch or two.

"There were fights. Sometimes your brother won, sometimes he didn't. Sometimes out in the jungle when the sergeant major wasn't there and the corporals were in charge, they'd gripe about his work and then make him keep working while the rest of us sat in the shade, drinking beer and watching. He put up with it though. He didn't have much choice, but he put up with it all right. They couldn't break him. It seemed to mean a lot to him, being a Legionnaire. Even if all he did was swing a machete in the jungle. After a while we left him alone. He became one of the crew.

"There was nothing to do on Mayotte when we were off-duty except sleep, sweat, drink in the barracks, or drink at the Legion's whorehouse in Dzaoudzi. You could always spend your pay on the whores but that was dicey. They were native girls, and the *corporal-chef* who ran the whorehouse liked them ugly. We called them the cannibals. Your brother used to come out drinking with us. He fit right in for a while. We decided we'd been wrong about him. He was an all right sort of fellow.

"But then he started disappearing. We'd be off-duty for a couple of days and we wouldn't see your brother anywhere. Turns out he was going over to the big island—he'd met a girl over there. We laughed when we heard. He'd gone native. It happened once in a while—a Legionnaire would get bored and start taking up with the natives. Your brother was touchy about it. We'd kid him about taking up with the cannibals and he'd start swinging. I guess he really liked the girl.

"The sergeant major told him to cease and desist, but he didn't listen. He kept going over there when he could. Then he didn't show up for *appel* one morning and the sergeant major sent ten of us over to the big island to find him. It took us two days but we tracked him and his girl down. She lived in a village on the west side of the big island, a place called Chiconi. Nothing much to it—a bunch of huts pushed together at the edge of the jungle. Filthy. Smelled of shit and coconut milk. Everyplace in Mayotte smelled of shit and coconut milk. We found him in a hut, sitting on the dirt floor. He said he'd gotten drunk and overslept, and when he realized he couldn't get back to the barracks in time for *appel* he got scared, didn't know what to do, so he stayed there. We said, 'Right. Let's go.'

"We took him back to the barracks. The sergeant major decided to teach him a lesson and charged him with desertion. The colonel gave him forty days in the detachment prison. It was run by a couple of corporals—a Spaniard and a Norwegian—who had a reputation for violence. We'd see your brother when they brought him outside into the yard for his exercise. While the corporals strolled around the compound, your brother was made to run in circles around them. If he didn't run fast enough, they made him crawl on his hands and knees. One day we walked by the prison compound and saw him lying facedown on the ground, with his hands tied behind him, while the two corporals took turns beating on the soles of his feet with a stick. Your brother hadn't run fast enough when they told him to run, so they decided that his feet needed toughening up.

"He did his forty days and then came back to the unit. But as a deserter he was bad luck now and no one wanted to associate with him. We turned our backs. He tried to get back into the swing but he couldn't do it. He couldn't keep his mind on the soldiering and his gear was always a mess. The sergeant major made life hell for him. Here was this young Legionnaire whose father had been at Dien Bien Phu and he'd gone and deserted—the sergeant major couldn't stomach that. Dien Bien Phu—that's a sacred thing to the old Legionnaires.

"We weren't surprised when your brother disappeared again. The sergeant major ordered us to find him, so off we went again to the big island. This time it wasn't so easy. We spent four days trudging through the jungle on the big island, all of us getting more and more pissed off.

"Finally we found him. He'd taken the girl from Chiconi and gone out into the jungle in the center of the island. He was hiding out, in a little village called Ouangani. We dragged him out of a hut and marched him up to the top of a nearby hill. We were hot and tired and completely pissed off. Your brother had put us to a lot of trouble and the corporal in charge—Corporal DeGreer—wanted his pound of flesh.

"At the top of the hill there was a small clearing in the jungle. De-Greer handed your brother a field shovel and told him to start digging. He wanted your brother to dig his own grave.

"No one said a word. We just stood there watching him dig his grave. When he was done DeGreer ordered him to lie down in it. Then DeGreer covered him over with dirt until only his head was above-ground. DeGreer ordered the rest of us to stand in a circle around the grave and sing the regimental song, 'Le Boudin.' So we started singing and kept right on, while DeGreer beat your brother senseless with the shovel head.

"Then we dug him up and dragged him back to Dzaoudzi and threw him back in the prison.

"He got another forty days for desertion. When he got out the sergeant major told him to pack his gear up. Your brother was a disgrace and the sergeant major didn't want him around. The sergeant major had put him in for a transfer to the Legion post at Aubagne.

"I saw your brother before he left the island. He swore he'd get even with us someday, all of us—DeGreer, the sergeant major, everyone in the detachment, everyone in the whole damn Legion. I shrugged my shoulders and told him to fuck off. He'd dug his own grave, so to speak. Now he was going to have to lie in it. But your brother didn't see it that way. He thought the Legion had let him down. He'd believed in the Legion but the Legion had turned its back on him, and he was going to settle the score one day.

"An hour later he was on the Transall, flying back to France. After he left the sergeant major ordered us never to speak of Legionnaire Hagen again. We never did."

Tate's voice drifted off. In the glow of the dashboard lights Hagen could see Tate's face contorted in pain. The Legionnaire swallowed hard, closed his eyes. Whatever else was wrong with him, he had lost a lot of blood. He must've been feeling it by now. Hagen glanced at the pistol in Legionnaire Tate's hand. He was getting ready to reach over and make a grab for it when the Legionnaire opened his eyes quickly, alarmed and disoriented.

"So what happened?" Hagen said. He wanted to keep the Legionnaire talking. Keep his mind off the pistol in his hand and his own fading awareness.

"What happened?" Legionnaire Tate wasn't sure where he'd left off.

"In Aubagne."

A pause. Then, "I don't know what happened in Aubagne. I was posted there a couple of years later. I saw your brother there a few times. They had him working in the motor pool. I didn't speak to him. He was a nonperson as far as I was concerned. I was surprised to see him though. I would've thought he'd have deserted again and made it stick. But he didn't. He finished his enlistment. It would've been better for the Legion if he'd deserted."

"Because he stole the hand?"

"Yes. Your brother stole the Hand of Danjou."

The Hand of Danjou—Hagen thought again of what his father had told him once. A long time ago. His father had been drunk and feeling bitter that night. His father had talked of the men he'd seen die at Dien Bien Phu. They hadn't died for a cause. They hadn't even died for a half-baked notion of God and country. They'd died for the Legion and the Legion alone. They'd died because the Legion had ordered them to never retreat and never surrender—like Captain Danjou. His father hadn't mentioned the wooden hand or the tale of Captain Danjou but Hagen made the connection now. Never retreat. Never surrender. March or die. *Légio patria nostra*—the Legion had been their God and their country.

And the myth of the Hand of Danjou *was* the Legion.

And Ronnie stole it. Ronnie stole the Hand of Danjou and brought it back to Las Vegas to sell it. To get even with the Legion for turning its back on him. For making him dig his own grave on a Mayotte hilltop.

"So you came here to find the hand," Hagen said. "And while you searched for it, Ronnie was killed. Which one of you killed him, Tate? Was it you?"

"Killed him?" Tate shook his head slowly. He grimaced with pain. His voice was weak and unsteady. "Legionnaire Hagen died and was buried on Mayotte. He just didn't have the good sense to lie down. Until now."

The cell phone beeped. Tate pulled it out of the pouch. His hand shook as he fumbled with the cover over the face of the phone.

"Tate here. . . . I don't know. . . . Almost—almost there. . . ."

Tate said to Hagen, "How far, to Searchlight?"

"Maybe five miles."

Tate repeated the information into the telephone, slurring a few words.

Tate told the caller he'd meet them in ten minutes or so, then hit a button with his thumb to end the call. As Tate tried to close the cover the phone slipped from his hand, fell down between his seat and the gearshift console. Tate stared for a moment at the spot where the phone had disappeared. His head swayed, like he was dizzy. Like he was fading out.

"Tate?"

The Legionnaire didn't respond. His eyes had moved to the steering wheel in Hagen's hands. He stared at the wheel, blinking his eyes, as though his vision was fogged over and he couldn't clear it. Then his eyes closed. His chin fell slowly onto his chest. The Glock in his hand fell to one side, limp fingers still half clutching the butt of the pistol.

Hagen waited a moment, to see if Tate came to again.

He didn't. Legionnaire Tate was unconscious.

Hagen slowed the car down and pulled off onto the side of the road. He reached over and pulled the pistol from Tate's loose grip. The Legionnaire slipped a little farther to one side, his head against the seat.

Hagen grabbed his wrist and checked his pulse. Weak, but steady. Legionnaire Tate wasn't dead yet.

Hagen set the Glock in his lap. He pulled back onto the highway and drove on.

A few miles south of Searchlight he spotted a dirt road leading off into the desert hills. He turned onto it, the car bouncing and lurching as it traversed the deep ruts and the rocks in the road. An old utility road. Where did it come out? The road curved. The headlights illuminated the bare dry earth, the creosote bushes, the sagebrush. The road wound around the base of a rocky hill and descended into a narrow valley and continued on. Up ahead in the headlights Hagen spotted an abandoned wooden shack that sat at the base of a hillside off to the left, fifty yards or so from the utility road. The wood was parched and weather-beaten. One wall stood crookedly, the roof sunken to one side.

Hagen stopped the car on the road, switched on the high beams to illuminate as much of the desert around him as possible, then got out. He walked around to the passenger side, opened the door. Propping the unconscious Legionnaire up in the seat with one hand, he reached down and picked up the Beretta off the floor, closed the door, returned to the driver's side of the car. Opening Ronnie's valise he removed a cotton shirt and used it to wipe the small amount of Legionnaire Tate's blood off the Beretta, then slipped it into his shoulder holster. Then Hagen picked up the Glock, removed the clip, pumped the round out of the chamber, dropped the clip into his pocket, tossed the loose round out into the darkness. He wrapped the Glock up in the shirt and tucked it under the driver's seat.

Hagen removed the blue bundle that contained the wooden hand from the bag. Ahead and off to the right, on the opposite side of the road from the shack, he could just make out a formation of boulders, and he carried the bundle over to the near side of the formation. At the outside edge of the light from the headlights he found two large rocks lying on the ground in close proximity to each other. Hagen searched the ground for a small flat rock. He found one and brought it over to where the larger rocks lay and used the flat rock to dig a shallow hole in the dry earth. He set the bundle in the hole and covered it with the loose earth, then pushed the two larger rocks together over the buried hand.

The hand was safe there. As safe as it ever would be. And the shack and the boulders would serve as good reference points when he came back to get it. The Legionnaires would have to play Hagen's game now. If they didn't, this hand would rot out here in the desert for years. But what was his game? Hagen didn't know. He only had one thought in his mind now, one overruling idea. And that was to talk to Colonel Zahn. Hagen would make a trade—the wooden hand for the Legionnaire who killed Ronnie. If Zahn wanted to leave Las Vegas with the hand, he'd have to leave that Legionnaire behind.

When Hagen returned to the car he found Legionnaire Tate sitting up in the passenger seat, his back against the door and the cell phone in his hand. A small thin voice on the other end of the connection called his name. "Tate? Tate?" Tate didn't answer. Tate's eyes were glazed over, staring at Hagen but not seeing him. Tate had regained consciousness and found enough energy to pull the cell phone out from where it had fallen and put a call through. But now he couldn't find the strength to speak.

Hagen reached over and took the phone from Tate's hand. Tate didn't seem to notice. Tate's breathing was faster than before—short sharp breaths with a raspy edge to them. How long was Tate going to last?

The voice on the other end of the phone, speaking in French— "Tate? Are you there?"

"Hello?"

"Tate? What's going on?"

Hagen answered in English. "Tate is indisposed. My name is Bodo Hagen. I want to talk to Colonel Zahn." Was this Zahn's number that Tate had called, or was it the pair of Legionnaires waiting up the road?

"Hagen?"

"Let me speak to Colonel Zahn."

Hagen sat there with the phone to his ear, watching Tate as the Legionnaire struggled to keep his head upright and his eyes open. The towel Tate had held to his side had fallen to the floor of the car. Tate's side was covered in drying blood from his armpit down to his trousers.

A new voice came on the line.

"Mister Hagen?" The voice was crisp and sure and spoke English with a strong French accent.

"Colonel Zahn?"

"Yes, this is Colonel Zahn. What has happened to Legionnaire Tate?"

"He took a bullet in the side back in Laughlin. He's not doing too well. I'm not doing too well either. But I have the Hand of Danjou. If you want it, we're going to have a talk first."

Pause. Then, "All right, Mister Hagen. What do you have in mind?"

"I want to know which one of you killed my brother."

"I don't think that's something I can help you with."

"I think you're wrong."

Another pause, longer this time. Colonel Zahn was weighing his options. Then, "I'll see what I can do for you, Mister Hagen. It may take some time. Can we meet face-to-face? Someplace that is convenient for you? Maybe we can do business then."

A meeting with Colonel Zahn—that was exactly what was called for. As long as it was on Hagen's terms. "That's fine. We'll meet."

"Where?"

"I'll call you when I get there. Give me your phone number."

Colonel Zahn gave him the number. "I look forward to seeing you, Mister Hagen."

"And, Colonel, tell your men to stay out of my way. I don't have the hand with me, and if your men give me trouble I'll make sure you never find it."

"I understand."

Hagen closed the cell phone.

"You'll have to hang on for a while longer, Tate."

Ten miles north of Searchlight on Highway 95 Hagen passed a blue Ford Explorer utility vehicle parked in a turnout on the northbound side of the road. In his rearview mirror he saw the Ford's headlights come on. The Ford pulled out onto the highway and gained speed. But the Ford didn't try to overtake him. The Ford stayed behind him, following him from a distance.

Five miles farther on a sedan traveling in the southbound lane slowed down as it approached Hagen. Once Hagen had passed by, the sedan made a U-turn and fell in behind the Explorer.

Two pairs of headlights now. Pacing him. Watching him.

Colonel Zahn was giving him an escort back into Las Vegas.

Hagen drove on. Every now and then a car came speeding up behind him. Hagen watched the approaching headlights carefully in the rearview mirror, prepared to hit the brakes as soon as the car came up alongside him and slowed down. A single pistol shot from a passing car—easy to do out here on a long quiet desert highway in the middle of the night. They might shoot a tire out and force him off the road. They might even shoot him as he drove. Get it over with, right off.

But no one in a passing car took a shot at him. The cars flew past Hagen and moved on up the highway while the Explorer and the sedan stayed behind him. Hagen kept his own speed down. He didn't want to attract the attention of any highway patrol units who might be cruising the highway. That would be a fine mess—a state trooper pulling him over for speeding, only to find a dying man in the passenger seat and a couple of high-powered pistols lying around. Better to keep the speed down, stay low-key. *Low-key*—that thought struck Hagen as grimly amusing. A band of well-armed soldiers from the French Foreign Legion tailing him, Harry Needles lying dead back in Laughlin and another man dying right beside him in the car and Hagen was worried about keeping a low profile.

Too late for that.

Legionnaire Tate had slipped back into unconsciousness again. He needed a doctor. Soon. But Hagen couldn't take him to the hospital. He'd give him to Zahn. He was Zahn's man—Zahn could take care of him. If Tate was going to die he could do it on Zahn's time.

It was another twenty miles before Hagen saw what he was looking for—a large parking lot outside of a business park on the outskirts of Henderson. The parking lot was well lit and empty. Hagen exited the highway, turned right onto a surface street, drove along for a hundred yards. When he reached the business park he turned in and drove to one corner of the parking lot, where a second entrance led out onto a side street. Hagen turned the car around, headlights pointed back at the main entrance, the second entrance a few yards off to his right.

A moment later the Explorer pulled into the lot, followed by the sedan. The sedan stopped near the main entrance, headlights pointed at Hagen. The Explorer drove to the opposite side of the lot and turned around.

Two sets of headlights pointed at Hagen. Three engines idling. And how many guns?

Hagen hit the redial button on the cell phone.

"Colonel Zahn?"

"Mister Hagen, are you at your destination?"

"Not quite. But your man Tate needs a doctor. I'm going to let you take him off my hands."

"How will we do this?"

First thing, Hagen wanted Zahn's two vehicles together, the sedan over with the Explorer. While Zahn kept Hagen on the line, the colonel used another cell phone to talk to his men in the sedan. A minute later the sedan drove across the parking lot, pulled up next to the Explorer.

Then Hagen gave Zahn the rest of the instructions.

As Hagen watched, a man climbed out of the sedan. He pulled his shirt up over his head and tossed it back into the car, then began walking bare-chested across the parking lot. Hagen pulled out the Beretta as he watched the man's progress. He was a short stocky man, his pale white chest covered with tattoos. He walked with his arms out from his side, like a Wild West gunslinger with his hands over his side holsters.

When he was fifteen yards from Hagen's car the tattooed Legionnaire stopped and turned fully around, so that Hagen could see that he had no weapon tucked into the back of his trousers.

Zahn on the phone—"How are we doing, Mister Hagen?"

"Just fine."

"Very well then."

The tattooed Legionnaire reached Hagen's car, stepped around to the passenger side. Hagen kept the Beretta pointed at him as the Legionnaire reached for the door handle. Tate fell backward slowly as the car door opened. The tattooed Legionnaire raised his knee and pushed it into Tate's back to hold him in place while he grabbed Tate under his arms. Then he pulled Tate out of the car and dragged him several feet, the heels of Tate's shoes scraping the concrete.

"Now close the door," Hagen said.

The Legionnaire did as he was told. Then he retreated to the prostrate figure of Legionnaire Tate and stood over his fallen comrade while Hagen sunk his foot into the gas pedal and sped out of the parking lot, tires screaming in the night.

16.

THE LIGHTS OF LAS VEGAS ahead of him.

The Ford Explorer behind him.

Only a few more miles.

Traffic picked up on Highway 95 as Hagen approached the city. It was half past two o'clock in the morning but that didn't matter. The city didn't sleep. He wasn't sure but he thought a second car was now following him, to replace the sedan that was taking Legionnaire Tate to a hospital. A bullet wound—there might be awkward questions at a hospital.

But maybe Colonel Zahn could handle those kinds of questions. He seemed to be a man of considerable resources. How many Legionnaires had Zahn brought with him from France or wherever the colonel had departed from? He seemed to have a small army with him. An invasion force of Legionnaires that had descended on Las Vegas for one purpose—to locate the Hand of Danjou and take it back to France.

The French Foreign Legion. A fighting force of men from all corners of the globe, led by an elite cadre of French officers. Tested for almost two centuries in the deserts of North Africa. Now fighting a war of attrition in a new theater of operations—the deserts of southern Nevada. And a war of attrition is what it was. Ronnie—dead. Sidney Trunk—dead. Gubbs and Harry Needles—both dead. And how many of them were out there right now with Hagen in their sights, waiting for the right moment to pull the trigger?

Eyes, everywhere in the night.

Hagen's headlights sped across the scarred surface of the highway.

Hagen thought of Ronnie and of how Hagen had felt when he heard that Ronnie had joined the Legion. The Legion—that had been their father's game, not Ronnie's. All his life Ronnie had only wanted to be out from under the iron fist of Wolfgang Karl Hagen, former Waffen-SS soldier, former Legionnaire. Then Ronnie turned around and joined the Legion. Why? Because Ronnie wanted to succeed where their father had succeeded. It was Ronnie's way of proving himself. He'd gone into the Legion to do battle with their father's ghost.

But Ronnie had failed. The Legion had beaten him down and spit him out. And in his defeat he struck out at everything that had made their father who he was. The honor and valor of the Foreign Legion. The code of the noble warrior. The memory of Dien Bien Phu. All those things were represented by the Hand of Danjou.

And Ronnie stole it. To spite the ghost of their father.

But Ronnie was dead now.

The ghost of their father had won.

Hagen drove down the Las Vegas Strip.

Lights. Money. A sea of roulette wheels, slot machines and cool fresh casino decks with slick surfaces and suicide jacks. A sea of winners well on their way to losing. Hagen felt like he was standing on the edge of that same precipice. Waiting for that one last deal of the cards. Waiting for that dead man's hand to come sliding across the green felt toward him and tell him that this game was over for good. Only he was playing for higher stakes than what he carried in his wallet.

He was playing for his life.

Hagen watched the casinos slip past. Mandalay Bay. Luxor. Excalibur. Up ahead he saw the MGM Grand, lit up in electric green and glowing in the night like a giant emerald. Hagen turned right on Tropicana Avenue and pulled into the parking garage behind the MGM. On the third level he parked the car near an escalator and jumped out. Running over to the escalator Hagen looked back and caught a glimpse of the Ford Explorer driving down a row of parked cars toward him.

On the ground floor Hagen jogged along a passageway lined with closed shops. Took an escalator up into the hotel, climbing the steps two at a time. At three o'clock in the morning the action inside the hotel casino was going strong. People at the tables, people at the slot machines. And all of it watched over closely by the surveillance cameras in the ceilings that kept track of every bet at every table, every deal of the cards, every toss of the dice. Hagen was grateful for the crowd. Safety in numbers. Hagen walked to a bar near a row of roulette tables and sat down, ordered a bourbon and soda from the bow-tied bartender.

Hagen took a long drink of the bourbon. Driving back into town a hunch had come to him. A hunch that had taken on force and clarity, the more he thought about it. Hagen decided to set some machinery in motion so that he could play the hunch if he needed to. He hoped that he didn't.

Hagen pulled out the cell phone and made some phone calls.

The last call was to Colonel Zahn.

Hagen was working on his second bourbon and soda and smoking a Benson and Hedges the bartender had given him when he spotted the short thin man walking across the casino toward him. Back straight, legs moving in a stiff starched gait. He wore a dark gray linen sport coat over a light blue shirt, white slacks with razor-sharp creases, freshly buffed dark brown oxfords. His angular face was leathery and his dark eyes moved quickly around the casino before coming to rest on Hagen at the bar.

Two other men had entered the casino behind him. One of them a short Japanese man with a shaved head, wearing a blue blazer and jeans. The other a tall young man with a sallow complexion, wearing a brown leather jacket. The two men broke off, the Japanese moving over to a bank of slot machines near the bar, throwing quick glances at Hagen. The tall one drifted around the edge of the casino, disappeared behind the crowds of people at the craps tables across the room.

The older man smiled as he approached the bar. The thin gray mustache over his lip looked like something that had been applied with a ruler, width and length measured out to the millimeter.

"Mister Hagen, good evening."

"Colonel Zahn?"

The man bowed his head slightly. Hagen thought he heard the heels of the man's shoes click together.

Colonel Zahn sat down next to Hagen. "What are you drinking?" When the bartender appeared Colonel Zahn ordered the same as Hagen. While the bartender mixed the drink a man with closely-cropped black hair and Arabic features sat down at the end of the bar. He seemed to be looking everywhere except at Hagen and Zahn.

"How many men did you bring with you?" Hagen said.

"A small number."

"I wouldn't try anything here. Security is tight in casinos. They tend to frown on fighting and gunplay."

"I am aware of why you chose this place to meet."

While Zahn waited for his drink he sized up Hagen with a sharp eye. Hagen knew very well that Zahn would've preferred a different kind of meeting, one where he had more leverage. A small quiet meeting, in an empty room somewhere, with Hagen tied to a chair and several of Zahn's men standing by to help drive Zahn's point home. This short thin man with the mannerisms of a effete drill sergeant was dangerous. Hagen hoped he never found out just how dangerous.

Behind them a cheer rose from one of the roulette tables. Zahn turned to survey the action.

"Do you like roulette, Mr. Hagen?" Zahn spoke English with a clipped French accent that seemed to bite the ends off his words.

"Never play it."

"A game of pure chance."

"It's a sucker's game."

Zahn smiled. "Just like life, no?"

"I suppose. If you're a sucker."

When the bartender returned with Zahn's drink, Zahn removed a wallet from inside his sport coat. Dropped a twenty-dollar bill on the bar. "I'll pay for my friend's drink as well," he said to the bartender, nodding at Hagen.

"Already taken care of," the bartender said.

"My mistake." Then, to Hagen, "I will owe you a drink."

Zahn picked up his glass and took a drink. Hagen noticed a long red scar running under Zahn's chin from one side of his neck to the other. Looked almost like someone had tried to cut his throat but hadn't quite gotten it right.

"I don't believe I've had the pleasure of drinking such good bourbon," Zahn said, holding his glass before him, inspecting the color of the drink. "I've been told that when one is in the land of bluegrass, bourbon is the drink of choice."

"You're two thousand miles from the nearest bluegrass."

"Two thousand miles? Well, that's as close as I've ever been."

"Then drink up."

The bartender returned with Zahn's change, fanned the bills out on the bar. Walked off to serve the Arabic man.

"Where shall we begin?" Zahn said.

"Tell me about the hand. How did my brother acquire it?"

"Ah, yes." Zahn ran his hand over his closely shaved chin. "The Hand of Danjou. Do you know anything about the Hand of Danjou, Mister Hagen? It belongs to the French Foreign Legion, did you know that?"

"That's why the Legion sent you here."

A sly look fell across Zahn's face. "In case there's any misunderstanding, let me just say that myself and my men do not represent the French Foreign Legion. Let us say only that the Legion's interests and ours are sometimes the same."

"All right. The Legion didn't send you here. They don't know anything about you. And if anyone says any different, the Legion will act shocked and appalled and issue an official statement denying any knowledge of you. Yes, I know how that works."

"I'm glad we understand each other."

"We don't understand each other at all, Zahn. Tell me what happened."

Zahn took a drink, then set the glass down slowly, fitting the bottom rim of the glass exactly onto the wet ring on the cardboard coaster. At the end of the bar the Arabic man looked startled as the bartender set some sort of frozen concoction in front of him—a large glass goblet filled with a bright blue mixture and crushed ice. A slice of pineapple rested on the rim of the glass and a straw protruded up from the depths of the goblet. The Legionnaire muttered something under his breath, sipped the drink through the straw, then looked over his shoulder with a wary expression, as though afraid that his colleagues might catch him with such a flamboyant beverage.

"Are you familiar with the history of France, Mister Hagen?" Colonel Zahn said. "Or the history of Mexico?"

"I get around."

Zahn raised an eyebrow. "Then perhaps you are aware that in the nineteenth century France took a great interest in Mexico. Napoléon the Third wished to administer the country for the benefit of France and proposed—through certain *intrigues,* shall we say—to place Archduke Maximilian of Austria on the Mexican throne for that purpose. Maximilian agreed to this proposal, but only on the condition that Napoléon provide him with a force of no less than ten thousand men to protect him from the Mexican republicans who opposed France.

"Napoléon gave him the Foreign Legion.

"The first Legion forces arrived in Mexico in 1863. They began military operations in the area of Veracruz. They quickly found that the Mexicans were a poorly trained enemy—nothing more than small bands of guerillas who fired on the Legionnaires and then ran off into the countryside. The guerillas were more interested in looting than in protecting their homeland. The real enemy for the Legion forces in Mexico was the yellow fever. Entire companies of Legionnaires died of the *vomito*—so called because one very visible symptom of the yellow fever is the vomiting of copious amounts of blood.

"Believing the yellow fever epidemic to be the result of living in the lowlands along the coast, the Legion decided to move their base of operations inland, to higher ground near the town of Córdoba. It was during this"—Zahn waved a hand in the air as he searched for the right words—"effort of retrenching, shall we say, that on April 30, 1863, Captain Jean Danjou led a Legion force of sixty-five men along a road near the town of Camarón, southwest of Veracruz. Danjou was a veteran Legionnaire who'd lost his left hand during an earlier Legion expedition. He employed a wooden hand in its place.

"As they traveled along this road the Legionnaires were attacked by Mexican guerillas on horseback. Danjou ordered his men into a fighting position and they repelled the Mexican attack. But these guerillas were more determined than their predecessors, and instead of running off they fell back and prepared for a second assault on the Legion position. Captain Danjou saw this and ordered his men into a nearby hacienda. The hacienda was surrounded by earthen walls that provided a great amount of protection to the Legionnaires, and very quickly the hacienda was turned into a fortress from which the Legionnaires prepared to do battle.

"When the Mexican force returned and surrounded the hacienda, the Legionnaires saw that the guerillas were now reinforced by several regiments of Mexican army regulars loyal to the republican cause. The Legionnaires were vastly outnumbered. But when the Mexicans attacked the Legionnaires fought valiantly. The attacks continued throughout the day, however, and with each attack the Legionnaires' position became less and less tenable. Captain Danjou, seeing the truth of his situation, ordered his men to swear an oath. They would fight to the death. There was to be no surrender.

"A short time later Danjou himself was shot and killed. But the dwindling number of Legionnaires fought on. The hacienda was set ablaze by the Mexican forces and still the Legionnaires continued their fight in the midst of smoke and flames. Hope no longer existed for them. It became clear that they would soon die. But there was no thought of surrender.

"Soon only five Legionnaires remained, including one wounded officer. Down to their last cartridges, they fired their rifles one last time, then fixed bayonets and prepared to charge the Mexican forces. One Legionnaire was shot dead before he'd advanced ten paces—he took nineteen Mexican bullets before he breathed his last. But before his brothers in arms could carry out their suicidal charge, the position was overrun by Mexican soldiers and they were captured. When the Legionnaires were taken before the Mexican commander, he was astonished to learn that only four remained. 'They do not fight like men,' the commander told his aides. 'They fight like demons.'"

Zahn paused. The bartender stood nearby, head cocked to one side, trying to follow the conversation. The captain threw him a harsh look and the bartender moved farther down the bar, busied himself washing glasses.

"And that, Mister Hagen, is the story of Camarón," Zahn said. "Captain Danjou's wooden hand was found in the ashes of the hacienda, and it was transported back to the Legion headquarters in Algeria, where it remained for one hundred years. In 1962, when the Legion moved its headquarters to Aubagne, France, the hand was taken there and placed inside the Legion museum that now stands beside the monument to all the Legionnaires who have died in battle. The Legion celebrates the battle of Camarón every year on April 30, and during these ceremonies Captain Danjou's hand is removed from its place of honor and paraded in front of the assembled Legion regiments. The Hand of Danjou has come to symbolize the glory of the Legion, and the words *'Faire Camerone'* have become the Legion battle cry. Because, you see, the greatest glory a Legionnaire can possess is to die fighting—for France and for the Legion—against hopeless odds and without thought of surrender."

"Like Dien Bien Phu."

"Yes, Mister Hagen. Like Dien Bien Phu. I understand that your father was there with the Legion, so perhaps you understand better than many about the glory of the Legion."

Hagen took a drink. The glory of the Legion? Dien Bien Phu was no crowning achievement—it was a bloodbath. But let the Legion believe what it wanted. Hagen didn't care.

"There are people who think this relic is worth thirteen million dollars," Hagen said. "That's a steep price for a wooden hand."

"Yes, that's true. A wooden hand—nothing more. And the Shroud of Turin is only a piece of cloth. Yet there are many people who would kill to possess it. Because to possess it is to possess history. One cannot put a price on history, at least not in terms of money. The value of history is measured in the blood of men, as every schoolboy knows."

"And the Legion is prepared to spill blood to get it back."

Zahn shrugged. "If you wish to look at it that way. But you have to understand, it is a question of proprietary interest. The hand belongs to the Legion. It is the Legion. And the Legion is prepared to go to great lengths to see that it is returned to its rightful place beside the Monument aux Morts."

The Monument aux Morts. Monument to the dead. A fitting place for a wooden hand that seemed to leave in its wake nothing but violence and death. Hagen thought again of the photograph his father had once shown him, the ranks of Legionnaires standing at attention under the sun, kepis starched white, red epaulettes clinging to their shoulders, looking sharp-edged and solemn as the wooden hand in its glass reliquary was paraded before them, surrounded by billowing battle flags and trumpet blasts. Had one of those Legionnaires in the photograph been Hagen's father—Legionnaire Wolfgang Karl Hagen, former Waffen-SS soldier, veteran of Dien Bien Phu? Had he saluted this wooden hand, just as he'd saluted the Nazi swastika years before? What price would Hagen's father have placed on the Hand of Danjou? Would it have been worth taking a life to him?

Colonel Zahn sipped his bourbon. He didn't seem to be in any rush. Hagen had expected him to show up here making urgent demands and angry threats, but Zahn was sitting here like an old chum, ready to shoot the breeze all night if need be, or so it seemed. Was Zahn playing for time? Was there some reason why he wanted to keep Hagen here as long as possible? Hagen couldn't see any reason why he should. As long as they sat here in the casino Hagen was safe. But Zahn must've given some thought as to how he could force Hagen onto a less level playing field. One where Zahn could bargain more quickly and violently, without the pleasantries thrown in.

"We've discussed ancient history," Hagen said. "Now let's discuss more recent history. How did Captain Danjou's hand wind up in Las Vegas?"

Zahn was looking down the bar at the Arab Legionnaire, who was eyeing a young woman who had sat down next to him. Zahn turned back to Hagen slowly, as though only half aware that Hagen had spoken. "That is a problem that has kept us very busy. You see, three months ago the hand was stolen from the museum where it is kept. Someone broke into the museum and employed a pry bar to break open the case in which the hand rested. For three months I have searched for some clue as to where it might be. Last week my efforts met with success.

"A man in Paris who is in the business of selling things that don't belong to him told me about a young man who came to him with a relic that he wished to sell. The man was at first interested—it is his business to be interested in such propositions—but when he realized what the relic was he prudently had second thoughts. He kept this information to himself for a time but finally saw that it was his duty to report the incident to us. He didn't know who the young man was, but it wasn't hard to identify him based on the man's description. The young man was your brother, Mister Hagen."

"The man in Paris—what's his name?"

"Georges Amarantos. I understand that one or two of his people have had dealings with you in recent days. As it happens, we know quite a bit about Monsieur Amarantos—enough to convince him that it was in his best interests to help us locate the hand and bring it home. My men are the best men in the world, Mister Hagen, but they do not possess the delicate sensibilities and the social graces that are needed to do business with dealers of rare and expensive things. Because it was these very dealers who we assumed your brother would go to to sell the Hand of Danjou, it was agreed to enlist the aid of Monsieur Amarantos and his operation. It seemed wise to have people on hand who knew the workings of the black markets. People who are familiar with that kind of terrain."

"And you kept the theft of the hand quiet because that made it easier to keep prospective buyers away from it while you searched for it."

"Yes, that's right." Zahn shook his head, affected a sad look. "Of course, these precautions would not have been necessary if we had caught up with your brother before he departed France. Unfortunately, your brother's contract with the Legion had just ended a few days before I learned that he was the man I was looking for, and he'd already left the country. I organized a detachment of men and sent them here to Las Vegas. I myself was detained in Paris for several days and only just arrived here today. But I gave my men orders to reconnoiter the situation. Their work has led me to you."

"And in the process of this reconnoitering, your men killed my brother."

Zahn pursed his lips, thoughtful. "That question presents a problem for me. You see, I don't have that piece of information. I've talked to my men and they do not know the answer either. It would appear that Legionnaire Hagen was murdered by people unknown to us."

"Bullshit."

"I'm afraid not, Mister Hagen."

"If you want the hand you're going to have to tell me who murdered my brother. That's the deal."

Zahn raised his hands in a gesture of resignation. "I cannot bargain

233

with something I do not have. But let me say this, and you can see for yourself how things are. Your brother was murdered last Friday morning, according to the newspapers. The first detachment of my men didn't arrive here until Sunday afternoon. So you will have to explain to me how they could have killed your brother, when your brother was already dead for over two days."

"All right, Zahn. Your men are only reconnoitering. And yet people keep turning up dead. I suppose your men didn't kill Sidney Trunk or Jack Gubbs either—or Harry Needles down in Laughlin."

"Sidney Trunk?"

"He died out in Boulder City the other night. Why did your men reconnoiter him to death and then burn his house down?"

Zahn responded to his glass of bourbon, as though it and not Hagen had just spoken. "I'm afraid Sidney Trunk is not a name that has been brought to my attention. As for this man Needles, Legionnaire Tate acted against my orders. He was told only to observe. Of course, I cannot blame him so much for taking the hand from you when he saw the opportunity to do so. But in the event, this man Needles was killed—an unfortunate accident and one that Tate will be reprimanded for.

"And my men cannot take credit for Mister Gubbs's death either. Two of my men came to believe that Mister Gubbs either had the hand in his possession or knew where it could be found. Last night—again acting without my consent—they entered his apartment while he was away and searched it. They found an envelope containing two photographs of the Hand of Danjou. But while they continued their search they were interrupted by Mister Gubbs upon his return to his apartment. Having no recourse, my men confronted Gubbs with the photographs and asked him to explain himself. After a certain amount of persuasion, Mister Gubbs admitted that Legionnaire Hagen had given him the photographs to distribute to parties who might be interested in brokering the sale of the hand. Mister Gubbs claimed to know nothing about the current whereabouts of the hand and my men, after a lengthy interrogation, left him in his apartment, slightly bruised but very much alive. We were all very sorry to hear that he died in the night. I had high hopes for Mister Gubbs."

Hagen considered what Zahn had just told him. An envelope containing photographs of the hand—Ronnie must've given the photographs to Gubbs to pass around. And one of those photographs had wound up in the hands of Winnie the Poof. Winnie told Hagen that it was Ronnie who went to his house and gave him the photograph. Hagen wondered now if it was Gubbs and not Ronnie who spoke to Wilson. If so, then Gubbs may well have known the value of the wooden hand from the start. But why would the Poof have lied about that? To protect Gubbs?

Hagen glanced over Zahn's shoulder. Over by the slot machines the Japanese Legionnaire was now talking to yet another Legionnaire, this one wearing a baseball cap and a black-and-white football jersey. Shit, how many of them were here? If Hagen got up and walked to the front door he'd have half the casino following right behind him.

Zahn was motioning to the bartender for a fresh drink. "Can I buy you one now, Mister Hagen?" Hagen declined. When Zahn's drink came he threw back a third of it in one gulp. Zahn was warming up to the bourbon. At the end of the bar the Arab Legionnaire had traded in his crushed ice concoction for a green bottle of Heineken. He seemed much more at ease now, glancing with interest at Hagen and Zahn. Just sitting there watching his boss work. His jacket was too large by a size—the easier to hide the pistol that was no doubt holstered underneath.

A cocktail waitress approached the bar, her tight-fitting costume and long tanned legs catching Zahn's eye. Zahn signaled to her and the waitress came over. Zahn pulled two twenties and a ten out of his wallet. Asked the waitress to buy him some chips. "I'm interested in a game of chance. Can you help me?" Zahn's eyes fell to the cleavage she displayed. The waitress knew quite well what Zahn was interested in. She smiled from under her blow-dried hair when he dropped another ten on her serving tray—"For your trouble, my dear." The waitress hurried off in the direction of the casino cage, Zahn's eyes following her until she disappeared in the crowd.

Zahn turned to Hagen. "So where do we stand, Mister Hagen? Have I told you what you want to know? Is there something else I can do for you? I can see that you are not convinced that we bear no responsibility for what happened to Legionnaire Hagen, but I don't know what else I can tell you. Let me say only this—if we had found your brother alive, we most certainly would have the hand now. But we don't have it. So what possible advantage would killing your brother have been to us? No, I submit to you that your brother was killed by others. Who, I do not know. Furthermore, it's none of my concern. It is a question you will have to answer for yourself."

"What does Marty Ray have to do with this?"

Zahn looked puzzled.

"The gentleman in the warehouse. What were your men doing there?"

"Ah, I see." Zahn nodded. "You have Mademoiselle Cosette to thank for that. She was on her way to talk to you at your hotel when she saw you departing with the two rough-mannered men. That was a stroke of luck for you, because the men I had ordered to watch you were elsewhere at that moment. Mademoiselle Cosette followed you and contacted me to tell me of your whereabouts. It appeared that you might be in some trouble and I was concerned. Legionnaire Hagen and Mister Gubbs were already dead. I didn't want you killed as well. So I ordered my men to go in and—what's the expression?—'pull your chestnuts out of the fire'? I wanted to give you every opportunity to locate the hand for us. I must say, Mister Hagen, that you haven't let us down."

Hagen doubted that Cosette's appearance at the hotel had been a coincidence. It was more likely that she or her partner had been watching the hotel, waiting for him to leave. Maybe they'd had a scheme of their own in mind, but Marty Ray beat them to it.

"Is Marty Ray dead?" Hagen said.

"Not at all. Very much alive. But I don't believe he will be putting his nose where it doesn't belong anymore. A bad dog needs a swift kick now and then."

"What if I don't give you the hand, Zahn? What if I call the police and tell them about you and your men?"

"You could do that, of course. Yes, you could do that. But aside from Tate's indiscretion this evening, I don't know that the police could do much with us. And even if they could, we are willing to take that chance. 'Faire Camerone,' Mister Hagen. 'Faire Camerone.' If I and my men do not succeed there will be fifty more Legionnaires right behind us, and fifty more after that, and on and on until the Hand of Danjou is returned to its rightful place. You cannot kill history, Mister Hagen. But history can most certainly kill you."

Zahn let the statement hang in the air for a moment. Then he waved his hand to dismiss the thought. "But this is all very morbid. Let's not get caught up in threats and accusations. The only question that remains is how do we want to complete this business of ours? I'm prepared to be reasonable. You have acquired the hand through your own diligence and I am prepared to reward you for that diligence. Let me suggest this—if you are prepared to give us the hand, we are willing to negotiate a small fee for your services. Would ten thousand dollars be sufficient?"

Ten thousand—wasn't that what Winnie the Poof had offered him? Hagen smiled. "I don't have the hand with me."

"But you can get it, certainly. So let's say I give you two hours— two hours to retrieve the hand from wherever you have hidden it and to bring it here to me."

"I'll take fifty thousand."

"As you wish. I think I can arrange that price."

"Or maybe a hundred thousand."

Zahn said nothing. The cocktail waitress returned. She handed Zahn a stack of five ten-dollar chips. Zahn raised a finger, bidding her to stay for a moment. "Would you be so kind as to place a bet for me?" He dropped the chips into her hand, asked her to set them all on a nearby roulette table—"Number six, please." The waitress gave Hagen an amused look, wondering if this was some kind of gag. It wasn't. She carried the chips over to the closest roulette table, spoke to the croupier. Set the chips down on the number Zahn had asked for.

"Let's see how my luck is," Zahn said.

While Hagen and Zahn watched from their seats at the bar, the croupier spun the wheel. The black ball bounced along the wheel, clicking against the metal rungs. The wheel slowed. The ball slipped into a cup. The croupier called the winning number, then pulled in Zahn's stack of chips with his paddle. The cocktail waitress gave Zahn an apologetic look. Zahn smiled, nodded to her.

"How quickly things change," Zahn said, turning to Hagen. "One moment I have a stack of chips, the next moment they are gone forever. When one takes chances, one can lose everything in the blink of an eye. Don't you agree? It seems to me that it might be more prudent not to tempt fate."

"Thanks for the object lesson."

Zahn drained his glass and set it on the bar. "You wanted to discuss things. Now we've had our little talk. Two hours, Mister Hagen. You have two hours' grace. Call me on the telephone when you are ready. If I do not hear from you in two hours, all the bets are off, as I think the saying is. And we will proceed to do what needs to be done."

Zahn raised his finger to the corner of his eyebrow—a parting salute. Then he got up and walked away. Hagen watched him disappear back into the crowd of gamblers. But the Arab Legionnaire remained seated at the end of the bar. And the Japanese Legionnaire—he was still watching Hagen from the bank of slot machines. Hagen looked around casually. The Legionnaire in the football jersey and the one in the leather jacket were both lying low now, and Hagen didn't see any other men who were obviously Legionnaires. But he knew they were there. Zahn had suggested that he had fifty men in Las Vegas. How many of them were in this casino right now, waiting for Hagen to step outside?

Hagen checked his watch, then ordered another bourbon. He worked on his drink, smoked another of the bartender's cigarettes, just sitting there, letting the clock tick. After twenty minutes the Arab Legionnaire left the bar and disappeared. Ten minutes later Hagen decided that it was time to leave too.

Time to play his hunch.

Hagen signaled to the bartender.

"Call security for me," Hagen said.

The bartender looked alarmed. "Is there anything I can help you with?"

"Yes, you can call security for me."

Hagen, walking briskly across a casino floor—

Off to his left, a tall slot machine in the shape of one of the pyramids of Giza. In front of him, Egyptian hieroglyphics covered the surface of a wall the color of North African sand. On his right, a cocktail waitress dressed as Queen Nefertiti served a tray of martinis to a table of businessmen making off-color jokes about needing a mummy.

When Hagen reached the long wide hallway he broke into a jog.

At the MGM Grand Hagen had slipped two casino security officers fifty dollars to escort him outside. He told them he'd won quite a bit of money and he was afraid that thieves might be watching him. Hagen wasn't taking any chances. Zahn's Legionnaires wouldn't dare to grab him inside the casino, but they might just be bold enough to grab him outside the door and throw him into a car. The two burly security men didn't buy Hagen's story about thieves but they didn't care either— fifty bucks was fifty bucks. They walked Hagen outside and watched over him as he climbed into a cab.

Hagen told the driver to take him to the Luxor casino. When the cab pulled up in front of the tall black pyramid Hagen tossed the fare to the cabbie, jumped out of the cab and darted inside. A dark-skinned man dressed in the white loincloth and webbed sandals of a Nile barge slave tried to hand him a brochure. Hagen brushed him aside and moved on, past a pair of stone renderings of the Egyptian king Ramses the Second, two stories tall, the sullen king seated and staring mutely out from antiquity. Hagen strode across the casino floor toward the far side of the building. The long hallway that led to the Excalibur casino was just where he'd been told it would be. He jogged down it and into the adjoining casino. Ancient Egypt was left behind and now he was surrounded by medieval jesters strumming lutes while old men and women with wizened faces dropped coin after coin into the rows of slot machines, their eyes dazed, their movements somnolent.

Out the front doors of the Excalibur, the parapets and towers of the fairy-tale castle rising up behind him, painted in cartoon colors and lit up like a three-alarm fire. A line of cabs stood out front. Hagen paused at a small patch of ornamental landscaping outside the casino doors, picked up a few small stones that he thought he might have a use for, then jumped into a cab. Fifteen minutes later the cab pulled up in front of the Circus Circus casino. Ancient Egypt to a Camelot castle to Barnum and Bailey—the city of Las Vegas had become one big costume party. Inside Circus Circus Hagen pushed through a crowd of middle-aged couples wearing matching T-shirts, the men with baseball caps pushed back on their heads, the women with fanny packs belted around their girth. Hagen ran bodily into a greasepainted circus clown juggling white plates, apologized as the plates crashed to the floor. Hagen saw an exit leading out to the parking garage. As he pushed open the door he glanced over his shoulder. The circus clown was giving him the finger—

The car was waiting for him. A green Chevrolet sedan. The headlights flashed on and off. The engine started.

Hagen walked up, climbed into the passenger seat.

McGrath sat behind the wheel.

"How did it work out?" McGrath said.

"I think I lost them."

As McGrath pulled out of the parking garage he dropped a pint bottle of sour mash whiskey in Hagen's lap. "You look like you could use a drink." Hagen twisted off the cap and drank. The whiskey went down like a hard dose of reality in a city of hallucinations.

At the MGM Grand Hagen had called McGrath before he called Colonel Zahn. He had asked McGrath to come meet him.

McGrath was reluctant, told him to call back tomorrow. It was the middle of the night, for god's sake. "Harry Needles is dead," Hagen said. McGrath woke up, all ears now. "I'm being followed," Hagen said. McGrath told him about the connecting corridor between the Luxor and the Excalibur. Go into one hotel and come out from another. A good way to lose a tail.

It worked. Or seemed to.

"What's going on, Bodo?" McGrath said as they sat in McGrath's car at a red traffic light on the corner of Las Vegas Boulevard and Sahara. Hagen suddenly realized he was tired and hungry. But there was still much to do tonight—this morning—before he could sleep.

McGrath pulled onto a side street and parked. Hagen handed him the bottle of Jack Daniel's. McGrath took a drink, handed it back. Then Hagen told him. About Harry Needles. About Colonel Zahn and his detachment of Legionnaires. About Ronnie's trouble in the Legion and the wooden hand that he brought back with him to Las Vegas. About the woman from Paris named Suzanne Cosette and about Legionnaire Tate and the long drive back to Las Vegas from Laughlin. McGrath rolled down the window, smoked one cigarette and then another while Hagen told him the story of the Hand of Danjou. McGrath's face was a stone mask. His blue windbreaker was badly wrinkled and smelled of cheap cologne.

"This man Zahn killed Ronnie?" McGrath said.

Hagen recalled what Zahn had said. He'd said his Legionnaires hadn't arrived in Las Vegas until Sunday, two days after Ronnie was murdered, but it wasn't that. Hagen wasn't sure he believed that. It was something else Zahn had said. *If we'd found your brother alive we'd have the hand now, but we don't have it.* Zahn had made some sense there. Or maybe it was only that Hagen had been thinking along those same lines. "I don't know if Zahn and his men ever met up with Ronnie. But I know they killed Harry Needles, and I think they killed Gubbs. Pick them up. All I have to do is call Zahn and tell him I've got the hand. Have your men stake out the meeting and arrest them. Then you can talk to Zahn yourself. Harry Needles is dead. That should be reason enough to arrest them."

McGrath didn't sound convinced. "I only have your word for it that these Legionnaires—if that's what they are—killed Harry Needles. How do I know you didn't kill him yourself, Bodo. And Gubbs too."

"Pick up Zahn," Hagen said, too loud and too angry. McGrath raised his hand—back off, Bodo, calm down. "You've got fifty men from the French Foreign Legion on the ground in Vegas," Hagen said, quieter now. "They're all looking for a wooden hand that Ronnie stole from them. I'd think you'd be interested in talking to them, no matter what you believe."

McGrath picked a piece of tobacco off the tip of his tongue, flicked it out the open window. "I'm interested, don't get me wrong. But I hope there's something to it. It's going to be bad for you if there isn't. You're a pretty good suspect too. Right now you're the best one I've got."

"That's why I'm telling you this."

"You're telling me something. I just wonder why."

"I'm telling you what you'd know yourself if you'd bother to do your job."

Silence fell. The hot ember of McGrath's cigarette grew bright, dimmed, grew bright again. The ticking of the warm car engine sounded like a countdown to an explosion.

"Stick around," McGrath said. "I'll show you how I do my job."

"I'm not going anywhere."

"That's right. You're not going anywhere." McGrath gave him a severe look. "You left this wooden hand out in the desert?"

"Just south of Searchlight. Let's go out there right now. See it for yourself."

McGrath glanced at his watch. Four thirty in the morning. "Maybe we'll do just that."

Southbound on Highway 95—one more long drive into the desert. In the east the sky was lightening with morning. The sun would be up soon. On the road ahead the white lines and black skidding slashes captured in the headlights looked like old celluloid film looping around and around, slowly tearing itself to pieces. Hagen had the feeling that he'd spent all day and all night running up and down this highway.

Not getting anywhere, just running.

Hagen asked McGrath for a cigarette. McGrath handed him the crumpled pack from his shirt pocket. The lights of a long-haul truck traveling in the northbound lane washed over McGrath's face. McGrath looked exactly like what he was, an old cop with too much on his mind. Hagen lit the filterless Pall Mall with the dashboard lighter, inhaled the strong cigarette smoke.

"Zahn said his men didn't arrive here until Sunday," Hagen said, thinking out loud. "It might be true."

"Then who killed Ronnie?"

"I don't know."

"You've got all kinds of ideas. Let's hear them."

Hagen tried to sort it all out in his mind, bit by bit. He had a rough idea of what might have happened. Hagen asked McGrath if he'd heard of the murder of a man named Sidney Trunk out in Boulder City a couple of nights ago. McGrath knew of Trunk's death, but only as an item on the police blotter.

"When Ronnie got to town he started looking for a fence," Hagen said. "He got in touch with a man named Dallas Martinez in Vegas right off, but Martinez thought the hand was bogus and handed it off to Trunk out in Boulder. At least that's what Martinez says. Trunk was interested and he put out some feelers in Los Angeles to see what kind of price he could get if the hand was real. Maybe he believed it was real or maybe he was thinking about working some kind of con, but he never had the hand. Someone thought he did though, and that's why he was killed."

"Who put you on to this fellow Martinez?"

"The Sniff."

"You've dragged the Sniff into this?"

"Only to ask around, see what he could find out about the hand."

Hagen went on, speaking slowly. Setting each small piece of the puzzle down and then adding another small piece, like a man taking small careful footsteps along the edge of a cliff. "At the same time Ronnie was shopping the hand to Martinez, he told Gubbs that he needed a fence. Gubbs told him about Winnie Wilson. Ronnie gave Gubbs some snapshots of the hand and Gubbs took one of those pictures to Wilson. Wilson must've told Gubbs what the hand was worth, or at least given him a good idea. Wilson told me that it was Ronnie he'd met with and not Gubbs, but I think that's bullshit. I don't think Ronnie ever met Wilson. It was all handled through Gubbs. It makes sense that way. Wilson is a professional. He'd want to deal with someone he knew. He didn't know Ronnie, but he knew Gubbs."

"Why would Wilson lie?"

"Maybe he was still hoping at that point that Gubbs could find the hand for him and he wanted to protect Gubbs from me. Maybe he was protecting Gubbs for some other reason, I don't know. You knew Gubbs better than I did, McGrath. What do you think?"

"I never got a chance to talk to him about it. Someone put a bullet in his head."

"Zahn's men."

"That's what you keep saying. Go on."

"Ronnie went out to Hoover Dam to meet someone. He was shot sitting in his car with the window rolled down, so whoever shot him was someone he knew and who he wasn't smart enough to be afraid of. I think it was Gubbs. I think Gubbs gave Ronnie some kind of story to get him out there with the hand—maybe that Wilson wanted to buy the hand and they'd all meet out at Hoover Dam to discuss a deal. Nice out-of-the-way place, and yet not so out of the way as to make Ronnie too nervous. So Ronnie drives out there. Gubbs shows up and shoots Ronnie, but when he searches the car he doesn't find the hand. Ronnie didn't bring it.

"So now Ronnie is dead but Gubbs still doesn't have the hand. But he knows it's got to be around somewhere. He also knows that Ronnie had been to see Harry Needles. So Gubbs starts working on Harry. Harry goes home, searches the bags that Ronnie left with him, realizes that he has the hand. He throws in with Gubbs and they decide to sell the hand out of town rather than bring Wilson into it—because Wilson would know that Gubbs had killed Ronnie to get the hand. But neither of them knew that the Foreign Legion was in town looking for the hand. Gubbs comes back to his apartment last night and finds a couple of Legionnaires tossing the place. They put the screws to him and then kill him."

"Who killed Trunk?"

"My guess is that it was Gubbs. I spoke to Trunk on the phone the night he was killed. He said he'd talked to Ronnie on the phone Monday night about the hand. Only it wasn't Ronnie. But Ronnie was staying at Gubbs's place when he first got into town. He might've been passing Gubbs's phone number around. I don't know what Trunk said to Gubbs on the phone, but it must've been just enough to give Gubbs the idea that maybe Trunk knew where the hand was. So Gubbs goes out to Boulder and Trunk winds up dead. Harry said that he only threw in with Gubbs yesterday—and Trunk was killed Wednesday night. So at the time Trunk was killed, Gubbs still wasn't sure where the hand was."

McGrath laughed to himself. "It's convenient to pin all of this on Gubbs. He'd be hard-pressed to deny it at this point. What's this wooden hand supposed to be worth?"

"Trunk thought it was worth thirteen million."

"Thirteen million?" McGrath let out a low whistle.

"That's what I'm told."

McGrath shook his head. "That's quite a story, Bodo."

"It's a start. I think there's some truth in it. Quite a bit. Pick up Zahn and his men. Pick up Wilson too. Once you get them sorted out I think you'll see that it falls together just about the way I've said."

"Anyone else you want me to arrest?"

"They'll do for a start."

"We'll have to see about that."

A road sign appeared—the turnoff where Highway 95 separated from Highway 93 and headed due south toward Laughlin. McGrath guided the car through the turn, hit the gas when the highway straightened out again. A mile farther on Legionnaire Tate's cell phone buzzed. Hagen flipped it open to answer the call, then closed it slowly, a puzzled look on his face.

Hagen glanced at McGrath. "Nobody there."

Dawn was breaking by the time they reached Searchlight. The roadhouse casinos looked closed up. The mobile homes scattered on the hillside stood at odd angles amid the sagebrush and rocks, the desert soil blown up against them in drifts.

South of the town Hagen pointed out the old utility road.

McGrath slowed, pulled over onto the shoulder of the highway. Eased the big Chevrolet sedan onto the dirt road and crept along. The car rocking side to side, a cloud of dust kicking up behind them. After a time the road curved and carried them around a hillside and then down into the narrow valley.

The wooden shack appeared up ahead. Off to the left, about fifty yards from the dirt road. And off to the right was the formation of boulders where Hagen had buried the hand.

McGrath stopped the car on the road, turned the engine off. They climbed out of the car. It wasn't even six o'clock in the morning but already the temperature was into the nineties. Soon it would be too hot to breathe in this desert. Hagen wondered who had built a shack out here. Whoever it was, they had wanted to live at the end of the world.

While McGrath leaned against the car smoking Hagen walked over to the boulders near the road. The boulders looked narrow and angular in the daylight. He found the rocks he'd left as a marker and he prodded them aside with his foot, then bent down and dug up the blue sweatshirt bundle from the parched earth and brought it back to the car.

Hagen set the bundle on the warm hood of the car. Unrolled the sweatshirt.

McGrath flicked his cigarette onto the ground, picked up the aged wooden relic. Turned it over in his hands, his forehead wrinkled with deep furrows. A wooden hand with a broken finger, found in the ashes of a burned-out hacienda in Mexico a hundred and fifty years ago. It had traveled from the deserts of Mexico to the deserts of Algeria and now finally to this desert. It had a life of its own—but no, Hagen knew that wasn't true. It only had the life that men had given it. And many men—Legionnaires—had given it their lives.

"Doesn't look like much," McGrath said.

He handed the relic to Hagen. Then McGrath turned away, surveying the sharp crags on the hill behind the crumbling shack. McGrath sighed. A long tired sigh. Hagen set the wooden hand down on the sweatshirt and began wrapping it back up. McGrath opened the car door, took his windbreaker off, threw it into the backseat.

Slammed the door shut.

Hagen looked up. McGrath was facing him. Standing with his legs braced. As though expecting a hard wind. McGrath held a .38 revolver in his hand. Snub-nosed, chrome finish—McGrath's police special. The short barrel was pointed at Hagen.

"What the hell are you doing, McGrath?"

A look of resignation had fallen over McGrath's face. "Set the hand down on the hood and step away from the car."

"You're out of your mind."

"Do as I say, Bodo." McGrath motioned with the barrel of the revolver. "Move."

For a moment Hagen couldn't move. Then he set the bundle on the hood of the car. He took three steps away from the car, keeping his hands out at his sides. McGrath waved the barrel of the revolver again and Hagen stepped farther away from the car. The sound of his footsteps scratching in the dirt seemed far too loud.

"By the way, Bodo, that piece under your coat—I think I'd like to watch over it for you. It occurs to me that there are far too many guns around here." McGrath pointed to the ground at his feet with his free hand. "Toss it over here. Use two fingers."

Hagen pulled the Beretta automatic he'd taken from the Englishman out from under his coat, using his thumb and index finger. He tossed the automatic and it landed on the ground a few feet to McGrath's left. Hagen studied the distance between himself and McGrath. Twenty feet. McGrath eased over and bent down, slow and watchful, keeping Hagen covered with the revolver. McGrath picked up the automatic. He tucked his revolver under his arm and quickly racked the slide of the Beretta to make sure that a cartridge rested in the chamber. Then McGrath turned the Beretta on Hagen while he tucked his own police special back into his leather side holster. McGrath transferred the Beretta to his right hand.

"What are you thinking, McGrath?"

"I'm thinking you figured this out pretty good, Bodo. But you missed one or two things."

"I didn't count on you."

"There's always one more son of a bitch than you counted on, isn't there, Bodo. That's a good rule to live by. Too bad you had to learn it this way."

"You shot Ronnie?"

"No, Gubbs shot Ronnie—you were right about that."

"You were in on it."

McGrath turned his head, spat onto the ground. The pistol in his hand was steady. "That's right. Wilson made the mistake of telling Gubbs what the hand might be worth, and Gubbs told me. I told him to get his hands on it and we'd make a little money for ourselves. So Gubbs got Ronnie to drive out to the dam—told him he'd found a buyer and they'd all meet out there. Ronnie was supposed to bring the hand with him but he didn't. Unfortunately Gubbs didn't find that out until after he shot Ronnie. Gubbs wasn't the sharpest knife in the drawer."

Hagen felt the sweat forming on his forehead, the back of his neck, the palms of his hands. "Then you killed Gubbs."

"I let him find the hand first. He thought Harry might know where it was and Harry did, but Harry needed to be convinced that it was worth his while to do business with Gubbs. It took a few days for Gubbs to bring him around. Might've been sooner but Gubbs got sidetracked by Trunk. You were right about Trunk—he called Gubbs's place the other night looking for Ronnie and talking about the hand. Gubbs got the idea that Trunk knew more than he was saying and he went out to Boulder to talk to the poor man. I guess the conversation turned sour and Gubbs started playing with matches. Like I say, Gubbs wasn't wrapped too tight even on a good day. But Harry finally decided to play ball and that put us back on track. Harry smelled money—" McGrath didn't bother to finish the thought. "I was going to let Gubbs string Harry along for a while and then we'd get rid of him, but things started getting a little out of control. Harry got scared. Gubbs got scared. You were running around asking difficult questions. And when these Legionnaire friends of yours beat up Gubbs night before last, I began to wonder what the hell was going on myself. Gubbs called me and told me about that, so I decided it was time to pay a visit to Gubbs. I had to get rid of him. I've known that for a long time but I've been putting it off. But the time was right."

"Because you could set me up for it."

"You've got the motive, Bodo. That's why I had you picked up. I've got two detectives now who think you probably killed him too. You thought Gubbs killed Ronnie, so you killed Gubbs. The gun Gubbs used to kill Ronnie was at his apartment. The gun that killed Gubbs will be found in your hotel room. It's going to look very simple."

McGrath was right. It was simple. And solid. Gubbs killed Ronnie. Hagen killed Gubbs. Harry Needles's murder and the death of Sidney Trunk in Boulder were loose ends but not ones that McGrath needed to worry about. He hadn't been directly involved. It seemed to Hagen that the only person still alive who could tie McGrath to Gubbs's deadly search for the Hand of Danjou was Hagen himself.

McGrath nodded at Hagen. "You'll disappear too, of course—but in a few weeks or months someone will find your body out here. There'll be an investigation but it won't lead anywhere because there's no place for it to go. These Legionnaires will be gone by then and even if they're not, so what? They don't know a thing about me. After a while you'll be just another cold case. No one will think twice about it. Yes, you've set things up for me nicely. With Gubbs out of the way I thought I was going to have to kill Harry myself to get the hand, but you found the hand and had the good manners to give it to me. I really do have to thank you, Bodo. You've walked right in. Now I'm going to close the door behind you."

Hagen saw it all clearly. McGrath and Gubbs working together— they must've been doing it for years. Gubbs fed information to McGrath and McGrath used it as he pleased. He had a badge and the power of the law to keep them both out of trouble. A nice little setup. No one at Metro would question it because Gubbs was a known informant. And it stretched back for years—all the way back to Jimmy Ray's murder. Maybe farther than that.

"Who killed Jimmy Ray, McGrath? You, or Gubbs?"

A grin spread over McGrath's face. He cocked his head to one side as though seeing Hagen in a new light. "Very good. You've been giving this some thought. It was Gubbs who told me about the money Jimmy Ray took home with him. The next night I was waiting for Jimmy when he got home. Gubbs never knew for sure that I'd done it, but he had a good idea. Not that he could've told anyone. If Marty Ray ever found out that Gubbs was a police informant, Gubbs would've found himself standing on the bottom of Lake Mead with a cement toilet seat around his neck. Yes, I had a good time with Gubbs. We had an understanding. He made a little money out of it and I made quite a bit of money. He knew enough about me to cause me trouble, but I've always known enough about him to get him killed. Funny thing is, he never thought I'd do it myself."

Hagen's throat was dry. His voice sounded cracked and brittle in his ears. "Ronnie didn't have anything to do with it."

"Ronnie was like you, Bodo. He set himself up to take the fall."

"You set him up."

McGrath looked off to Hagen's right, toward the shack at the base of the hillside, one eyebrow raised. As though he'd just seen something over there, out of the corner of his eye. Hagen glanced across his shoulder. Noticed a bird, looked like a prairie falcon, circling above the shack. The bird flew off after a moment, disappearing around the side of the hill behind the shack. McGrath continued. "I did what I had to. I wound up working the Jimmy Ray case myself and I needed to throw suspicion away from Gubbs. When Ronnie left town I started throwing it in his direction. I asked Marty Ray and his friends just enough questions about Ronnie to make them wonder what I knew about him and wasn't telling. Ronnie was long gone—Marty Ray wasn't going to chase him down overseas. It's too bad that Ronnie came back. Too bad for him and too bad for you.

"Now, Bodo, let's take a walk over behind that shack."

Hagen stayed where he was, his eyes on the Beretta in McGrath's hand. "I didn't come back to Vegas to die, McGrath. At least not in your company."

McGrath motioned with the pistol. "It's too late for tough talk, Bodo. Get moving."

Hagen nodded in the direction of the shack. "Maybe it's not as late as you think."

"And why is that?"

"For one, I've got a friend posted over there in that shack. She's got a rifle sighted in on you. And when she pulls the trigger, she won't miss. Not at this range. So drop the pistol, McGrath."

McGrath looked in the direction of the shack. A slow smile spread across his haggard face at the thought of Hagen pulling an obvious feint. "Bodo, you're a bigger fool than I thought."

Hagen turned to look at the shack. He waved his right arm in a short arc. Hagen shouted, "Peach? Our friend doesn't believe you're out there. Why don't you squeeze off a round, show him how wrong he is."

Hagen studied the crumbling structure that stood fifty yards away. A morning shadow crept out from the edge of the shack, seemed to be reaching out to Hagen with a long crooked finger.

There was no response from the shack.

No sign of movement.

No rifle shot.

Nothing.

The shack and the desert around it was still and silent in the early morning light. The only sound Hagen could hear was McGrath's labored breathing. Or was that his own breathing? Hagen turned back to look at McGrath. McGrath looked like a stick figure in the sunlight. A tall thin scarecrow, propped up here in the desert to watch over the barren soil where nothing lived for long. But the smile on the detective's face had grown larger. And the Beretta was raised higher. McGrath had turned sideways to Hagen and was now aiming down the barrel of the pistol, aiming squarely at the center of mass of his target.

McGrath had decided to shoot Hagen where he stood.

Twenty feet of empty space separated them—Hagen was sure he could make it. His chances were good, he told himself. And even if they weren't as good as he wanted to believe, he knew it didn't matter now. There was nothing else he could do. There was nothing else to think about now. Hagen's body tensed and he exploded forward, moving fast and low. He would knock the gun aside and hit McGrath hard and throw him backward onto the ground. Hagen expected a reaction out of McGrath that might give Hagen an extra second or two, but McGrath didn't look startled. He didn't flinch. He didn't raise his head. The pistol in his hand didn't waver. As Hagen came toward him, McGrath's finger tightened on the trigger, the pistol barrel rose a millimeter or two, and before Hagen could reach him the gunshots echoed through the hills.

17.

THERE WERE TWO of them.

They stepped out from behind an outcropping of rock far up on the hillside behind the shack and walked down the hillside slowly, cutting to one side and then the other. Their dust-covered boots dislodging rocks and soil as they moved along.

Neither of them spoke. The first one had taken off his white T-shirt and tied it around his head, the tail of the T-shirt falling onto the back of his neck. His sunglasses caught the sunlight and flashed as he turned his head, searching the landscape around the shack. He held a large rifle in his hands. A long-barreled sniper rifle, with a telescopic sight.

The one behind him carried a pistol. A pair of black binoculars hung from a thin strap around his neck. He walked stiff-legged. His foot slipped on a patch of scree and he started to slide. He caught himself and moved on. The sound of the scree sliding down the hillside continued for a moment. A faint rustling sound, somehow peaceful, like the sound of rain falling on a roof.

The man with the rifle reached the bottom of the hill first. He paused, the rifle barrel swiveling from left to right as the man studied the landscape. Nothing moved. There was no threat here now. When the second man reached the base of the hill he removed a cellular phone from his belt and spoke into it quietly, then put the phone away.

A third man appeared, from the shadows behind the shack. He carried not one but two rifles. One of them slung over his shoulder, the length of the rifle resting against his side, and a shorter, more compact assault rifle that hung from a strap over his other shoulder and that he carried with the rifle barrel pointed forward and his hand on the rifle's grip.

His other hand held Maxine Peach's arm as he guided her ahead of him, out into the early morning sunlight.

Peach's hands were bound behind her. The front of her thin brown shirt and heavy padded shooting pants were covered with dirt. She walked hesitantly, seemed to lose her balance once or twice, as though her legs had cramped up after sitting in an awkward position for a long while.

The four figures joined up beside the shack. Then the man with the binoculars stepped out in front and they approached McGrath's car, the three Legionnaires holding their weapons at the ready.

The body of McGrath lay facedown in the dirt, five feet from the side of the car, along the edge of the dirt road. Arms outstretched, one leg cocked to the right, as though the corpse was trying to burrow straight down into the ground. Blood collected in pools in the parched soil around his shoulders and head.

Hagen stood beside the car with his arms raised, watching Colonel Zahn and his Legionnaires approach with Peach under guard. The automatic that McGrath had planned to shoot him with now lay several feet to the left of where Hagen stood. McGrath's own police special remained tucked away in the detective's side holster. Hagen didn't dare make a move in the direction of either of the pistols.

Not that the Beretta would have done him much good.

It was jammed.

Hagen had jammed it himself.

The rigged pistol was part of the setup Hagen had put together back at the MGM Grand, before his meeting with Colonel Zahn. If McGrath had been clean, he would never have known about the ploy. But Hagen had acquired some doubts about McGrath. Nothing solid, just a feeling that things didn't quite wash. Certain things. McGrath not telling Hagen about Jimmy Ray's murder, or the possibility that Ronnie had known something about it, that was one thing. And the idea that Gubbs had told McGrath that Ronnie was looking for a fence, but hadn't told him why, that was another. Gubbs had known about the wooden hand from the start—or at least the photograph of it that Ronnie had given him. It didn't make sense for Gubbs to mention a fence to McGrath without mentioning why a fence was needed. It seemed to Hagen that if Gubbs had been trying to hide the situation from McGrath, he would've hidden the whole thing, not just half of it.

So McGrath should've known about the wooden hand. But McGrath had played dumb, and later sent two detectives to strong-arm Hagen and accuse him of Gubbs's murder. It was a heavy-handed move, but it gave McGrath the opportunity to throw suspicion on Harry Needles, so that Hagen would be sure to go after Harry himself. With Gubbs dead, McGrath decided to let Hagen find the wooden hand for him.

Yesterday Hagen had thought that everything tied back to Jack Gubbs. Over the course of the night Hagen had come to see that there might be one more link in the chain, stretching from Gubbs to the man who stood behind him, pulling his strings.

John McGrath.

But Hagen had also seen that time was running out. The Legionnaires were closing in. If Hagen wanted to know what McGrath's angle truly was, he'd have to take some action soon. Sitting there at the MGM casino bar, he'd made three phone calls. One to Zahn. One to McGrath.

And one call to Peach.

She'd said she wanted to help him. He decided to take her up on the offer. Hagen told her about the utility road off Highway 95, just south of Searchlight. Told her about the shack out in the desert. Told her to take her target rifle and drive out there and get set up, out of sight. He'd told Peach to give Tate's cell phone a call, use a one-word signal so that Hagen would know that she'd reached the shack and was in position, waiting. Hagen even killed time after meeting with Zahn at the MGM to make sure the sun was up when Hagen and McGrath arrived out in the desert. And as a further precaution, Hagen jammed the Beretta, using one of the small stones he'd picked up in front of the Excalibur casino. Before meeting with McGrath in the Circus Circus parking garage, Hagen had cleared the pistol's chamber, then removed the first three cartridges in the magazine and wedged the stone down into it, below the point where the reloading mechanism would shave off the next round. The magazine still had weight, and a person could still rack the slide to chamber a round. But they wouldn't know there wasn't a round in the chamber until they tried to fire the pistol. Hagen had felt certain that if McGrath wanted to get rid of him, McGrath would rather use Hagen's pistol than one that could be traced back to him.

The whole thing had been a hunch, that's all. A gambler's hunch. And Hagen had played it.

But the Legionnaires had had a hunch too.

And they'd gotten here first.

When Colonel Zahn reached McGrath's car he stopped, slid his pistol into his shoulder holster. Zahn studied the blue sweatshirt bundle lying on the hood of the car for a long moment. Finally he reached out and picked it up. Hefted it in his hand. Like a man unsure of what he'd just bought.

Hagen smiled at Peach to reassure her. She tried to smile back but it was a grim, tight-lipped smile. Her eyes were watchful and afraid. Trails of sweat snaked out from under her hair, running down the sides of her face, disappearing under her jawline. Her forehead was covered with sweat smeared with dirt. There was a nasty bruise forming low on one cheek, a cut above her right eye, and more bruises and small abrasions on her bare arms. The Legionnaires had been rough, but Hagen was sure that Peach still had some fight left in her.

Hagen turned back to Zahn, watched as the old Legionnaire unwrapped the bundle and inspected the wooden hand of Captain Danjou, then wrapped it back up again, taking great care, using the sleeves of the sweatshirt to tie off the bundle.

Zahn tucked the bundle under his arm. Stepped over to McGrath's body. He prodded the body with the toe of his boot. Nodded to himself, as though pleased with the quality of the sniper's work. The other two Legionnaires broke off, one of them taking up a position to Hagen's left, the other moving to the right. Hagen recognized one of them. He was the Legionnaire that Hagen encountered in front of the High Numbers Club—the German Hagen had thrown against the car. That memory seemed to belong to a time long ago. Another life perhaps. The third Legionnaire Hagen hadn't seen before. A thin young man with black hair, flattened nose, large plastic sunglasses tinted dark blue. The rifle he held in his hands was much smaller than the German's sniper rifle, looked like a modified FAMAS assault rifle. The rifle slung over his other shoulder must've been Peach's target rifle. Small-bore, lightweight gray frame, high-tech telescopic sight.

Now Colonel Zahn looked up from McGrath's body. Looked directly at Hagen for the first time.

"Who was he?" Zahn said.

"A cop," Hagen said.

Deep creases appeared on Zahn's forehead. "Is that so?" Zahn nodded again, this time with a judicious frown. The dead man at his feet was suddenly more interesting. "Why is he here?"

"He found out what the hand was worth. He wanted to sell it."

"Indeed." Zahn made soft tsk-tsking noises with his tongue. "An unfortunate idea."

Hagen glanced at the German. "*Gruss Gott*," the German said, sarcastic, patting the butt of his rifle with his hand. The sun glinted off the glass face of the telescopic sight. The other Legionnaire reached down and picked up the Beretta that lay near McGrath's body, then removed the revolver from McGrath's side holster. Tucked both pistols into the waistband of his trousers.

"How did you find this place?" Hagen said.

"Not so difficult," Zahn said, looking around him as though he'd just noticed where he was. The corner of his thin mustache twitched.

"Perhaps you'll remember, this morning I had a vehicle positioned just north of this town"—Zahn pointed vaguely off in the direction of the highway—"what's the name of it? Searchlight? Tate talked to the men in the vehicle from somewhere just south of that town. A few minutes later he called again. He was in no condition to speak at that point but he was able to convey to us that you had driven off the highway and into the desert. So wherever you were, it had to be a place only a few miles north or south of the town. Now why would you leave the road and drive into the desert?" Zahn waved a dismissive hand in the air, as though the question hardly needed asking. "A short time after Tate called us, my men spotted your car and followed you. They kept you under observation all the way back into Las Vegas. They even saw you leave Tate's vehicle when you arrived at the casino where we spoke. You had nothing with you when we met, and while you were inside the casino talking to me my men searched the car. The hand wasn't there either. So it was a very simple deduction—you drove off the road and hid the Hand of Danjou out here.

"I still had a few men operating in this area, and after I spoke with you this morning, I ordered them to take up spotting positions north and south of the town. I knew you'd come back. It was only a question of time. My men were prepared to sit out here for a week if that was what it took. But I was sure it wouldn't take that long." Zahn nodded at Peach. "When your friend's vehicle was observed leaving the highway we followed and approached this location on foot, and when we saw that she'd brought a rifle with her we confronted her. Unfortunately, she couldn't tell us where the hand was, much as we tried to convince her otherwise. So we took up a position on the hillside and waited for you to arrive. Very simple. It required a bit of work but not so much."

"Sweat saves blood," Hagen said, recalling the phrase his father used to repeat. The old Legionnaire motto.

Zahn looked surprised to hear it. "That's right, Mister Hagen. Sweat saves blood. In this case it saved yours." Zahn glanced at the corpse on the ground, one eyebrow raised. "Not that I am concerned about your welfare. But I don't like to see a man killed in cold blood. There are certain rules, Mister Hagen. Soldiers must live by them too."

"I appreciate the thought."

"I hope you do."

"If it means anything to you, the pistol he wanted to shoot me with was jammed. And I knew it was jammed."

Zahn shrugged. "Well then, I suppose that makes his death doubly unfortunate, wouldn't you say?"

In the distance Hagen heard the high-pitched whine of an engine traveling in low gear. A moment later a utility vehicle appeared on the dirt road. A white Range Rover. It drove down into the narrow valley, moving slow. Zahn watched it approach. The Range Rover stopped on the road. Zahn raised his hand. The driver rolled down the window, waiting, the engine idling.

"You've been lucky for us, Mister Hagen," Zahn said now. "You led us to the Hand of Danjou quickly and, if I may say so, decisively. But it remains to be seen how lucky you are."

"What do you mean?"

Zahn patted the bundle under his arm. "We have what we came for. Now we are leaving. Within three hours most of my men will be out of the country. By tonight all of them will be gone. Let me advise you of this, Mister Hagen—there will be no evidence that we were ever here. The names on our passports belong to people who do not properly exist. And of course the Legion will disavow any knowledge of what has happened here. Officially, the Hand of Danjou has never left Aubagne. Any inquiries made by your police or your government will go no further than that. So, Mister Hagen, let's hope that your luck continues. We are going to leave you here with this dead policeman. I suspect you may have some explaining to do."

"I'll take my chances."

"Let's hope it's not the kind of bet that is—what do you call it?"

"A sucker bet."

"That's right. A sucker bet. Good-bye, Mister Hagen."

Zahn motioned to the other two men, then turned and started off toward the Range Rover. As soon as Zahn's back was turned the German Legionnaire stepped up to Hagen with his rifle held at port arms. Hagen saw his own reflection in the German's sunglasses.

The German smiled.

The butt of the rifle shot out. Slammed into the side of Hagen's face.

Hagen fell to the ground, dazed. Sharp pain shooting up the side of his head and down his neck. With the German standing over Hagen, the third Legionnaire knelt and patted Hagen down, took Hagen's wallet and Tate's cell phone. As the third Legionnaire moved off, the German leaned in the open car window of McGrath's Chevrolet and removed the ignition key. The German hurried past Hagen, and a moment later Hagen heard the doors of the Range Rover slam shut and the popping sounds of loose rocks under the tires as the vehicle turned around. He raised himself up onto his elbow. Shook his head. Spit blood out onto the ground, his fingers gingerly feeling his jaw. Peach dropped to her knees beside him and together they watched the Range Rover drive off down the dirt road.

"Are you all right, Peach?"

"Don't worry about me, Bodo. I'm in need of some untying, that's all."

When the Range Rover disappeared over the hill Hagen picked himself up off the ground and set to work untying Peach's hands. The Legionnaires had used a length of what looked like communications wire for the purpose, and it was a few minutes before he could work the knot loose. When he was done, Peach massaged her wrists and fixed him with a sorrowful look. "I'm sorry, Bodo. There was nothing I could do. I didn't even see them in the darkness until it was too late."

Hagen stepped up and placed his arms around her, kissed her on her dirt-smeared forehead. "Nothing to be sorry about. You did exactly as I asked. Now, where did you leave your car?"

"Around the other side of the hill," Peach said, motioning toward the hillside behind the shack. "But it's not going to do us any good. They took my keys. They took my phone too."

Hagen set to work searching the dead man's pockets and the interior of the Chevrolet, but he found no cell phone, no police radio, nothing that might help them. There was nothing left to do but begin the long walk out to the ribbon of highway that led back to Las Vegas. As they stepped around McGrath's body Hagen paused for a moment, looking down. Hagen heard McGrath's voice—*There's always one more son of a bitch than you counted on, Bodo.*

So true, McGrath. So true.